SIX DAYS
TO LIVE

OTHER BOOKS

BY KENNETH M. PAGE:

A Father's Blessing: The Power and Privilege of the Priesthood

How Will Christmas Find Us? (contributor)

SIX DAYS TO LIVE

a suspense novel

KENNETH M. PAGE

Covenant Communications, Inc.

Published by Covenant Communications, Inc.
American Fork, Utah

Printed in the United States of America
First Printing: January 2018

24 23 22 21 20 19 18   10 9 8 7 6 5 4 3

ISBN 978-1-52440-338-6

To the incredible men and women of the U.S. Air Force Survival School for their dedicated and professional service in training more than 20,000 aircrew members annually. This critically important training has saved countless lives during both peacetime and war. The school's motto, "Return with Honor," describes the commitment of any downed aircrew member, especially those shot down behind enemy lines.

ACKNOWLEDGMENTS

Special thanks to Alicia Knight Cunningham, Esq., for your crucial insights into the overall structure of the book and your thoughtful recommendation on dialogue and character development. Thanks to Ali Monson for your terrific copyediting and other suggestions on the final draft, which made this book complete. Both of you have contributed significantly to bringing this project to fruition. And many thanks to Kami Hancock and the whole team at Covenant Communications—professionalism in action.

CHAPTER 1

DAY 1

EDDIE ANGHELONE SAT IN HIS car across the street and a block away from Harvest Savings Bank, the warm June sun beating through the dirty windshield. He hated his car, a nondescript 1990-something Chrysler New Yorker. The paint was a faded black that looked more like the dirty smoke from the local lumber mill rising into the leaden sky of a fall day. The carpet was matted down and stained from a combination of dirt, food, and who knew what else.

He could see the bare metal floor in the hole in the carpet where his right heel rested when he worked the gas pedal. The seats were leather, or what used to be leather, with a spiderweb of cracks in the middle and outright tears where the thread was unravelling along the seams. He was certain the eight-cylinder engine now ran on only five or six cylinders, like a rough and uneven version of a coin-operated vibrator bed that might be found in a cheap hotel.

And when the engine was running, the noise pounding from the rusted-out muffler attacked his eardrums like a toddler banging on pots and pans with a serving spoon while playing on the kitchen floor. As he thought about it, he couldn't explain why the car still ran at all. *Won't be long before it gives up the ghost altogether,* he thought.

Eddie glanced down at his watch. It was nearly 5:00 in the afternoon. It was a beautiful midsummer day, but Eddie hardly noticed. The bank would be closing soon, and he planned to make his way through the front doors just before the rent-a-cop locked up for the day. He reached up and rubbed the side of his face as he mentally ticked off each step of his plan. His coarse salt-and-pepper whiskers reminded him he hadn't shaved or, for that matter, showered in quite a while—exactly when, he couldn't remember.

Eddie was not the fastidious type, but even he could smell himself after a few days without soap and water. Whether it was body odor or the smell of his dirty clothes, he honestly couldn't tell. Then again, he really didn't care. If he had two quarters to rub together, he might consider a laundromat, but that wasn't exactly his highest priority.

He had moved to Spokane three months ago and was living in a flophouse a couple of blocks from the bus station in the low-rent part of town. He was a scavenger, really—a lazy ne'er-do-well who reluctantly took the occasional odd job to pay the rent and buy a rare hot meal. He didn't really think of himself as a bum but rather as carefree—no longer tied down by the vestiges of his once suburban-family lifestyle.

In truth, he was a prisoner of his past and a slave to alcohol, having lost all he once considered precious in life: a home, a respectable job, and his family. With that thought, he lifted a bottle of cheap wine, wrapped characteristically in a plain brown paper bag, and took a long pull. The sweet liquid slid smoothly down his throat, sending a warm, comforting sensation through mind and body.

He would need this liquid courage to follow through on his latest get-rich scheme. Plus, he figured, a little "hair of the dog" would help numb the pounding headache and nausea that came with every hangover. Every day. And today was no different. He took another long drink to empty the bottle then tossed it over the seat into the back.

Eddie knew he needed to have his wits about him if his plan was to succeed. He also knew he needed the alcohol to function even at the most basic level. It had become, for him, almost medicinal. At least, that's what he told himself. So, he closed his eyes and breathed deeply in and out a few times, trying futilely to sharpen his permanently dulled mind. He laid his head back against the headrest to relax and was softly snoring seconds later.

He awoke with a start, his heart racing. Eddie squinted at his watch, trying to focus his reddened, puffy eyes on the small instrument. It was 4:52—time for him to get going. If he didn't hurry, he'd be late. He reached across the car, opened the glove compartment, and grabbed a chrome .38-caliber Smith and Wesson revolver. It felt cold in his hand, and heavy, just like his mood.

He stuffed the Saturday-night special into the right-hand pocket of his dirty gray hoodie, covering it lightly with his hand to conceal its bulging shape. Then, taking another deep breath to steady his resolve, Eddie slipped the hood up over his head. He pulled on a scratched pair of sunglasses then reached for the door handle.

Wait just a dang minute, you fool. Now you look just like a bank robber.

Since it was a warm afternoon, he decided to pull the hoodie back but keep the sunglasses. He even unzipped the hoodie to vent his body heat. Satisfied, he climbed from the car.

Eddie hurried up Sprague Street toward the bank as he nervously looked around for any signs of the police. As he walked, he realized that no matter his past life of petty theft, he was about to cross a big line into felony territory. Yet, he didn't know what else to do. Life, he reasoned, had dealt him a bad hand, and he had little choice but to play it out.

As it was, he could barely make ends meet, and the wine—he always had to have the wine—quickly drained him of any money he managed to collect. Of course, none of this was his fault. It just happened despite his best efforts to the contrary.

Fate, probably.

With the proceeds from this bank heist, he'd finally be on easy street, at least for a while, and could get out of the crummy motel-room-turned-apartment he called home. Might even be able to afford three squares a day and some decent clothes.

Proceeds. He chuckled to himself. *Sounds like a business transaction. That's pretty much what it is, I guess.*

Absentmindedly, Eddie stepped into the street to make his way over to the bank entrance. Suddenly, a horn blared and brakes screeched, startling him back to the present. He retreated just in time to avoid being hit by a passing car, the angry driver shouting at him as he sped past. This was not the beginning he'd planned. He really needed to focus on the task at hand and leave the thinking for a dark alley and a full bottle of wine.

Eddie pushed through the front door a minute before closing, looked around, and then got in line behind an elderly lady at the only open teller's station. Behind him, he could hear the rent-a-cop locking up the door and turning the "Open" sign to "Closed." Time seemed to slow down as he waited to make the biggest withdrawal of his life.

Suddenly anxious, he crowded up closely behind the woman and whispered into her ear.

"What's taking so long, lady?"

Finally, the old lady turned to leave, nodding to him politely yet unable to hide the look of disgust on her face at his less than comely appearance, body odor, and obvious lack of good manners. Eddie grinned at her in response, showing his uneven, tobacco-stained teeth, and then paused to watch her make her way out the door. He turned and stepped up to the counter with all the confidence he could muster.

"How can I help you today?" the teller asked pleasantly. Her softly curled auburn hair caressed the sides of her face, and the corners of her mouth turned up slightly in what she apparently hoped would pass for a smile.

Eddie glanced at her nametag—Madelyn Jemison—and could tell immediately she was a relatively new teller. He chuckled to himself as he watched her struggle to maintain her "customer-friendly" face and attitude while trying to hide her repugnance for the man standing before her.

Eddie pulled a crumpled-up plastic grocery bag from his back pocket and pushed it across the counter. Then he leaned in close to the teller, speaking barely above a whisper.

Madelyn leaned forward. "I'm sorry, could you please say that again?"

"I said, 'Gimme all the cash in the drawer. Just bills. No coins. And make sure you don't add no dye bomb or trigger the alarm.'"

Madelyn looked stunned and simply froze in place. She'd clearly never been robbed before and probably assumed it would never happen to her.

"Now!" Eddie hissed, turning slightly to his left and pulling the gun out just enough so she could see it but no one else could.

Madelyn snapped back to reality, and though she was shaking, she grabbed the bag and quickly began emptying her cash drawer. Eddie smiled for the first time since entering the bank. He figured she didn't want to give him a reason to use his gun.

As she handed the full plastic bag back to him, she said, "This is all I have." She lifted up the drawer's slide-in cash bin for him to see.

Eddie grabbed the bag, stuffed it in his hoodie, and looked over his shoulder. The guard was eying him suspiciously and walking toward him. "Is everything all right, Maddy?" the guard called out, his hand loosely on the Glock 9mm handgun resting in its holster.

Eddie turned back to the teller. "No alarm. If I hear anything, I'll blow a hole in you big enough to drive a Mack truck through!"

Madelyn gasped and fell back a step as Eddie turned to confront the guard.

Without warning, Eddie lunged at the guard, knocking him to the ground in his rush toward the exit. "Stop!" the guard yelled as he reached for his sidearm.

Eddie turned back and saw the guard kneeling on the floor, fumbling with his weapon. "Don't do it!" Eddie shouted. But the guard still worked to un-holster his gun. Not thinking of the potential consequences—nothing new for Eddie—he pointed his Saturday-night special, still in his pocket, in the general direction of the guard and pulled the trigger.

Eddie heard Madelyn scream at the sound of the discharged gun. He looked at the guard's stunned face then watched as he crumpled to the floor without a sound. *No. No! I wasn't even aiming for him!* Eddie unlocked the front door and pushed through it at a full sprint into the street.

He ran back up the sidewalk until traffic cleared enough for him to dart across the street. Once safely across, he slowed to a walk and pulled his hoodie over his head. He didn't want to draw attention to himself. All he wanted to do was make it back to his car and then join the afternoon rush-hour traffic heading out of town. He even hoped the guard would be all right. *I'm not a violent man,* he thought, trying to convince himself.

Eddie reached his car and paused, looking to see if anyone was watching him. It didn't look like it, so he opened the door and climbed into the front seat, stashing the bag of money underneath it. He even took time to put on his seatbelt before starting the car. He looked over his left shoulder for a break in the line of cars and then pulled out into traffic. That's when he heard the bristling sound of a siren as the police began to converge on the bank.

Just in time. He sighed. *I knew my mama didn't raise no dummy. She didn't raise no genius either.* He chuckled.

Safely away for the moment, Eddie turned his full attention to driving. He couldn't deal with a fender bender right now—or worse, getting pulled over for a traffic violation. His best bet was simply to blend in with the cars leaving the city center. As he pulled to a stop at a red light, he glanced in the rearview mirror. No flashing lights. That was a relief, but he was only a couple of blocks from the bank.

I just might pull this off.

CHAPTER 2

LESS THAN TWO MILES WEST of the bank, Eddie was trying with all his might to drive at or under the speed limit and obey the other traffic laws. The last thing he needed was to draw attention to himself before he could dump his car for another. He didn't know if anyone would be able to tie the car to the bank heist or not, but he wasn't taking any chances. Abandoning this worthless car would at least slow the cops down. He hoped.

A bead of sweat trickled down Eddie's forehead and into his left eye, causing a stinging sensation, and a loud expletive escaped his lips. He wiped his eye with his shirtsleeve as he turned north onto Washington Street toward the city's beautiful and popular Riverfront Park.

The evening rush hour was in full force as the city began to empty for the day. Eddie tried to look like any other tired and bored commuter heading for his home in suburbia. The stop-and-go of downtown traffic eased a bit, and Eddie finally spotted the park up ahead.

His hastily thought-out plan was to pull into the parking lot across from the park's famous, larger-than-life children's slide in the shape of a traditional red Radio Flyer wagon. That's where most visitors parked, and Eddie figured it would be easy pickings to find a car to steal. People forgot to lock their cars all the time. His biggest challenge would be keeping his cool and waiting for the right opportunity. Knowing every cop in the city was looking for him didn't help.

Eddie turned into the parking lot and pulled into an empty space. He dragged the plastic bagful of cash from under the front seat and his old blue-and-red backpack from the back seat, and then shoved the money into the pack and zipped it shut. He reached into the glove box and grabbed his car registration and an old screwdriver.

He climbed from the car and calmly walked to the back, where he knelt on one knee and removed the license plate. He knew it wouldn't slow down the cops much, but even a few minutes could mean the difference between a clean escape and years in prison.

He tossed the license plate into his pack and looked around as he got to his feet. Nothing looked out of place. Eddie started walking up and down each row, looking for an unlocked car, hopefully with the keys still in the ignition. He strolled along several rows without success. *Not a single unlocked car! Not a single key left in the ignition! What's wrong with people around here?*

Eddie could feel the pressure building with each step. He was wary of what others might think if they watched him searching row by row, so he paused for a few minutes at the end of each row to relax and nonchalantly check his surroundings. When the coast was clear, he'd head down the next aisle. If he didn't find a car soon, he might explode.

He turned down the next-to-last row. Looking up, he spotted a group of women and children heading back to the parking lot from the park, laughing and hollering. He swore under his breath. *Now I gotta wait for them to leave! Or maybe not.* Eddie decided to change tactics. *If I can't break into a car, I might as well carjack one.* When the group passed by, he quietly fell in behind them, hanging back and looking as disinterested and nonthreatening as possible. He waited patiently for his chance to strike. He even felt strangely exhilarated.

His pulse quickened like that of a sprinter anticipating the crack of a starter's pistol. *Which of these women will become my prey?* Like a large African cat, he stalked the herd, anxiously seeking the weakest animal or one lagging behind the herd, upon which to pounce. *Should I grab a kid instead? No way! Some things you just don't do, and snatching a kid is one of them.*

The group arrived at their cars and began to divide up. Eddie hoped to single out a woman traveling alone. That would simplify his job considerably. At last, an attractive blonde woman, probably in her early twenties, walked past the others and approached her car, a taupe-colored Nissan Murano. Eddie smiled as he admired her trim figure and slender legs. She must not have had children of her own since she was traveling alone. As she searched her purse for the keys, Eddie silently made his way behind her.

He looked around. The other women were too distracted getting their children into their car seats to notice him. When the woman found her keys and pulled the door open, Eddie attacked. He shoved her into the car and climbed in behind her. He quickly pulled the door shut, pinning the woman against the console between the two front seats. She tried to scream but could barely breathe with Eddie lying across her.

He grabbed her by her long blonde hair and pulled her face close to his. She went white with shock at the realization of what was happening. Eddie knew then that he had her. He thrust the barrel of his gun firmly up under her chin. He didn't want her to misunderstand what he was about to say.

"Gimme the keys, and don't make a sound. If you scream or try to get away, I'll shoot you before you or anyone else can open the door. Understand?"

She nodded without uttering a word as she thrust the car keys in his direction.

"What's your name?" he asked.

"Addison Roberts," she replied, her voice quivering.

"Well, Addison, you can call me Eddie. I'm your new best friend. If you do exactly as I say, nothing bad will happen. I know you're scared. Heck, I'm a little jumpy myself right now. But I ain't gonna hurt you. I just need to borrow your wheels for a while to put some distance between me and the cops. When I get to a good spot, I'll let you go. Got it?"

"Yes," she whimpered.

"Good." He let go of her hair. "Now get into the other seat and put your seatbelt on. I don't want you trying to signal nobody or getting no stupid ideas about being a hero. I shot the last fool that tried that just about an hour ago and left him lying in a pool of his own blood. You don't want me to do the same to you, do you?"

"I'll do what you want, just please don't hurt me," Addison responded as she flopped over the console into the passenger seat.

Eddie tossed his pack into the back seat, and just as he snapped his seatbelt, Addison shoved her door open, trying to get out before he could respond. But the cramped parking space slowed her down. When she pushed the door open, it slammed into the side of the pickup truck parked next to them, leaving her only a narrow escape path. The precious seconds she lost trying to squeeze through allowed Eddie to lunge at her before she could get away. He grabbed a handful of hair again and yanked her back into the seat, slamming her head hard into the dashboard.

"Ouch!" she screamed, grabbing her head. "Okay, I'm sorry! Just stop hurting me."

"Shut the door, and put your seatbelt on like I said! This is your only warning. If you try that again, it'll be the last thing you ever do!"

Addison fell back into her seat and pulled the seat belt around her with trembling hands.

"That's better," Eddie said. He could see there was no blood but noticed a large red knot swelling up near her hairline. "I expect you got yourself a pretty good headache. Goes to show if you don't follow instructions, bad things happen. I'll only hurt you if you force me to. That's all on you."

Addison put both hands over her face for a moment and then rubbed her eyes as though to keep from crying.

Satisfied that Addison was now compliant, Eddie began to relax some and switched the gun to his left hand so he could keep it pointed at her while he finished getting ready to leave.

"That's the right attitude," he said softly. "Now, get out your cell phone. I know you got one."

Addison reluctantly removed her phone from her purse and tried to hand it to Eddie. He wouldn't take it.

"Crack open the case and take out the battery. When you're done, open your door and toss the phone right behind the wheel. Then hand me the battery." Eddie didn't know much about kidnapping, but anyone who'd ever watched an episode of NCIS knew smartphones could be tracked electronically—and that was something Eddie was determined to avoid.

With his gun still pointed at Addison, he started the car and backed out of the parking space in the direction of the other women. He made sure to run over Addison's phone in the process and then turned the wheel and drove away from Addison's group. With a little luck, none of them would notice anything suspicious. He checked his rearview mirror as he drove toward the exit. No one was watching. No one suspected a thing. So far, things were going his way.

Eddie pulled out of the parking lot and turned right onto Washington Street then made a quick left on Spokane Falls Boulevard. He easily merged into the last of the afternoon traffic heading to the western suburbs. *That wasn't as bad as I expected. Now I just gotta get outta town and hide 'til things quiet down.*

Eddie settled back into his seat, took a deep breath, and began to let his mind unwind. The tension of the last few hours began to drain from his body like water emptying from a kitchen sink. He glanced at Addison to make sure she was behaving and then turned on the radio, hoping to hear something—anything—on the bank heist.

Mostly, he was worried about that stupid bank guard and wondered if he'd killed him. He hadn't—couldn't have—even aimed the gun at him since it had still been in his sweatshirt pocket. So he might have wounded him but seriously doubted he'd killed him. But still, not knowing for sure bothered him. *I reckon I'll find out soon enough. What's done is done. I just gotta focus on the drive out of town and into my new life.*

Eddie wasn't certain where he would end up but planned to head north toward the safety of the mountains to hide out for a while. He had spent much of his free time there since moving to Spokane and had even cached some camping gear and dried food there.

In this part of the country, a person who knew what he or she was doing could disappear in the vastness of the mountains for months without seeing another soul. And even if he did bump into someone accidentally, it wasn't as if they'd recognize him.

Up ahead, Eddie spotted an old strip mall with more vacancies than tenants. Graffiti covered any open space fronting the vacant stores. He abruptly pulled into the parking lot and then around behind the mall. He climbed out and hustled around to Addison's side, keeping his gun trained on her the whole way.

Opening the back door behind Addison's seat, Eddie grabbed his pack, which he kept loaded with odds and ends he might need in an emergency. He reached inside and pulled out two pairs of flex cuffs—the long white plastic zip-ties popular with police departments. The uses for such a simple device were nearly endless. He also grabbed a folding knife and dropped it into his front pocket, and then tapped on the glass with his gun barrel and motioned for Addison to roll down the window. She did as instructed, her face filled with apprehension.

"I'm gonna add a little security system to make sure you don't cause me no more trouble."

"You don't need to do that," Addison said. "I won't cause any trouble. I just want you to let me go, like you said. I don't even care about the car. Just take it and go."

"Oh, I plan to let you go, on my terms. Them cuffs will make sure of that."

Eddie handed Addison one set of cuffs through the open window and told her to secure them around her ankles, checking to make sure they were tight. Then he reached through the window and fastened the other cuff around her right wrist and the armrest of the door.

"That should stop any thoughts of you escaping."

Eddie locked her door, climbed back behind the wheel, and stowed the gun under his seat. He wouldn't need it with Addison restrained.

"Roll up your window," he barked. "I hope you know there's no way for you to escape now. But if you're a good girl, everything's gonna be just fine. I got enough on my plate to take care of without having to drag you along much farther."

Eddie clicked on the window lock so Addison couldn't roll the window back down, then pulled back onto the road. Four-and-a-half miles later, he stopped at a red light at the intersection with Nine Mile Road. He nervously tapped his fingers on the steering wheel while waiting for the light to change. In a few more miles, the cityscape would fade to countryside as Spokane receded in his rearview mirror. The thought brought a smile to his face.

Eddie was bright enough to know he wasn't too bright. Still, he was confi-dent in his decision to stay away from Interstate 90 and the other major arteries, which he figured would be crawling with cops. It would take them days to find his old car abandoned across from Riverfront Park and figure out who owned it. Right now, only he and Addison knew they were leisurely heading out of town like old folks on a lazy Sunday-afternoon drive.

Before the light turned green, Eddie glanced to the left as another car pulled up to the light. *I don't believe it—a dang cop! Take a deep breath and relax. There ain't no way he knows who he's stopped next to.* The cop looked his way and nodded. Eddie smiled and nodded back. Sensing what Addison must be thinking, Eddie turned toward her.

"Don't even think about it, Addison. I already shot a man today. Might have even killed him. So, it won't make no difference if I kill you too. They can only execute me once. I'm pretty sure you're not looking to end your young life today." Addison just kept staring ahead. The light turned green, and Eddie slowly accelerated through the intersection as the police car turned left.

"Now, that's what I'm talking about!" Eddie shouted excitedly. "Ain't nobody gonna put old Eddie behind bars!"

Even as he was rejoicing in his good fortune, Eddie could see Addison slump back into her seat with her head against the window. He could tell she was frightened and on the verge of tears.

"Aw, come on now. It ain't that bad. If my luck holds, so will yours. You'll be free in no time."

Addison didn't move or even acknowledge that Eddie had spoken. That just enflamed his already mercurial temper. Unable to control himself, he slammed his fist down hard on the center console, causing Addison to jump.

"I said I'd let you go, and I meant it! Don't go getting all weepy on me. I ain't good at dealing with crying women. You best be happy or at least pretend to be. Ticking me off ain't gonna help you none."

CHAPTER 3

It had been half an hour since Eddie had carjacked Addison. They were just past the outskirts of the city and making their way north, toward the mountains. The traffic thinned, and Eddie's confidence grew with each passing mile. And finally, with time and distance, he was able to shed most of the enormous stress of the day.

He glanced over at Addison and really took stock of her for the first time. Her natural blonde hair was long and thick, with soft curls stretching from top to bottom. Her eyes were emerald green and glistened in the light of the setting sun. *She's a beautiful woman,* he thought, and for a fleeting moment, he was sorry he had dragged her into this mess. Then he looked down at her left hand, checking for a ring. *Dang.*

"Look, Addison, I know you're scared, and I'm sorry I had to grab you, but I didn't really have no choice. Truth is, I robbed a bank and shot the guard, and now I'm running from the cops. But like I told you, I don't mean you no harm."

Addison looked over at him and nodded slightly.

"Well, we got another hour or so of driving, so we might as well make the most of it. I see you got a ring on your finger. Tell me about your family."

Addison looked at him then hesitantly began. "I just got married a few months ago. It's just the two of us. We don't have children yet but plan to."

"What's his name?"

"Chase."

"Well, I bet you and Chase make a fine couple. How'd you meet?"

"Why are you asking me all these questions?"

"Just trying to make some conversation. Lighten the mood a little. You got a problem with that? You too good to talk to the likes of me?"

"No, not at all. I'm just scared. When are you going to let me go? It'll be dark soon."

"I told you already! Don't rush me. I don't like to be rushed! You're just like my ex. 'Do this; don't do that.' I'll let you go when I dang well feel like it. Now don't go asking me no more!"

In that instant, all the tension from earlier returned.

It was Addison who broke the silence. "I'm sorry, Eddie. I'm just nervous. I don't know what I'm saying half the time. You can understand that, can't you?"

"I reckon so."

"I know you don't intend to hurt me, and I hope you know I'll cooperate with you until you decide to let me go."

The two sat quietly for another five minutes. Then Addison continued. "Wisconsin. We met in Wisconsin. I was helping clean out my grandparents' house after they passed away. My mother and I were in a bad car accident there, and she was seriously hurt. Chase was the paramedic that responded and helped save her life. While Mom was recovering in the hospital, Chase stopped by to check on her, and we just hit it off."

"You from Wisconsin, then?"

"No. My family lived in Maryland at the time, so we were just visiting. My father was in the air force, and he retired out there. But my mother was from Wisconsin. I know you were married before, but are you married now, Eddie?"

"No, just once to my ex, but she left me and took the kids. I don't want to talk about that now though. It'll just make me mad. Besides, you already know more than you should about me."

The conversation faded into an uneasy silence as the miles wore on. The sun edged downward, reaching for the horizon. Eddie was tired. And thirsty. He hadn't had a drink in hours, and his head was pounding. The stressful afternoon was taking a toll on him, and he began to nod.

"Hey!" Addison yelled. "Stay awake, or you're going to get us both killed!"

Eddie swerved to get back into his lane just as an oncoming car sped past. The irritated driver in the other car laid on the horn so Eddie would know just how he felt.

Eddie let loose with a string of his favorite curse words. "Guess I'm tireder than I thought."

"You want me to drive?"

"No way! I ain't gonna sleep while you drive us straight to the cops. I'm wide awake now, but I need you to keep talking so I don't doze off no more. Now, where was we?"

"You were telling me about your ex-wife and children."

"We're not going there. Where'd you say you was from?"

"Maryland."

"That's right. How come you're out here, then?"

"Well, Chase was in ROTC in college, and when he graduated he became a second lieutenant in the air force. He worked as a paramedic until it was time for him to go on active duty. His first assignment was pilot training, where he learned to be a rescue helicopter pilot. After graduation, he was transferred out here. We got married between pilot training and moving to Spokane. It's all been such a blur."

"Chase is an air force officer?"

"Yes."

"And he works out at the base?"

"Yes."

"I done me some time in the army, but I was just a grunt. Infantry. Where's your lieutenant now?"

"He's flying home from a mission," she said, looking down at her watch. "It won't be long until he discovers I'm missing."

"Well, that ain't no good."

CHAPTER 4

As THE AFTERNOON SUN BEGAN to settle in the west, Chase looked out the Bell helicopter's window, awed by the beauties of the nature in which he was privileged to work. At twenty-five, he was a little older than the other lieutenants in his unit, but his rugged good looks, wavy brown hair, brown eyes, and outgoing personality erased any age issues with his colleagues. He was comfortable where he was and felt like he fit in.

Chase was flying as the UH-1N's copilot. Known as *Hueys*, these helicopters were the modern version of the army's workhorse of the Vietnam era. Chase was coming off a three-day shift at Cusick, the remote U.S. Air Force Survival School staff site. It was located just east of the town of Cusick and situated on more than six hundred acres in the Coleville and Kaniksu National Forests, about two hours north of Spokane.

The school used this land year-round for survival and evasion training. Helicopter crewmembers, like Chase, rotated through three-day alert periods at the school's log cabin mountain headquarters. The rustic building, nestled in the mountain forests, included bedrooms, hot showers, a kitchen, and a recreation room with satellite TV.

The helicopters flew in and out of a nearby helipad to support the training program and were continuously on alert in case of medical emergencies. Between Chase's rotations to Cusick, he spent his time back at the base engaged in flight and ground training, studying to learn his new job and performing his assigned nonflying duties.

Chase couldn't wait to get back home to Addison. He hated being away from her, even for a few days, but knew his air force career would demand many such separations, some for as long as a year. The air force had become much more of an expeditionary force in the past decades than it once was, a reflection of the shrinking number of bases around the world and the ever-present requirement to project U.S. forces to remote parts of the globe.

As the miles back to the base ticked down, he thought of little else than the upcoming reunion. He knew Addison would welcome him with open arms and a delicious, hot meal. *I wonder what she has planned for tonight. I'm starving,* he thought.

He and Addison both missed their families, of course, but starting out together in their new life was exciting. They loved the northwest in general and Spokane specifically. The people were friendly, the conservative farming values that permeated the population felt comfortable, and they both enjoyed being out of doors. *So far,* he thought, *life is treating us pretty well.*

Chase was startled from his thoughts when the aircraft commander called for the Before-Landing Checklist. As copilot, one of his duties was to read off each step as the aircraft commander accomplished it. Checklists were the bread and butter of aviation and a key facet of safe flying. The control tower cleared them to land as they turned on final approach. They would be on the ground shortly.

After landing, shutting down the helicopter, and completing the post-flight paperwork, Chase carried his flight gear into the hangar and stowed it in his locker. He joined the rest of the crew in a small conference room. The aircraft commander led them through the debriefing checklist; he was the only thing standing between his crew and their families.

"Okay, we've covered all the basics, and I know everyone wants to get home, but I'd like to discuss anything not covered by the checklist that any of you feel is important. Chase, I think this was only your second time on alert up at Cusick. How do you think it went?"

"Well, I don't really have much to compare it to, but I think it went well overall. The weather was great, and we were able to accomplish all of our required training for the students. I guess the only thing that stood out to me was that I was a little rough in the higher hovers when we were hoisting students. I'll keep working on that."

"Good observation, and you're spot on. It'll come, with practice. Just relax and sense the movement of the helicopter early and apply a gentle touch to the controls to compensate. Anything else?"

Silence.

"All right, let's get out of here. Have a great day off, and I'll see everyone when we're back in the office."

Chase called out his goodbyes as he headed for his gray Ram 4x4 quad-cab pickup. The drive home was a short five minutes. Living on base made for short commutes. Chase rounded the corner onto his street and took in the normalness of the evening. Kids were playing outside in the warmth of a beautiful afternoon. Men and women were pulling into their driveways, returning home from another day of work. Some of the adults were doing yardwork or playing with their kids. He saw his neighbor, Scott Johnsen, playing catch with his boys and waved as he drove past.

Chase pulled up to park at the curb in front of his house and hit the button on the garage door opener strapped to his sunshade. He hated carrying keys, so the garage had become his main access to the house. As the door rose, he noticed Addison's car was gone. He wondered where she was but didn't think too much of it. He walked up the driveway and entered the house through the garage.

He looked around for a note from Addison but couldn't find one. *Oh yeah, she did say she was going out with some of her new friends for the afternoon. She must not be back yet.* He opened the pantry, grabbed a couple of store-bought cookies to hold him until dinner, and then headed to the shower.

He dressed quickly after toweling off and checked the clock on his way past his nightstand. It showed 6:45 P.M. *Addison should be home by now.* She usually met him at the door when he'd been gone for a few days. *I wonder if the honeymoon is starting to wear off.* He laughed to himself. *I hope she gets home soon.* He'd been looking forward to their reunion all day. *And,* he thought, *I'm starving.* Chase walked to the living room, felt for the light switch, and flipped it on.

He crossed to the large picture window and looked outside. The soft light of early evening created the mellow atmosphere Chase loved. This was his favorite time of day. He smiled. It would be dark before long. Chase sat down in his recliner, reached for his cell phone, and punched in Addison's number. The call went immediately to voicemail. *That's strange. Maybe she's busy and doesn't want to be interrupted.* He ended the call and sent her a quick text message.

Hi, honey. I'm back from Cusick. Starting dinner now. Hope to see you soon. Call me when you can.

Well, if I'm making dinner, I'd better get moving. Chase wasn't a half-bad cook. He searched the fridge and pantry for options, then decided on something simple, the single man's best friend—spaghetti. He browned some hamburger on the stove and added in a can of tomato soup, diced onions, tomato paste, and some fresh garlic. This was his mother's recipe—simple yet delicious. He would eat it two or three nights a week, if Addison would let him.

Next, he dumped the pasta into a pot of boiling water. While it was cooking, he tossed some frozen garlic bread into the oven and a mixed vegetable steamer into the microwave to round out the meal. Dinner was ready in no time. It smelled great, and his growling stomach reminded him just how hungry he was.

Chase looked at the clock above the oven. It was nearly seven-thirty, and Addison still wasn't home. He checked his phone for the third time. Still no reply to his text. He'd been reluctant to call her right away, not wanting to look like he was checking up on her.

As a new husband, he was cautious about appearing overly protective or controlling. Besides, Addison could take care of herself in just about any situation. That was one of the things that had originally attracted him to her.

By 8:00, a rising tide of concern caused his neck muscles to tense and creases to appear on his forehead. The first signs of a headache began to take shape in the form of a dull but throbbing pain in the back of his head. *Where could she be? We hardly know any of our neighbors yet. Why hasn't she called? She has to know I'd be worried about her. This isn't like her.*

Chase took a couple of deep breaths and tried to relax. Now was the time for patience, not panic. *I'm sure everything is all right. She's probably just running late and didn't think to call. Or, more likely, her cell phone battery died and she couldn't call or text.*

He dialed her cell phone to check, but it again went straight to voicemail. *Hi, Addison. Please give me call as soon as you can. I love you.* Another thirty minutes ticked by, with him pacing the floor and watching out the window for her car. Now he was really worried. Chase called a few neighbors and friends from their Latter-day Saint ward to see if they knew where she was.

On the third call, he hit pay dirt.

"Hi, Melissa, this is Chase, Addison's husband."

"Oh, hi, Chase. We sure had fun with Addison today."

"That's great. Where did you go?"

"We took our kids to Riverfront Park, downtown. They had a blast."

"I'll bet they did. When did the group get home?"

"Oh . . . five, maybe five-thirty. Why, isn't Addison there?"

"No. I got home about six-thirty, and she wasn't here. I'm starting to get worried. Did she leave the park the same time as you?"

"Yeah, we all walked back to the cars together. I was so focused on getting my kids into their car seats and getting home, I really didn't notice Addison leaving. I don't think she carpooled with anyone. I hope she's okay."

"That makes two of us. Can you please tell me who else went to the park so I can check with them?"

"You bet. There were six of us there: Amie, Melanie, Elise, Kristin, Addison, and me. Try Kristin first. They spent the most time together. I'll give you their phone numbers if you don't already have them."

He programmed the numbers into his phone and said, "Thanks, Melissa. You've been a big help."

Chase called the other women, but the story from each was the same: the group had left at the same time, and most were back home by five-thirty. No one recalled seeing Addison actually drive away. This wasn't what Chase wanted to hear, but at least he had been able to gather some useful information.

By the time Chase wrapped up the calls, it was nearly nine o'clock. He couldn't just sit there and wait. He thought it was too early to involve the police, and not knowing what else to do, he decided to trace Addison's most likely routes to and from the park. Like most military officers, he was action-oriented. He thought if he could just find her car, that would be huge. So he put the uneaten dinner in the refrigerator, left a note on the kitchen counter in case she came home, and then drove slowly along their usual route into town. He headed directly for the parking lot where he was told the women had parked. No sign of their Murano anywhere.

Strike one. Trying to keep calm, Chase thought through the likely scenarios. *Since the car's not here, she could have left for home. I doubt if she stopped anywhere that would have taken her three hours. Her car wouldn't have been stolen, or she would have called the police and one of her friends for help.* He didn't even want to think of what else could have happened.

Chase circled the block and began an ever-widening search pattern. It was dark now, making it harder to distinguish between cars. After thirty minutes of driving, he was convinced her car was not downtown. *Strike two.* He decided to take an alternate route home but still came up empty-handed. *Strike three.* Chase's already bad mood continued to darken. He choked back the growing anxiety as he returned to his empty house.

The smell of spaghetti and garlic bread still wafted through the kitchen. Chase had been starving when he'd prepared it, but his appetite had long since disappeared. He pulled the food from the fridge and warmed it up anyway and then took his plate to the table. He tried to eat, but mostly he just stirred the food on his plate. He just couldn't eat with Addison missing.

He didn't know what to do. He didn't think the police would even take a missing person report for twenty-four hours. He started to dial Addison's mom but didn't want to get her and Addison's father all worked up when he didn't have any real information to share. He stood and started pacing. He knew he should just be patient, but this was killing him.

He checked his watch—ten-thirty. He wracked his brain for the hundredth time, trying to figure out where she might be and what he should do next. He walked back and forth, wringing his hands in a meager attempt to control his anger and frustration. The hair on the back of his neck rose, and a sense of foreboding settled on him like a cold, wet blanket, chilling him to the bone. He shivered, despite the warm temperature in the house.

Chase could stand it no longer. He'd worked through every possible explanation and listed in his mind every conceivable place Addison could be. Every avenue he pursued was a dead-end. He finally knew what he had to do and grabbed his phone.

Chase paused for a moment to think through the call he was about to make and then dialed the Spokane Police Department. A female officer answered on the second ring. "Police Department. This is Sergeant Monson."

"Hello, this is Lieutenant Chase Roberts, from out at the base."

"What can I do for you, Lieutenant?"

"My wife has gone missing. She should have been home more than four hours ago, and her cell phone has gone immediately to voicemail every time I've called. I know I'm supposed to wait a day before I report it, but I'm really worried and not sure what to do."

"It's a common misconception that you have wait twenty-four hours. You did the right thing to call. The sooner we get involved, the easier it will be to find her. We get missing person calls more often than you'd think, and most of the time, everything turns out just fine. Maybe she's out of cell tower range or her battery died. Have you checked with her friends or family?"

"She was with her friends at Riverfront Park this afternoon, but they all left for home before dinner. No one has seen or heard from her since."

"Let me take down some basic information, and then we'll get to work on finding her right away." Sergeant Monson ran Chase through the missing person report process so they could document the vital information. The report would then be provided to the detectives assigned to the case.

"Okay. That's it, Lieutenant. We'll get this moving right away. Do you have any other questions I can answer for you?"

"Can you at least check to see if her car was in an accident?"

"Sure. What's the plate number?"

Chase gave it to her, along with the make and model of Addison's car, his and her names, and his phone number.

"Please hold while I check the police blog."

This took less than two minutes. "Lieutenant, I've checked our list of accidents, and her car was not involved in any of them. I'll put out an all-points bulletin when we're done so all of our officers will be on the lookout. If it does turn up, I'll call you right away."

"Is there a way for you to check on 911 calls to see if anyone might have responded to an emergency involving her?"

"Sure, it'll just take a few minutes for me to tap into the fire department's 911 log." There was a longer pause, and then Sergeant Monson said, "Sorry again, Lieutenant. There's no record of her calling in or someone else calling in on her behalf."

"Okay. Thanks for your help."

Chase ended the call feeling even worse. *Addison, where are you?*

Not knowing what else to do, he decided to call his commander, Major Brad White. Although he was a no-nonsense commander, Major White was also compassionate and put his people first. He was a pilot's pilot and someone his subordinates trusted completely. He answered on the second ring.

"Hello."

"Major White?"

"Yes?"

"Sir, this is Chase. I hate to call you this late and at home, but I need some counsel, and I don't know where else to turn. Have you got a minute?"

"Of course. What's on your mind?"

Chase explained the situation briefly. "I'm not sure what to do next."

"You did the right thing by calling the police and then me. Give me a few minutes to touch base with the Security Forces Squadron commander, and I'll get back to you."

Chase sat with his phone in his hand, his index finger tapping out each second in rhythm with the large wall clock that hung nearby. The waiting weighed heavily on him. No one, especially Chase, liked being dependent on others to solve their personal problems. Just when it was becoming unbearable, the phone rang. He answered before the first ring ended.

"Yes, sir?"

"Chase, you were right to start the missing-person report process with the police. Since our Security Forces have a great working relationship with the Spokane Police Department, the police will keep our guys posted on the investigation, but they have jurisdiction. As I'm sure you know, the SPD is going to put out an all-points bulletin on your wife's car, so law enforcement in the area will be looking for it overnight. If Addison contacts you or comes home, call me immediately—no matter the time so we can turn the search off. If you don't hear from her, be in my office tomorrow morning at seven, and we'll decide how best to proceed. Okay?"

"Yes, sir. Thanks for your help. It means a lot. I hope to talk to you sooner rather than later."

"Me too. Now try to get some sleep. You need to bring your A game if Addison's still missing in the morning. We'll find her."

CHAPTER 5

EDDIE REACHED THE EDGE OF town where commercial buildings and strip malls gave way to suburban homes. The Murano blended right in to the flow of afternoon commuter traffic heading home. Before long, he merged onto U.S. Highway 395 toward the small town of Deer Park.

He took a deep breath and exhaled loudly, a smile on his face. They were well outside Spokane city limits, with an open road in front of them. Eddie's worst fear was a roadblock. He hadn't seen any yet and didn't think they'd have any this far out of town, but time would tell.

"I'll just bet you're hoping we hit a roadblock, ain't ya? I imagine you're dreaming about getting rescued and being back home for supper tonight." He chuckled. "Well, don't get your hopes up. The farther away we get, the better the odds of me getting away."

Addison just looked at him, disgust in her eyes, but kept quiet. After a moment, she turned her head back to the side, staring blankly out the window.

"Awe, come on. I'm just funning with you a little. You need to lighten up some. The way I see it, not running into a roadblock is what's best for you. That way, I can let you go like I said I would. But if we run into the cops, I'll have to hold you hostage. That's gotta be worse, don't you think?"

"Yeah, I guess you're right," Addison responded, with no conviction in her voice.

The last remnants of daylight faded as the traffic thinned—each passing vehicle reduced to a pair of headlights anonymously streaking past. With the onset of darkness, Addison's mood followed suit—even as Eddie's mood brightened. He actually hummed along with the radio music as he drove.

"We oughta hit Deer Park in a few minutes. Then I think we're pretty much home free," Eddie said. "And that's something worth celebrating, right?"

Getting no response from Addison, he tried another approach.

"Penny for your thoughts?" Eddie offered.

"What?" Addison replied.

"What are you thinking about? You've been way too quiet. You must be thinking about something."

"I'm thinking about my family. I'm thinking how scared they must be. I'm thinking how scared I am. And I'm wondering where you're taking me. It's hard to concentrate on anything else."

"No need for you to be scared now. I told you I ain't gonna hurt you so long as you follow orders. You been downright perfect since we left the park."

"Earlier, you said you'd drop me off somewhere. We're way outside of Spokane now, and it's dark outside. Can't you just let me out along an empty stretch of road? I have no idea where you're going, so I can't give the police any information that could hurt you."

"I will drop you off . . . just as soon as I find the right spot. Too many cars on this road, and farmhouses. I can't drop you where you could call the cops right away and rat me out. I'm more concerned about putting distance between me and the cops. Once we get past Deer Park, the traffic will die down, and most of the land up there is owned by the government, so there ain't near as many houses as there is here. And if the cops manage to catch up with us between now and then, I can use you as a bargaining chip, so just hold your horses a little longer."

"Sorry."

"Don't be sorry. I know you're worried. Heck, I would be too if our positions was reversed. But, you strike me as a pretty tough girl, and smart. Am I right?"

"I don't know. I guess so. My parents raised me to take care of myself, if that's what you mean."

"Not really." Eddie paused to think how he could put it. "I guess what I'm trying to say is, I'm sure you done some tough, hard things in your life, right?"

"Yeah."

"Okay, what's the hardest thing you ever done?"

She looked at him quizzically. "Why are you asking me that?"

"You'll see. Just play along. What's the hardest thing you ever done?"

Addison thought about it for a few minutes before replying. "Well, I guess it was when I was a little girl—about four years old. My family was visiting my grandparents' farm in Canada, and I was playing outside. I fell into an uncovered well. I don't know how deep it was, but I remember it being dark and cold and wet. Even standing on my toes, the water came up to my chin. I was really scared. I tried to call for help, but it seemed like my voice was just swallowed up by the well. Nobody knew I was in there. I thought I was going to die."

"But you didn't die. You just held on until you was found, right?"

"Yes. My dad found me."

"That's my point! Just hang on now. You'll make it."

"If you say so."

"I do." He smiled, proud of his sound and comforting advice.

Eddie looked over at the clock. It was almost seven o'clock. The news was about to come on, so Eddie reached over and turned up the volume on the radio. As he waited for the barrage of commercials to end, he replayed the day's events over and over in his mind. When the commercials ended, he listened closely, hoping for any kind of news but preferably good news. But it was just the opposite. He learned that the bank guard, a man named Ross Glover, had died at the scene.

He slammed his fist into the steering wheel, startling Addison. He cursed. "Why'd that idiot have to go for his gun, anyway? All I wanted was the money. Didn't want to hurt nobody."

"Was that the man you shot, Eddie?" asked Addison.

"Of course it was! I told you that already. But I weren't sure I hit him, let alone killed him, 'til now."

"I . . . uh, just thought you were trying to scare me. I can't believe he died."

"Well . . . nothing I can do to change it now. What's done is done."

Disgusted with the situation, Eddie turned off the radio and slumped back into his seat, a scowl on his face. They drove in silence until arriving at the edge of the small town of Deer Park. Eddie slowed down to match the new speed limit then looked down at the gas gauge.

"We gotta get gas," he growled as he pulled into an old Conoco on the near side of town.

Eddie slowed to a stop, with the passenger door away from the cashier's kiosk. "Don't get no fancy ideas, Addison. You can't get loose from them flex cuffs, and the cashier can't see you from where she's sitting. If I see you trying anything stupid, I'll knock some sense into you, and it ain't gonna be pretty."

He reached over and grabbed Addison's purse, hoping to find enough cash to fill the tank. He knew from watching NCIS that cops could track credit cards, so he planned to use Addison's cash first and then tap into the bank cash later if he had to.

Eddie found some cash, opened his door, and got out, quickly making his way to the kiosk to pay in advance. Once he got the gasoline flowing, he stooped down with his face close to Addison's window and tapped on the glass. She looked at him, and he just smiled back at her. She shivered.

Eddie filled the gas tank and then returned to the kiosk, where he bought a pack of cigarettes, two hot coffees, and a couple of granola bars for the rest of the trip. It was getting late, and he needed to stay awake. He paused a few seconds to look around the area before heading back to the car. Not a single soul around them except for the kiosk lady, and she was too busy with her romance novel to notice Addison anyway. Eddie climbed back into the car and deposited his Styrofoam cup in one of the holders in the console. He handed the other cup to Addison.

"No, thanks. I don't drink coffee."

"What? Who don't drink coffee?"

"I just don't like the way it tastes, but thank you anyway."

"Suit yourself. You paid for it. You want a granola bar?"

"Yes, please. I'm pretty hungry."

"Here you go. It ain't much, but it'll help."

Eddie started the car and pulled onto the street. He moved slowly through town until he saw a sign for Milan then turned right. It didn't take long to hit the eastern edge of Deer Park. In another three or four miles, they turned north again onto Newport Highway toward the tiny town of the same name. They passed fewer and fewer buildings, and the number of vehicles on the road dropped substantially.

Eddie slowly cooled off after his last emotional outburst. He might even say his spirits were starting to rise a little since there wasn't a cop in sight and he didn't expect any. It felt good to be heading back toward the mountains where he felt more comfortable and safe. They were rapidly closing in on the spot where he usually camped and had hidden his supply stash.

Ten minutes later, they passed the quaint welcome sign for Newport. They cruised by the decrepit buildings passing loosely for a downtown and then turned left onto State Highway 20. They were now paralleling the Pend Oreille River. Eddie knew it was a beautiful river in the daylight, but tonight, it was visible only by the absence of light where it wound its way through the valley.

He reached for the radio again and turned up the volume. He figured the eight o'clock newscast would be longer and more detailed. He was right. After a couple of minutes of national and world news, Eddie heard what he was hoping for.

"And in local news, law enforcement agencies are still searching for leads in the bank robbery that took place just before closing at Harvest Savings Bank and which resulted in the death of security guard Ross Glover. Witnesses described the gunman as a white male, mid-forties, and disheveled. He was wearing a gray hoodie, sunglasses, and well-worn jeans. He is believed to have fled the crime scene by vehicle. Police are unsure if any other people were involved. Law enforcement agencies statewide are setting up vehicle checkpoints and urging people to lock the doors to their vehicles and homes. Anyone with information is asked to call the Crime Tips Hotline."

Eddie turned the volume back down. A smile creased his cheeks. They hadn't connected Addison's disappearance with him yet and had no idea he was driving a Murano. *How cool is that? Another few minutes and we'll be safely tucked away at my camp.*

They pulled through a four-way stop that marked the town of Usk, unnoticed by any of the local residents, most of whom had apparently already turned in for the night. Eddie and Addison continued up Highway 20, past the tiny village of Cusick. There were no other vehicles on the road.

The river still flowed darkly and quietly on their right, and Winchester Peak loomed large on their left. A setting three-quarter moon hung like a chandelier just above the peak.

The road bent sharply to the right around the base of Ruby Mountain. As they curved back to the north, the road straightened out. Suddenly, flashing blue and red lights appeared in the distance, instantly grabbing Eddie's attention. *That could be one of them checkpoints!*

He instinctively slammed on the brakes and skidded to stop. He had to quickly decide what to do. He looked up at the cop car. It was hard to tell how far ahead it was or if it was a roadblock or just someone the cop had pulled over. *I could just keep driving and take my chances. If the cop has someone pulled over, no problem. But if it's a roadblock, I could be toast. They don't know I'm driving a Murano—at least, I don't think they know. But Addison just might say or do something to mess things up.*

As Eddie crept closer to the flashing lights, he saw his way out and took it. He turned left onto an unmarked dirt road, which followed a draw up into the mountains. He kept looking over his shoulder to see if the cop car moved. *So far, so good. Just stay put, man!* Eddie killed the headlights and slowed to a crawl, squinting to see the road in the dim moonlight as his eyes adjusted to the dark.

"Where are we going now?" Addison asked.

"Away from that cop, duh! You think I'm stupid enough to risk running into a roadblock?" he shouted.

"No. I don't think you're stupid at all," she responded quietly.

The flashing lights remained stationary and soon passed from sight as Eddie followed the road into the wooded foothills. That either meant the cops hadn't seen them or they weren't going to follow them. *Guess he could be waiting on backup, but it don't matter none—we're committed now.*

As they bounced along the dirt road, the terrain steepened and the road became more deeply rutted, forcing him to slow down even more. "I can walk faster than this!" Eddie growled. Up ahead, they emerged into a small clearing where the road forked and both lanes disappeared back into the woods.

Eddie took the right fork for no reason. *When you ain't got a clue where you're going, any road will get you there,* he thought. They crawled along slowly, relying on the moonlight knifing through the trees to light their way. A few minutes later, he pulled to a stop.

"Stay here," he snarled.

Eddie got out of the car and walked back down the road, carefully listening for the sound of an approaching vehicle. It was quiet except for the chirping of crickets and the occasional rustling sounds of night animals searching for food. Finally, satisfied he wasn't being followed, he returned to the car.

"Well, I guess we're gonna park here tonight. You might as well get comfortable."

"I have to go to the bathroom. Can I at least get out for a few minutes?"

"Yeah. But stay right up against the car," he said, cutting through her restraints. "Don't worry, I won't look."

After she finished her business, Addison stretched and walked around. She stayed close to the car but seemed reluctant to get back in. Eddie indulged her for a while and then pulled another flex cuff from his backpack and nodded in the direction of the car. Addison slowly climbed back in. Eddie reached over to tie her arm to the armrest but left her legs unbound.

"There," he said smiling. "Now I can get some rest knowing you ain't going nowhere." He climbed into the back seat, folded his body as best he could in the cramped space, and then closed his eyes.

***

Chase sat motionless in his easy chair. The TV was on—an attempt to crowd out the silence—but he was oblivious to the programming. He could only think of one thing—Addison. After checking his watch for the tenth time in so many minutes, he decided to put the matter into God's hands and hope for the best. Chase dropped to his knees and made a passionate plea for help, and then he returned to his chair to continue his vigil.

He knew the police were already on it, at least in the form of an APB for Addison's car. Finding that would be a big win by itself, but the leads that may come from it could be pivotal to finding Addison. Chase's biggest challenge, though, remained the waiting. Not knowing when or even if results would come seemed like a slow, torturous process.

His mind wandered back to the time he and Addison first met. Although their meeting grew out of the strenuous circumstances of a car crash and a lifesaving surgery for Addison's mother, his memories of that time were mostly fond. He smiled to himself as he thought of how carefree and exciting those early moments in their romance seemed. He wasn't sure he believed in love at first sight, but their romance was pretty close. It seemed like a lifetime ago, and Addison hadn't even been gone a full day. He just hoped she was okay—wherever she was.

CHAPTER 6

DAY 2

BY TWO O'CLOCK IN THE morning, sleep finally overcame Chase, and he slumped in the chair. He adjusted his position frequently, checking his watch each time before slipping back into a fitful sleep. Somewhere in the recesses of his mind, he knew Addison was in trouble, but after praying, he had also received the comforting assurance that all would be well in the end. This eerie combination of nightmare and dream left him simultaneously unsettled yet calm.

Eventually, a shaft of morning sunlight broke through a gap in the curtains, warming Chase's face after what seemed like the longest night of his life. A few moments later, he stirred, realizing the new day was upon him. He checked his watch. It was 6:35. He stood up, stretched, and tried to work out a kink in his neck. Then he hurried back to his bedroom, cleaned himself up, and changed into his uniform. He was out the door in less than fifteen minutes.

At the office, he paced outside his commander's door, waiting for a chance to see him. It was only seven o'clock, but the military always began the day early. His commander had probably already been here for an hour or so. For that, he was especially grateful this morning. The door opened and his commander, Major Brad White, paused to say goodbye to his guest. Chase looked at him anxiously.

Major White was an up-and-comer in the helicopter world. On the basis of some daring and successful combat rescues, he'd been promoted early and given command of the detachment in which Chase worked. By all accounts, he was still performing well above average. He put the detachment's mission first, but his people were a very close second. Taking care of them and their families had earned him both respect and intense loyalty.

"Chase, no news yet on my end. How about you?"

"None, sir. And, it's driving me crazy!"

"I'm sure it is. Come in and shut the door. I know we didn't have a lot of time last night to talk, so I'm anxious for more details. Then we'll check in with Major Saxby."

Chase sat down in the chair facing his boss's desk and laid out the events of the last fourteen hours.

"I hate to ask you this, Chase, but is there any reason Addison would leave you, even temporarily? Did the two of you have a fight? Is she missing her family? Is there any explanation you can think of for her leaving voluntarily?"

"No, sir. She misses her family, but we're still in the honeymoon phase of our marriage and can hardly stand to be apart. None of her things are missing except her purse, cell phone, and the car. The fact that she didn't pack a bag tells me this isn't voluntary. She's never done anything like this before or threatened to leave."

"That's just what I'd expect, but I'm going to ask the question differently, just to make sure we're communicating. Is there anything at all you aren't telling me? I'd hate to find out about something that discredits us or the air force after the fact."

"Absolutely not, sir!" he almost shouted, his anger boiling near the surface.

Major White raised his eyebrows at Chase's sudden outburst.

"Sorry. I'm a little on edge. I know you're just trying to help."

"I understand. Don't worry about it. Go on."

"I called around to some of her friends and found out she'd been to Riverfront Park with them yesterday afternoon, but none of them actually saw her get into her car when the group split up in the parking lot to head home. I drove downtown last night, and her car's not where the women said she'd parked. I've talked to everyone I can think of, but that's all I've been able to come up with."

"Have you called Addison's parents to see if she's there or if they know where she is?"

"No, sir." Chase frowned. "I didn't want to worry them last night. I know I should have."

"That's for sure. Why don't you step into the hall and call them now. Come back in when you're through." Before Chase was out the door, the major called after him, "And call your parents too. That's an order."

Chase was back in less than five minutes.

"Did you talk to them?"

"Yes, sir. Addison's not there, and they haven't heard from her. They're going to fly here as soon as they can find a flight."

"How about your parents?"

"They're in Europe at the moment and didn't answer when I called, so I left a voicemail."

Major White nodded and then turned in his chair to the credenza behind him, picked up the phone, and dialed a five-digit, on-base extension. When it rang through, Major White put the phone on speaker.

"Good morning. This is Major White for Major Saxby, if he's available."

He tapped his fingers on the desk while the secretary got her boss on the line. Major Saxby was the new commander of the Security Forces Squadron—the air force's police force. Major Saxby was in his mid-thirties, with dark, rich ebony skin. He'd been a highly regarded collegiate athlete in the Big Ten but had chosen public service over professional sports. He still carried a deeply embedded competitive spirit and never met a challenge he didn't defeat.

"Hey Sax, this is Brad. I'm calling to follow up on our conversation last night."

"Lieutenant Roberts, right?"

"That's right. He's here with me, and I've got you on speaker. Have you got a minute to discuss the situation?"

"I can do better than that. I've got ten minutes, and then I have to run to a meeting. Lieutenant, I'm sorry your wife has gone missing. We'll put every resource we have on it, at least to the extent the Spokane Police Department will allow."

"Thank you, sir."

"I spoke with the police chief just before you called. She said you reported your wife missing last night. That's the most important thing you could have done. Are you available to sit down with our desk sergeant this morning and bring him up to speed?

"Yes, sir. I can come right now."

"Good. That will get us all on the same sheet of music."

"Mind if I tag along?" Major White asked.

"Not at all. That's right where you should be."

"My thoughts exactly. Thanks, Sax. Talk to you later."

"I wanted to make sure I understood the process since it's not every day someone in the unit goes missing," White said.

"I understand, sir, and thanks for letting me listen in."

"Let's get moving. You can ride with me. When we're done, let's head to the police station and see if we can talk to the detectives handling the case. They'll want to talk to you soon anyway."

As the two left the office, Major White paused at his secretary's desk. "Please cancel my morning appointments. I'm working on a family emergency."

The two made the short drive to the Security Forces headquarters in grim silence. When they pulled up, Major White led the way. "Chase, follow my lead once we get inside. Part of my job is breaking down barriers and greasing the gears of the bureaucracy. Your job is to provide the detailed information when asked."

"Yes, sir."

They quickly found their way to the desk sergeant, the noncommissioned officer managing the day's security-forces activity on the base. He sat behind a bulletproof window that looked similar to a drive-through teller's booth.

"Hi, I'm Major White, and this is Lieutenant Roberts. We're here to file a missing person report."

"Yes, sir. I'm Technical Sergeant Veliz. Major Saxby let me know you'd be here. Please step around the corner, and I'll let you into the office. You'll be meeting with Senior Master Sergeant Whitmill, the senior NCOIC, today. I hope you're not in a hurry. This could take a while."

"This is the only thing on the calendar this morning," Major White replied.

The two men walked toward the reinforced security door, which opened from the inside as they approached. They were now inside the twenty-four-hour command post for all law enforcement matters on base, and entry was tightly controlled. In addition to the senior noncommissioned officer in charge, two NCOs and an airman worked inside the vault.

Sergeant Veliz led them to the conference room, where Sergeant Whitmill welcomed them. "Have either of you gentlemen ever been here before?" Both Major White and Chase shook their heads. "That's not unusual, and it's probably a good thing. Let's sit down at the table and get to work. First, let me say how sorry I am for your wife's disappearance, Lieutenant."

"Thank you."

"I've taken the liberty of pulling your records so I could get a head start on the paperwork. I know you've already provided the police most of this information, but the redundancy will allow for better collaboration with them in the future. Sir, could you please review what I've entered so far, for accuracy?"

He removed a set of forms from a file folder and passed them across the table to Chase. He and Major White both slowly read the entries and nodded their approval.

"Great. I'll need your help to fill out the rest of the forms. This part of the process is intentionally slow and repetitive, but we want to make sure we don't overlook anything that could help us find your wife, so I'd appreciate your patience. When we're done, I'll pass it along to the OSI."

The Office of Special Investigations was the air force equivalent of police detective bureaus. Chase felt a measure of comfort knowing that they would be part of the investigation. *Finally! Things are starting to move forward.*

The sergeant continued. "The SPD will take the lead on the case and coordinate with us on the investigation. I've requested an agent be here in an hour so you can get all of your interviews out of the way in one visit. Any questions, sir?"

"No," Chase replied. "Let's get started."

CHAPTER 7

AFTER WHAT HAD SEEMED LIKE an eternity of darkness to Addison, the first rays of the rising sun settled on the car like a soft morning dew, barely perceptible at first, then gradually embracing her consciousness. It had been a long and uncomfortable night. Despite her fatigue, the flex cuff strapping her right wrist to the armrest kept her from sleep. The sharp edges dug into her skin so that any time she moved, a bolt of pain shot up her arm, making sleep impossible.

As minutes turned to hours, the chafing transformed the irritated skin into an open wound, leaving the armrest red with blood. As if that wasn't enough, her mind kept racing as she wondered what the new day would bring and if it would be her last. As scary as that thought was, Addison forced herself to consider her options and pull together a plan on how she would respond to whatever Eddie might throw at her the next day.

As she sat awake, her mind flooded with a myriad of memories on self-defense and how she should act if she were ever taken hostage or assaulted. *I wish I'd paid more attention during those college classes.* Like everyone, Addison knew bad things happened but couldn't possibly have imagined them happening to her. She scoffed wryly to herself. Then a thought popped into her mind. Whether it was inspiration or just a random thought, she couldn't tell. But it seemed to be just what she needed.

She remembered a lesson from girls' camp about how to face difficult situations. She couldn't remember who had taught it or what most of the workshop was about, but she did remember one phrase that stood out to her at the time: *In most dangerous situations, it is better to act than to react.* What a simple yet profound concept. She knew she couldn't openly challenge Eddie without getting hurt, but in that moment, she vowed to look for opportunities to make good things happen and resist the typical victim's more compliant role.

She also decided she'd try to humanize herself in the eyes of her kidnapper. *Who knows? If he sees me as a human being, he might even soften up a little.*

These two thoughts weren't much, but they formed the basis of the plan she decided to follow, and that gave her hope. Even without much sleep, she was energized and wide-awake. And, most importantly, she was ready to face this new day, no matter what it might bring.

Eddie stirred a short while later then sat up and stretched. Addison remained motionless, with her eyes closed. Notwithstanding her growing confidence, now that Eddie was awake, she just couldn't face him quite yet. She heard him open the back door and slam it shut as he left. Curious, Addison cracked an eye open and could see him heading into the trees, probably to relieve himself.

He returned less than two minutes later, grabbed his backpack and slammed the door shut again. This time, Addison had to sit up straighter to see him. He was walking up the road in front of the car. *What on earth is he doing? He can't be leaving me strapped inside the car!*

To her relief, he stopped along the side of the road and looked up at a rock outcropping that stood about fifteen feet above the road. He took off the backpack and set it down then climbed to the top. As she watched, Addison realized that Eddie was trying to see over the trees. *He must be trying to figure out where we are.*

She watched him climb back down, grab his backpack, and start walking back toward the car. She couldn't tell if he was pleased with what he saw or disappointed. *I guess I'll find out soon enough.* Eddie covered the distance rapidly. When he got back to the car, he pulled open the rear door and tossed his backpack in.

"Morning, sunshine. I hope you slept good last night. I sure did. Slept like a baby, as a matter of fact. And, it's a beautiful morning—sun's up, air's fresh, and ain't nobody nowhere near us to help you out, not even the cops."

Addison just glared at him.

"What? Cat got your tongue? You can't even be polite to old Eddie?"

"Can you let me out, please? My wrist is raw from the plastic strap, and I need to go to the bathroom."

"Sure thing. I wouldn't want you wetting yourself or nothing like that." He laughed.

Eddie walked around to the other side of the car and pulled the door open, nearly dragging Addison out in the process. The plastic flex cuff cut deeper into her wrist, causing Addison to scream at the sudden jolt of pain shooting up her arm. Tears formed instantly in her eyes, and she held her breath against the throbbing as blood flowed freely from the open wound.

"Oh, sorry about that. I don't know what I was thinking." He chuckled.

He pulled out a pocketknife and sliced through the flex cuff, freeing Addison's arm for the first time in more than seven hours. Addison bit her lower lip to keep from yelling at Eddie. As hard as it was, she felt her chances of survival were better if she tried to befriend him. It was an important part of her new plan.

"Thank you," she whispered. "Can I have some privacy now?"

Eddie laughed aloud again but moved slowly around to the other side of the car as if to make sure Addison knew who was in charge.

"You know the rules."

When Addison reemerged, Eddie tossed her one of the prepackaged food bars he'd brought along in his pack.

"Hope you like your breakfast."

"I'm so hungry, I'll eat anything. Thank you."

After a couple of bites, Addison thought she'd take a chance with Eddie. "I noticed you climbed onto some high ground and looked around. Did you see what you were looking for?"

"I seen some of what I was looking for but not all of it. I'm pretty sure I know where we is and where we's heading, but it'll take most of the day to get there. More important is what I didn't see—and that was signs of civilization and cops. Ain't many folks up here in this part of the national forest, even this time of year. I expect we'll be all by ourselves most of the day."

"Are you planning to take me with you or leave me like you promised?"

"That's the big question of the day, but I ain't for certain yet."

"But Eddie, you can just leave me here. It'll take me all—"

In the blink of an eye, Eddie brought a fierce backhand across Addison's face, knocking her to the ground. She stayed down, holding her fists and forearms up to protect her face, like a boxer being pummeled. Thankfully, Eddie didn't come at her again. While she laid there, she struggled to get her wits about her. As her head cleared, she pushed herself into a sitting position.

"Why do you keep hitting me, Eddie?"

"Because this ain't no democracy, and you don't get no vote! You do exactly what I say, no more and no less. If I say we walk, then we walk. I don't want to hear nothing out of you trying to tell me what I gotta do. You got that?"

"Yes."

"Now get back into the car and put your seat belt on."

Addison climbed in and pulled the door shut while Eddie walked around the car and climbed in behind the wheel. She wondered why he didn't zip-tie her to the armrest again. Eddied started the engine and drove up the road to where the terrain dropped away steeply on the right side. After finagling the car sideways on the narrow road, he finally got the front pointed toward the edge.

He put the car in park but left the engine running. He grabbed his back-pack, gun, and the rest of Addison's cash before he climbed out of the car.

Suddenly, Addison thought Eddie planned to send her over the cliff with the car. Her hand began to shake as she took hold of the door latch in case she would have to jump.

"Time to get out, Addison, unless you want to ride the roller coaster over the edge. It ain't as big of a drop as I'd like, but it'll do. It's time to say goodbye to your car."

Addison breathed out a big sigh of relief as she climbed out of her car. "But why do this, Eddie?" Addison asked before remembering her last mistake. "I know; I don't get a vote."

"That's a fact. You and me both know by now the cops is looking for you and your car. They might even have tied me and you together. That's why we gotta dump it now in a way that makes it hard for prying eyes to see. I don't want nothing showing the cops where we been or which way we's going."

Addison felt her hope sink as fast as a loose anchor in a deep lake. Her shoulders slumped, and her head dropped as she studied the ground around her feet, trying hard but failing to keep her emotions under control.

Eddie, on the other hand, was like a little kid at an amusement park. Addison looked back up to see a big grin on his face. He reached inside the car, shifted it into drive, and then jumped back. The car lurched forward and the front wheels shot over the edge, but it came to a quick stop as it high-centered. It teetered back and forth until Eddie ran at it from the back and pushed until it tipped downhill and slid off the road. It crashed through the underbrush and new saplings before coming to an abrupt halt at the base of a big pine tree. It sat with the back up in the air and the car tilted to the right.

"Woo-hoo! That's something I've always wanted to do. Never thought it would happen like this though. That was awesome!"

"I guess it depends on your perspective."

"Oh, don't be such a party pooper. Come on. You can help me cover it up."

"Great."

They slid down the embankment to where the car was smashed up against the tree. The engine was still running, and steam was shooting out from under the hood. The radiator must have cracked on impact. Eddie reached inside and turned the ignition off then threw the keys as far into the woods as he could.

"Grab some loose brush, Addison. I want you to pile it up against each wheel. Then I want you to scoop up as much dirt as you can and toss it up on top, especially on the back window. I'm gonna cut some saplings to lay up against the sides and on top when you're done."

Addison did what she was told but worked slowly. Not only was it hard to trash her brand new car, but if the police were ever going to find her, this was the biggest clue they'd have. She didn't want to make it harder for them than she had to.

Eddie was back a few minutes later with half a dozen young saplings he was able to cut down with his folding knife. He laid a couple across the back of the car. Then he laid another one on top of the car, with the branches hanging over the back window. Finally, he leaned the rest diagonally along the car's more exposed side.

He stepped back to inspect their work. "We ain't done half bad, Addison. I doubt the cops will find this anytime soon. But even if they do, it'll still give us a good head start."

Addison just shook her head.

CHAPTER 8

CHASE AND HIS BOSS SPENT the better part of two hours at the Security Forces Squadron, where he completed the missing person report and was then interviewed by Mr. Mike Stoker, an OSI agent. Chase hated the experience but was respectful and completely honest in his answers. He hoped he had nothing to worry about.

"I think we're finished here, Lieutenant. I'm sorry to have to put you through the process, but I'm sure you understand it's important to eliminate you as a suspect quickly," explained Mr. Stoker.

Chase was well aware that in the case of a missing adult, the spouse was almost always considered a prime suspect. He nodded. "I just hope you can now focus your efforts on finding Addison."

"We will. The SPD has the lead on this case since Addison's last known location was not on federal property. I'll follow their investigation and give them whatever support they may need from the air force. The good news is they have far more resources than we do and coordinate well with the other law enforcement agencies in the area."

"And the bad news?"

"I'm afraid they'll run you through the same question mill I just did. It's more about bringing them up to speed than anything else, so it's important that you cooperate with them, just like you did with me, to allow them to get on with the investigation."

"I understand. I'll do my best. Thanks for the advice."

"Would you like me to set up an appointment with them?"

"Please do. We planned on going there next anyway. I assume you'll send them a copy of this interview as well?"

"Yes, sir. Give me a second, and I'll make the appointment."

Fortunately, Mr. Stoker was able to get an appointment for Chase at the police department for just thirty minutes from then. Chase and Major White left the Security Forces building and walked to the parking lot.

"Sir, I can handle the police interview myself. I doubt if they'll ask anything different than Mr. Stoker asked. I don't want to tie you up any more than I have already."

"I don't mind going with you, Chase. Finding Addison is more important than anything else on my plate."

"I know, and I really appreciate it. I'll call you if I need anything during the interview, and I'll follow up with you afterward. Is that okay?"

"Of course. But I want you to know, I'll be immediately available day or night for you. It's no imposition. I want to be as involved in finding Addison as possible. Got it?"

"Yes, sir. And thanks again."

"And one more thing, Lieutenant. I imagine the police will turn your life upside down over the next day or two. Patience and courtesy are your two best friends. Let the police do their jobs as they investigate you, and be careful not to offend or alienate them. You'll need them on your side going forward."

"Patience isn't one of my strengths, so I'd better work on it."

Midday traffic was light, and the drive downtown only took fifteen minutes. Chase pulled into the police headquarters parking lot, found an open visitor's space, and parked his truck. He took a moment to compose himself, breathing in deeply and exhaling, and then headed through the front door to check in at the desk.

"Hi, I'm Lieutenant Roberts from the air force base. I have an appointment with Detective Strickland to report a missing person."

"Good morning, Lieutenant," the woman at the desk said. "We've been expecting you. If you'll follow me, I'll take you to him."

The desk officer met him at the door leading from the lobby into the working area of the department and led Chase to an open interview room. Two detectives joined them shortly, and the officer excused herself.

"Hi, I'm Ted Strickland, and this is my partner, Floyd Bateman."

They shook hands and exchanged nods as the three men sized each other up. Ted had the grizzled look of a seasoned professional, if not a bit old-school. He was dressed in a rumpled suit with his shirt collar unbuttoned and the knot of his tie loosened. He had short, salt-and-pepper hair and carried two pens in his handkerchief pocket to go with the small notebook on the table in front of him.

Floyd looked a few years younger than Ted and was dressed in a sport coat, slacks, and an open-collar dress shirt. His thick brown hair was longer than Ted's and was neatly parted on the side. Only a few gray hairs at his temples. There was a tablet on the table in front of him, sitting next to his cell phone.

"Have a seat," Floyd said, pointing to the chair at the end of the table. "We're sorry to hear about your wife, Lieutenant," said Floyd. "We talked to the desk sergeant at the base and the OSI agent you met with this morning. We've worked with Mr. Stoker before. He's a good man. We already have copies of your missing person report and the OSI interview, along with the information you provided over the phone last night. We'll be working with the OSI, but I think they told you we'd be taking over the case."

"Yes, I understand."

"Good. First, we apologize for the redundancy, but we need to hear your story straight from your mouth, and then we'll see where we go from there. All right?"

"I'm all yours, Detectives."

The three of them huddled together for the next ninety minutes, covering and re-covering every element of Addison's disappearance: who Chase had called, what they'd said, and where he had searched. No detail was too small, and no one wanted to leave any stone unturned. If this turned out to be an abduction, the first forty-eight hours would be crucial to a successful outcome, and half of that was already gone. The meeting wrapped up just after noon.

"Sorry again to have to put you through the wringer when you are worried about your wife, but any little piece of information can potentially break the case wide open," Floyd said.

"I get it. I wouldn't want it any other way. I know time is of the essence, so I'd appreciate your best efforts, and I promise I'll help you in any way I can, day or night. I'll gladly give you access to any of our personal information, my cell phone, and our computer—anything you think might be useful—so you don't have to wait on a warrant and so you can move beyond me and focus your efforts on finding Addison."

Ted extended his right hand and grabbed Chase's left arm as they shook.

"Thanks, Chase. I'm sure Floyd and I will have more questions as the investigation unfolds. We appreciate your candor this morning and your willingness to cooperate with the SPD. Oh, and if you can get us one of Addison's recent photos, we'll use it to enlist the public's help in finding her."

"No problem. I hope you'll keep me posted if you uncover anything useful. Just sitting at home not knowing what's going on is killing me."

"We'll do the best we can, but you know, we don't comment much on open investigations. We cut the families a little slack when we can, but we want you to have the right set of expectations."

"Yeah, I know. I'm just saying I'd appreciate anything you can share with me. Addison means more to me than anything in the world, and I want her safe and back home as soon as possible."

The detectives walked Chase back to the lobby, where they parted. Chase left, climbed back into his truck, and headed home, more depressed now than ever. *Patience and courtesy. Patience and courtesy. I guess my ability to employ both is about to be tested to breaking point.* He didn't know what to expect, but if they were about to turn his life upside down as Major Saxby said, he knew he had to be ready for just about anything.

When Chase arrived home, he was determined to be as proactive as he could. For the next couple of hours, he went through all of their files, setting aside anything that the police might request in the coming days. He figured they would be investigating him first, and probably more invasively than anyone else in the near-term since he was the best and only suspect at the moment.

By the time he finished up, he had compiled a folder that contained all their financial, social media, and email account information, with usernames and passwords. He included the latest statements from every company they currently did business with and produced a list of immediate family members and his and Addison's closest friends with their contact information.

That should do it, he thought as he pushed back from his desk. He hoped this would not only give them a head start on Addison and him but that it would help him win the trust and confidence of the police. *Then they can find Addison.*

CHAPTER 9

EDDIE WAS HAPPY WITH THE results of his and Addison's camouflaging efforts, and his disposition turned a little more pleasant. He was energized by their clean getaway and was anxious to keep moving. The morning was nearly gone, and the temperatures were on the rise as the sun neared its pinnacle.

He turned and bounded back up to the embankment to retrieve his backpack. He pulled out a compass and a topographical map and studied both. Then, pulling out a pencil, he oriented the map to true north and drew a line between his current location and his cache. Then he laid the compass next to the line and computed the correct heading to take them there.

So far so good, Eddie thought to himself. *Now all I got to do is get back to my cache and do what I do best—relax, have a drink, and enjoy Mother Nature.* He had enough food, water, and wine stashed there to keep him happy for a couple of weeks. *Plenty of time for things to quiet down.*

He heard Addison trudge up the hill behind him and soon saw her looking over his shoulder.

"Where are we going next, and how far away is it?" Addison asked.

"I figure my camp is six or seven miles from here on a heading of, oh . . . 350 degrees. We might could cover that distance before dark if we get moving, and the terrain ain't too bad."

"Look, Eddie, why don't you just leave me here? It will take the cops a long time to find my car, if they ever do, and it will take me hours to hike out to a road and probably longer to flag down help. That would give you a big head start. And you could move much faster without me. I won't be able to hike very fast in the shoes I'm wearing."

"Hmm. That ain't a bad idea. But I've grown quite fond of your company. I'll tell you what though. If it starts looking like things are staying quiet and the cops ain't got a clue where I am, I may tie you up and then call the cops with your location after I'm safely away. Besides, you just seen my map and where I'm going. You can't expect me to just turn you loose. Anyway, now ain't the time to negotiate—it's time to hike! I'll lead; you follow—but if you try to run, I'll catch you and beat you like you were one of Mike Tyson's punching bags. That's if I don't just shoot you. Understand?"

Addison bowed her head in resignation. "Yes. I won't try to run."

The first hour wasn't too bad. The terrain was hilly and steep at times, but there was little underbrush to get in their way, and the trees provided partial shade from the midday sun. They stayed true to the course Eddie had set, and before long, they had put two hours and maybe three miles behind them.

"Can we take a break, Eddie? I'm starting to get blisters on my heels. Do you have a first aid kit with you?"

Eddie looked at his watch then up at the sky.

"Yeah, we can stop for a few minutes. I've got some Band-Aids in my pack."

They sat down to rest while Addison tended to her blisters. Eddie pulled out his canteen, took a couple of long swallows, and then passed it to Addison. She looked disgusted but wiped off the spout and drank until Eddie grabbed the canteen. They were up and hiking again as soon as Addison applied the bandages.

"Eddie, these Band-Aids are going to come off pretty fast, and my heels will really start hurting. I'm not trying to slow you down. Just stating the facts. You'll be able to move much faster without me."

Eddie turned around suddenly, boiling with anger.

"I already told you no!" he shouted. "Is you deaf or just stupid? Bring it up again and I'll hurt you bad! And that will be on you! Now just shut up and walk."

* * *

The sun was still high in the summer sky but clearly past its zenith. The heat beat down on them through the sparse pines, with little shade to be found. Addison had fallen behind Eddie by about twenty-five yards. Not having her hiking shoes was tearing up her feet. She looked up and watched as he crested yet another of the seemingly endless ridges and paused to look around while he waited for her to catch up.

Addison looked at her watch—the one Chase had given her last Christmas. Oh, how she missed him and worried about him. They'd been walking for nearly four hours. *We have to have traveled at least six miles. And if that's true, Eddie should be able to make out some familiar landmarks by now.* But that didn't seem to be the case, and it worried her. *I don't know if it's better to be lost in the woods with a killer or at his camp where he might decide he doesn't need me around any longer.* The thought made her shudder. She crested the ridge and saw Eddie standing there, looking at her.

"How much farther 'til we get to your camp?" Addison asked as she slumped to the ground next to where Eddie stood.

"Can't say."

"Can't or won't?"

Eddie gave her a withering look.

"Can't, just like I said!"

"Why not? Are we lost?"

"I ain't lost!" he bellowed. "I know we're getting close, but I don't recognize nothing around here. I expect it just looks different coming from this direction."

Addison sucked in as much air as she could and rested her raw, bleeding feet.

"Stay put. I'm gonna take a look around. I'll be back in a couple of minutes."

Addison watched as Eddie headed up the ridgeline in search of a better view. While she rested, Addison tried to decide what to do. *Dear Lord, help me know what to do next and bless me with the strength and wisdom I need to survive.* She didn't know how long Eddie would be gone, and she didn't think she could outrun him, given the condition of her feet. Hiding was nearly impossible with the lack of underbrush.

She never thought she'd be glad to be lost, but at that moment, she was. *At least that should buy me some more time.* She wasn't sure he would ever let her go, so if she didn't escape before they got to his camp, she doubted if she'd ever see Chase again or have a family. *Or,* she thought, *even see another sunrise.*

As hard as it was, Addison stood back up and looked around for anything she might use as a weapon. There were a few old tree branches on the ground, but they were too dry and rotted to use. Any of the rocks might have worked in the heat of a moment, but she couldn't really hide them from Eddie, and she was certain she didn't want to carry any more weight.

As she stood there scanning the ground, Addison's eyes settled on something white peeking through the dirt. She bent to pick it up, but it was stuck. She grabbed a small stick and began digging around it, quickly prying it loose.

It was some type of small animal bone—a leg bone, maybe. The ball end that fit into a hip socket was about the size of a marble and was what had caught her eye. The long, narrow part of the bone extended about three inches and was sharp and jagged at the end. Addison cleaned the dirt off on her pants and then turned it over and over in her hand. *This is perfect. It's better than anything I could have made myself.*

Suddenly, she heard a stick snap under Eddie's foot as he returned from his walkabout. Addison hurriedly stuck the bone into her back pants pocket as she turned to face him, hoping he hadn't seen it. Eddie slumped down against a tree to catch his breath.

"Could you see anything that looked familiar?" she asked politely.

"Naw, just more of the same. I'm sure we're close; I can feel it in my bones. I guess we should keep on the same heading for another hour or so to make sure we've gone far enough. If I don't see nothing by then, we'll make camp for the night."

They sat there in silence for a few minutes while Eddie's breathing slowed to normal. Addison's mind was racing, trying to think what she might do to reach Eddie's softer side, appeal to his humanity. She decided it was worth risking another violent outburst.

"Eddie, I was just wondering, you seem so comfortable in these mountains; did you grow up around here?"

"No. I grew up down south along the gulf. My old man worked on the oilrigs. We moved wherever the jobs were, mostly in Mississippi, Louisiana, and Texas. Why?"

"No reason, really. How many brothers and sisters do you have?"

"A couple of sisters. Younger."

"Are you still close to anyone in your family?"

"Not really. My old man ran out on us when I was in high school. I enlisted in the army as soon as I could to get away from them. I call my mama a couple times a year, but we ain't close."

"Most people never think about robbing a bank or kidnapping someone. You don't seem like the kind of person who would do something like that. How did you end up here?"

"Why you asking me all these personal questions? Can't you just shut up for a while and let me rest?"

"I'm sorry, Eddie. I was just interested in who you are. I didn't mean any harm."

Addison stretched out into a prone position and turned away from Eddie. She closed her eyes, hoping to recharge her batteries while she had the chance. Even in the shade, she could feel the heat of the day taxing her energy. Her leg muscles were tightening up, and her hips were beginning to ache. *I never knew I could be this tired. Chase, where are you? I know you're trying to find me. Please hurry!*

"Jenna," Eddie said softly. "Her name is Jenna."

Addison rolled over to face him.

"Who's Jenna, Eddie?"

"My wife. I should say my ex-wife."

"Where are Jenna and your kids now?"

"I don't rightly know. I guess she's back home in Louisiana, but she don't want nothing to do with me."

"How old are your children?"

"Hmm. They must be about five and three now. Named 'em Ruth and David. Good Bible names."

"Those are nice names. I like them both. When was the last time you saw them?"

"I ain't seen 'em since she took 'em two years ago. Probably for the best. I worked my hind end off but never could stay ahead of the bills. And by the end, I was spending as much money on booze as I was on food. No way to treat a family. They're better off without me."

"I'm truly sorry, Eddie."

"Well, sorry won't get us where we're going. Come on, let's get moving. The sun ain't standing still."

An hour later, they were startled to hear a loud clap of thunder overhead. They both instinctively looked in the direction of the sound. They hadn't noticed the gradual afternoon buildup of cumulus clouds over the mountain peaks.

As they stared up at the rapidly darkening sky, the first gust of wind from the thundercloud's violent downdraft struck them, nudging them slightly off balance and tugging at their clothes. Moments later, they were blinded by the ultra-bright flash of lightning no more than a hundred yards away.

When the intensely loud boom followed, Addison opened her mouth to scream, but nothing came out. It was as if the thunder had sucked the air right out of her lungs. The thunderstorm was right on top of them. Seconds later, a heavy, drenching rain hit them hard, soaking them before they could scramble for shelter.

"Come on!" Eddie shouted as he ran down into a draw. Addison followed closely. Their immediate threat was getting struck by lightning, standing up on a ridge. They looked for any type of shelter as they ran.

In the bottom of the draw, they spotted what looked like a small cavity under a large slab of rock that jutted up out of the ground. It wouldn't provide much protection, but it was the best they could find in a hurry. The space was tight, forcing Addison to press in close to Eddie to get out of the rain. That was awful, but at least the forced shower helped temper his normal stench. *Thank goodness, Heavenly Father, for small blessings, even this one,* Addison thought.

Lightning continued to flash around them. The thunder seemed to come from the very top of the mountain high above them and then roll down through the canyons and valleys, echoing as it went. Their proximity to the storm only intensified the force of Thor's hammer, which rang ever louder in their ears. Hail soon followed the rain, pelting the earth all around them.

Huddled together under the ledge, they watched in stunned silence as the marble-sized balls of ice bounced off the ground on every side. The temperature dropped rapidly, causing Addison to shiver. She was still wearing the clothes she had on at the park—short sleeves and capri pants. The wind swirled around them, growing ever stronger but constantly changing direction. *I'd give nearly anything for a warm, dry jacket.* She couldn't believe how fast it had gone from hot to freezing.

Addison shouted over the roar of the storm, "I've never seen weather this violent before!"

"There's something about the mountains that really gets 'em stirred up. Can't say why, but I seen others worse than this. It sure grabs your full attention. Lightning is the most dangerous part of the storm, so we should be fine under this rock."

After a few minutes, the hail stopped as fast as it had started, followed by another heavy downpour. Eventually, the wind calmed and the intensity of the rain faded as the thunderhead drifted away. And then it stopped. An eerie darkness enveloped them. It was like a brown twilight one might expect on another world.

The silence was deafening. It was as if the birds and animals had disappeared. No more wind whistling through the trees. Just silence. They crawled out from under their hideaway and looked around.

Something wasn't right, but Addison couldn't put her finger on it. The hair began to stand up on the back of her neck, and goosebumps formed on her arms. The atmosphere was electric. She and Eddie stared at each other in wonder, as if trying to anticipate Mother Nature's next move.

Then they heard it.

CHAPTER 10

A WALL OF WATER CAME crashing down the draw directly toward them. The flash flood raced with incredible speed as the mountain swiftly shed the water from the towering thunderstorm. They looked in horror, unable to turn away and powerless to move their feet. The leading wave was on them in an instant.

The raging torrent hit Eddie and Addison chest high and drove them from their feet. They were lost in the sheer violence of the moment as they were hurled down the rocky draw along with anything else that stood in the water's way. Small trees, mud, rocks—all were held captive by the torrent of water, pounding against the ground, bouncing off trees, scraping against boulders.

Addison screamed as she struggled to right herself. She was being pushed downhill on her back, headfirst, unable to see where she was going. The water kept pouring over her. She gasped for air. Instinctively, she threw her hands out to each side, scratching for anything that might slow her down.

Abruptly, Addison's hands caught hold of an exposed tree root, which spun her around before she lost her grip. At least now she was moving feet first and was able to dig her heels into the ground. Finally, her feet gained purchase as the frontal wave passed her by, and her momentum slowed to a stop. She sat there completely stunned for a few minutes as the residual floodwaters flowed harmlessly around her.

She laid back in the muddy aftermath, breathing in deeply. Her hair was a muddy tangle, much of it hanging down in her face. She absently pulled it to the sides as she checked herself for injury. Scrapes and bruises seemed to be the worst of it. As she tried to process what had just happened, Addison was jolted back to the reality of her situation.

Where's Eddie? Is he hurt? What should I do? She frantically looked around, trying to assess her situation. She saw no trace of Eddie, so she quietly got to her feet and looked around again, now from a higher vantage point. Still nothing.

Fear drained from her quickly. She knew if Eddie was unharmed, she only had a few moments to act. Almost without thinking, Addison started moving slowly and as quietly as she could downhill along the streambed. *Ouch!* She'd lost a shoe and hadn't even noticed. She stood still and looked back uphill and then downhill and saw her shoe, caught against a log.

Addison let out a long sigh of relief. She hurried over to the log and grabbed her shoe, turning it upside down to empty the muddy water. She used her shirttail to wipe out the inside and then put it back on her tender foot. She didn't dwell on the pain. In an instant, she was up again and moving downhill. The going was easier, and gravity seemed to carry her along almost effortlessly.

As she worked her way down the draw, something red caught her eye. She strained to see it better, but she couldn't decide what it was. Curious now, she hustled over to the side of the draw where she'd seen it. It was a small blue-and-red backpack caught in the low branches of a tree. *Eddie's pack.* Just seeing it frightened her, and her heart pounded in her chest. She wondered if he was down below her.

Addison untangled the pack and opened it. Inside she saw the map and compass Eddie had used, his mostly empty canteen, and an opaque, tan plastic grocery bag. She pulled it open and discovered wads of cash. *The money from the bank robbery. Oh no.* She knew he'd be furious when he realized it was missing. *If I take it, he's bound to keep chasing me until he gets the cash. If I leave it here, he may actually get away with honest people's money.*

After taking a few minutes to weigh the options and potential consequences, she grabbed the pack, slung it over her shoulder, and started back down the hill. Addison wondered if she was making the right decision, but she wanted justice. Besides, Eddie might not assume she had his pack—for all he knew, it could have been washed away in the floodwaters.

As she walked down the draw, she realized she hadn't really decided where to go but was just walking down the path of least resistance. That bothered her, but not knowing where Eddie was kept her from a more rational decision. Still, what she was doing felt right to her. Then it dawned on her—something Chase had shared from his survival training.

"If you ever get lost in the mountains," he had told her, "follow a stream or streambed downhill, because it will likely lead to a larger stream, a lake, a trail, or a road that will take you out of the hills toward more populated areas where you can find help."

Okay, she thought. *That's my first decision to take control of the situation.* Suddenly, she felt a burst of confidence. Moving forward decisively proved to be empowering for her. It was a small victory, but a victory nonetheless.

As she walked, Addison stayed in the streambed, hoping to cover her tracks. Her head was on a swivel, continuously looking for Eddie. *He has to be nearby, but where?* The stress was palpable. Five minutes passed, then ten without incident. She gradually picked up her pace, only to slow again as the streambed cut sharply to the right. Her eyes darted left and right, looking for any sign of Eddie. Seeing nothing unusual, she resumed her pace, moving lightly but quickly down the draw.

The sun was setting behind the mountain peaks; dusk settled on the area like a soft and cozy blanket, but with the sinking sun came a corresponding drop in temperature. A chill coursed through her body, causing her to shiver. Her wet clothes offered no insulation. Addison checked her watch. It was only 5:20. *That can't be right.* Then she realized the sun set much earlier on the eastern slopes of the mountains.

She cautiously rounded another bend and saw that her path was blocked by a small cliff. Walking close to the edge, she cautiously looked over. It dropped straight down about fifteen feet. It would have made a beautiful waterfall during spring runoff, but right now it was just another obstacle to overcome in her escape. Dismayed, she doubted she had the strength or energy to get to the bottom.

As she stared over the cliff, she began to softly cry. *I'm alone, running from a murderer, and everywhere I turn, my way out of this mess is blocked. This can't keep getting worse. Something has to change soon.* Then a thought popped into her head. *You've gotten this far; now isn't the time for a pity party. Do something! Press ahead with your plan. Standing still gets you nowhere.*

Addison shook her head back and forth as if to clear the cobwebs. *Okay, now, how do I get down this cliff in one piece? It's not that steep, so it can't be that hard.* She walked to the right side and looked for a pathway around the cliff. Nothing. She walked back to the left side of the cliff and did the same. This side was shallower and had some small trees and bushes on the slope she might be able to use as handholds.

She approached it carefully. She told herself again that it wasn't all that far down, but in the gathering darkness, it seemed worse. Before starting her climb down, she paused again to search her surroundings. She was deathly afraid of being followed. She had to get moving if she intended to get past the cliff before dark.

Satisfied that she was not being followed, she turned around to face uphill and grabbed ahold of a small tree. It bent easily, so she used it like a rope, working her way down the side of the cliff, carefully moving her feet and hands from one hold to the next. Reaching the bottom, Addison took a last step backward, looked up to where she'd just come from, and then turned to resume her trek.

Without warning, Eddie lunged at her from a small cavity behind the dry waterfall. Scared half out of her mind, Addison jumped away and tried to run, but Eddie lunged again and caught her foot. Down she went, hitting the ground hard. Eddie was on top of her in an instant, pinning her to the ground faceup.

Addison was in better physical condition, but Eddie was stronger and heavier. He grabbed for her hands and shifted his weight directly over her abdomen. She struggled for breath even as she fought back with all the strength she could muster. She turned from right to left, unsuccessfully trying to knock him off her. Then she bucked up and down with the same results.

I refuse to give in, no matter what happens!

CHAPTER 11

"You stupid piece of—"

"Get off of me, Eddie!"

"You trying to steal my money behind my back, is that it? Trying to take advantage of me 'cause of the storm? I ought to clock you one right now!"

"Just try it!"

Addison fought with all her might to get away, but Eddie kept her pinned to the ground on her back. The weight of his body exploded the air from her lungs. He quickly sat upright across her diaphragm as Addison gasped for air. She pushed at him in a vain attempt to knock him off, but he punched her hard in the face, bruising her cheek and splitting her lip.

"How do like that, you little witch?"

The warm blood tasted vaguely like copper in her mouth, but she didn't care. She still fought off Eddie's attempts to grab her arms. Addison was not about to let him control her. She focused all her concentration on breathing and defending herself.

Just when Addison started to feel faint, Eddie shifted his weight, and she gulped in air as fast as possible. This gave her newfound energy and a renewed will to fight off her attacker. She pushed hard against his chest, but Eddie responded by grabbing her left wrist and trying to get ahold of her right wrist. Addison spit in his face to distract him and then frantically felt around her for a weapon. She couldn't reach the animal bone in her hip pocket, but her right hand bumped against a rock, which she quickly grabbed. Eddie wiped the spit from his face in disgust and instinctively pulled back his free fist.

The moment he brought his fist downward, Addison countered with the rock to Eddie's left temple. The sound of the rock hitting flesh and bone would normally have sickened her, but not now. It was, instead, the sound of freedom. Eddie instantly slumped to the side, the momentum of her attack knocking him off her.

Addison lay there for a moment trying to catch her breath, but the fight or flight impulse kicked into high gear. *Move! Get up and run!* She sat up, pushing Eddie the rest of the way off her leg. Now was her best opportunity to escape, and she had to make the most of it. She jumped to her feet and ran full speed down the draw, Eddie's backpack bouncing up and down with every step.

With adrenaline streaming through her body, Addison's legs pumped up and down like the pistons in a finely tuned engine. Any thoughts of her bleeding feet or tender muscles vanished. Harder and harder she ran, never looking back and never second-guessing her decision. It felt good to pour every ounce of her being into her escape. The physical exertion would eventually putter out, but right now, she felt intense exhilaration coupled with the fear of being caught again.

* * *

Addison finally stopped when it became too dark to run anymore. She leaned over, hands on her knees as she panted. A soft breeze brushed against her skin as the cool evening air drifted down the mountain slopes. She had no idea how long she had been running or how far she had come. She tried to plan her next few steps but couldn't seem to focus her mind.

One question gnawed at her, and she knew she somehow had to address it before she could move on. *Did I kill Eddie when I hit him with that rock, or was he just unconscious?* There was no safe way for her to know. But if he was still alive, she was afraid he would still be coming for her or for the money. It really didn't matter which.

For a second, she allowed herself to question her immediate decision to run from him, thinking that she should have first taken the time to check his condition. Maybe even help him—or hit him again. But the thought was fleeting. *Focus, Addison! Stay on track, and keep moving!* She knew she was smarter than Eddie and in better physical condition, so she had every confidence in the world she could beat him at this game. But only if she stayed focused.

Darkness meant running was no longer possible. It was simply too dangerous. The last thing she needed was a sprained ankle, or worse. Addison looked around to get her bearings, putting one foot in front of the other as she felt her way along the uneven ground.

"Ugh! Now what?" Her right foot was suddenly wet. Addison had stepped into the small stream meandering down the draw. She hadn't noticed it before and wondered if it was residual rainwater from the flash flood or if it was spring water. She stooped down and scooped up a handful of water. It was cold and clear. *I guess it's fresh.*

Without thinking further, she cupped her hand in the water and brought it to her mouth. The cool water soothed her dry mouth as she swished it around to clean away residual blood from Eddie's punch. She came to her senses before swallowing and spit the water out, gagging as she did so. She had remembered the warning from her parents whenever they'd gone camping together, not to drink untreated creek water, because of Giardia, the parasite that could cause cramps and diarrhea. She hoped she had not just made a serious mistake.

Mad at herself, she sat down in the grass beside the stream, overcome by her predicament. In the moment it took her to begin feeling sorry for herself, she slammed shut the door to self-pity. It certainly wouldn't help her. And she knew it would put her on the slippery slope to defeat, something she wasn't about to let happen. She laid back in the soft grass, closed her eyes, and tried to still her mind with thoughts of Chase and happier times.

Before she knew it, her mind was lost to the past as she relived the first time she ever saw Chase and their whirlwind romance and long-distance relationship. She had been a student at Brigham Young University, and he had been commissioned as second lieutenant and was off to pilot training. She remembered exactly how she'd felt when she first knew he was the one she wanted to spend this life and forever with. She watched in her mind's eye as he proposed and later, as they were married. Why did the last two days have to be so different from that day?

The gentle breeze floated across her body, chilling her skin. She shivered in the darkness as her body temperature dipped. Instinctively, she hugged herself in the attempt to stay warm.

The gentle babbling of the water as it raced over and around the rocks soothed her. It even blocked out the other sounds that seemed to come alive in the darkness of the woods—sounds she might otherwise have found a little frightening. But she wasn't afraid at all. Not now. She knew she would survive. *I've come this far. I can make it the rest of the way.*

Worried she'd fall asleep, Addison opened her eyes and propped herself up on her elbows. She looked up at the night sky, awed by the vast array of stars so vibrant, she thought she could reach out and touch them. She had forgotten just how beautiful the night sky could be without the ever-present night pollution that enveloped Spokane or, worse, the Maryland suburbs of Washington, D.C.

The moon was up now, fully above the horizon to the east, so Addison knew she'd been traveling in the right direction. The moon would be brighter as it rose, so she'd be more vulnerable, but she'd also be able to move faster. If she could see better, so could Eddie, but she know she could outrun him.

As Addison lay there, she finally relaxed enough to think more strategically, rather than reacting impulsively in the heat of a moment. She hadn't noticed it before, but her subconscious was queuing up the more important issues for her consideration. For instance, she hadn't thought much about the daylong survival orientation she and other new military spouses received when they first arrived on base. But now, the tips she'd learned that day seemed to be flooding her mind. *I wish I had listened better. I didn't think I'd ever need to know that stuff.*

The bits and pieces of the course material began to fit together like a jigsaw puzzle in her mind. *When evading the enemy, whether during the day or night, stay in the shadows to avoid exposure.* Another hit her. *In hilly or mountainous areas, walk along the middle ground, between the hilltop and valley. Walk too high, and you'll be silhouetted against the sky. Walk too low, and you end up right where a pursuer would naturally look.* Amazed at what she'd remembered, she jumped up and adjusted her path as she started hiking again. Her confidence grew with every step, and she gradually quickened her pace as she continued downhill toward what she hoped would be more populated areas.

The hours ticked off as the moon climbed to its zenith and then continued toward the western horizon. Addison somehow managed to plod on. The adrenaline rush had long since faded, and fatigue wrapped its soft, comfortable arms around her body. Her mind wandered as she trudged along. Finally, near total exhaustion, she collapsed. *I can't take another step tonight.* She was just too tired to go on and knew if she was going to make it, she had to get some sleep. With her last ounce of energy, she crawled into a small stand of young pines just up the hill from the stream and laid down, using Eddie's pack as a makeshift pillow.

Before drifting off to sleep, Addison's mind wandered to the good times she'd had on family campouts. She'd always loved camping in the mountains and listening to the wind sing gentle lullabies as it moved through the pines. Oh, the pines! There was nothing like the aroma of lodgepole pines. And the ever-present burble of river water rushing over the rocks. She could see her dad now, fly fishing in the cool, still morning of another perfect day.

Addison bounced from one sweet memory to the next, until she pictured herself with Chase, camping on their cross-country trip to Fairchild Air Force Base after their honeymoon. They'd camped to save money so they could furnish their first home when they arrived. It seemed so vivid to her, as if she were experiencing it for the first time all over again.

She'd smiled to herself as she stood in her new backyard beside a beautiful tamarack tree. Along the side of her new home, mountain laurel bridged the transition between house and lawn, its brilliant pink blossoms in full bloom. She had planted flowers in the shrub beds and along the sides of the concrete patio in their backyard. She could almost smell their sweet scent on the morning breeze. She could hear the sounds of children laughing as they played nearby. Oh, how she longed for her own children someday. And then she was gone, sound asleep.

CHAPTER 12

DAY 3

FOLLOWING ANOTHER RESTLESS NIGHT, CHASE finally woke up for good at five-thirty. Rather than jump up and get ready for work, he just lay there for a while thinking about Addison and what he should do that day to try and find her. Suddenly, he heard the slamming of multiple car doors, which struck him as odd for so early in the morning. The doorbell rang, and he heard pounding on the front door.

He flew out of bed and threw on a T-shirt and pair of sweatpants before running to answer the door. It was Mr. Stoker, the OSI agent who had interviewed him, with half a dozen other law enforcement officers from the base and the SPD.

"Good morning, Lieutenant. Sorry to surprise you like this, but we have a warrant to search your house and vehicle. Please stand aside."

"Like I told you, Mr. Stoker, you're welcome to search everything. I pulled together a stack of documents I thought you'd need, along with contact names and phone numbers—even a recent photo of Addison. They're sitting on the kitchen table. So I'm not sure why you needed to barge in here at this time of day."

"This is standard procedure in cases like this. Step aside, sir, or we'll have to forcibly remove you from the premises while we search."

"I'm sorry. I was just startled by the pounding on the door. Please, do what you need to do." Chase retreated from the doorway while motioning the officers inside.

"Just sit here in the living room, Lieutenant, and stay out of the way. We'll finish this up as quickly as possible."

"Can I at least get my cell phone first?"

"Where is it?"

"On the kitchen counter, charging."

"As you can see in the search warrant, your phone is also subject to the search, so I'll have to confiscate it until our technical unit has a chance to scrub it."

"Scrub it for what, exactly?"

"You're the first person of interest we need to investigate and, hopefully, eliminate as a suspect. I'm sure you want us to be thorough, and unfortunately, that includes this search."

"Okay. Can I call my commander on my home phone?"

"You won't need to. He'll be here momentarily."

Chase was somewhat relieved that as his military commander, Major White, had been informed of the search ahead of its execution and had apparently been invited to be present. The major carried great weight on all matters affecting his people, and Chase knew he would be intimately involved in the judicial processes.

But he was also frustrated. Chase paced back and forth in the living room as he watched and listened to the police turn his house upside down. He knew deep down they wouldn't find anything incriminating, but still, the whole process was intimidating and a little frightening. He opened the curtains to let the morning light in and noticed some of the neighbors already looking on in curiosity.

Isn't that just great? Now my reputation with our neighbors is shot. People almost always assumed the worst, especially without knowing what was going on.

Another car pulled up out front, and the driver got out. *Good!* Relieved, Chase met Major White at the door, and they both stepped out into the front yard.

"Hi, Boss," Chase said dejectedly.

"I'm sure sorry about this Chase, but I couldn't warn you. Remember, patience and courtesy. If you think about it, this is a good thing since you'll be officially cleared, and this part of the investigation will just be another unpleasant memory."

"Yes, sir, I know, but it's still a terrible way to start the day. I really thought I could avoid this by offering them anything they wanted without a warrant. I guess not. They're a bureaucracy after all."

"It won't take them long. Let's go sit in my car where we can talk privately." As if reading Chase's mind, he added, "Unfortunately, we'll still be in full view of your neighbors."

Major White told the young Security Forces sergeant at the door what they were doing, making it a statement rather than a request.

The two settled into the major's car. Thankfully, it was still cool outside, so keeping the windows up in the car wasn't as uncomfortable as it would have been in a couple of hours.

"I know this is hard on you, Chase, but it has to happen, so just suck it up and make the best of it. It'll be over soon, and I'll stay here until they leave."

"Thanks, sir. Is there anything else you can tell me about what's going on with the investigation?"

Major White let the question hang in the air, looking as if he were deciding how to respond.

"I don't know much, but I'll share it with you. And, it's imperative you keep it completely confidential. If this gets out, neither one of us will get any more information. Do you understand?"

"Yes, sir. But, if possible, I'd like to be able to share it with Addison's parents. They're flying in this morning. Her father is a retired air force colonel, so they will keep this quiet. I'd hate to have to hide important information about their daughter from them."

"Just make sure it stays between the three of you. No other family members or friends."

"Understood, sir. You have my word."

"First, let me ask you if you've heard anything directly from the police."

"Not a word. It's like I'm living in an information vacuum. I can appreciate that now; they hadn't yet executed this search warrant. Maybe they'll be more forthcoming after I'm cleared."

"Ha! Don't count on it. Like I said, I haven't heard much myself. I didn't expect the police to share much of anything with either of us, so I called Major Saxby back and asked him to poke around, just one cop to another, thinking the SPD would take him into their confidence."

"Yes, sir, that makes sense."

"Here's what I've been told: They think the guy who robbed the bank downtown two days ago and killed the guard might, and I emphasize the word *might*, have carjacked Addison."

"What?! What are they doing to find him? Do they really think he has—"

"Before you jump to any conclusions, there may not be a connection. There's no solid evidence, at least none that I know of yet, but that's their working theory at the moment. Apparently, they found the robber's abandoned car across from Riverfront Park—the same place Addison's car was parked."

"That's quite a coincidence." Chase groaned, the threat of nausea looming large.

"The bank robbery took place about the same time Addison and her friends would have been about to leave the park according to her friends you spoke with."

Chase just sat there silently for a few minutes. Major White seemed to know he needed the time to process it and didn't say anything further. After the famine, this seemed like an information feast.

"That's a lot to take in," Chase finally said. "What if it's true? Do the police have any idea who the robber is? And what if Addison's with him? Or worse, what if he's hurt her? I can't even think ab—I can't . . ." Chase trailed off, his voice catching.

"Slow down a little." The major put a hand on Chase's shoulder. "Keep in mind that the police don't have any corroborating evidence. They're pressing ahead on the *assumption* that the robbery and Addison's disappearance are connected unless and until they find hard evidence to the contrary. I'm sorry it's not what we hoped to hear."

Chase shook his head. "I'd rather know than be kept in the dark. Thanks for telling me, sir." He asked again, "Do the police have any idea where he and Addison might be?"

Major White paused, and it was just long enough to upset Chase.

"Sir, if you know anything at all, you *have* to tell me. Please!"

"All right, all right. The police are working around the clock to clear you as a suspect. They've gotten a ton of tips about the robbery and have been working their way through them as fast as they can. Two of them, so far, have led them to believe Addison and the perp might be near Deer Park. One tip came from a gas station attendant from up there who reported seeing a Murano with a man and a woman in it the night of the bank robbery and Addison's disappearance. The man fits the description of the bank robber. She didn't get a good look at the woman."

"And the other?" he asked, choking down the rising bile.

"Is much more of a long shot. The second tip came from a state police trooper manning a roadblock north of Cusick that same night. While he had a vehicle stopped, he noticed another vehicle turn up into the mountains a couple miles south of the roadblock. It seemed odd to him at the time, given the late hour, but he was busy at the checkpoint and didn't report it until the end of his shift. Since it was dark at the time, all he really saw was a set of headlights turning off the road."

"Has anyone followed up?"

"They have a police chopper searching the mountains just east of there for your car. We got a heads up from SPD asking our aircrews to keep our eyes open and report anything suspicious."

"And?"

"Nothing so far. But I have asked our guys to do some search pattern training in the area," he said. "I've also told them to use their FLIR sensors on every flight."

Chase nodded. He'd used the forward-looking infrared sensor in his own training to pick up heat radiating from humans or large animals he wouldn't have been able to see in the dark or through thin clouds—in the air force, the FLIR was essential for nighttime searches and low-level flights, but Chase knew the sensor was cost-prohibitive and therefore rarely installed in police choppers. Mingled with his growing fear for his wife's safety was a sense of gratitude for Major White's help.

"One more thing, Chase—and this is the most important part of our discussion. I don't want you going anywhere near the search area under any circumstances. You could get yourself hurt or even get Addison killed if you get in the middle of this and screw something up. And I shouldn't have to mention you could be charged with obstruction of justice. Do you understand?"

"Can I at least fly onboard the aircraft as a spotter? You know how important an extra set of eyes can be."

"Absolutely not. Did you doze off and miss what I just told you? You're not getting anywhere near this case. We're already blurring the boundary of the law by joining the search. I did call the JAG, and they said the limited scope of our participation was fine but we couldn't be directly involved in apprehending the perp. If you get caught chasing this guy yourself, that could create a real heyday for the press and way too much oversight from my boss."

"I understand," Chase said quietly as he sat back in his seat. "I really should stay with Addison's parents anyway. They're devastated, too, and I'll need to take care of them. But please call me if our guys spot anything or if you hear more from Security Forces."

"I will. You do your part, and I'll do mine. We'll find Addison, Chase. Just make sure you stay out of it."

"Yes, sir. What about an identity on the bank robber? Have they figured that out?"

"Again, this is a maybe, but they ran the VIN of the abandoned car and it connected to a guy named Eddie Anghelone. He has a couple of shoplifting and drunk-and-disorderly priors on his record but nothing violent. They don't know if he's the guy, but they've checked with his landlord and any known associates. No one has seen him since before the bank heist, and the police haven't been able to track him down. You can draw your own conclusion."

"Thank you so much, sir. Knowing something, even if it's bad news, is better than not knowing anything at all."

"Now, is there anything else we could be doing that we've missed? How about getting Addison's picture out to the public on TV and in newspapers?"

"When I met with the police, they offered to do that. I just gave Mr. Stoker a photo of her before you got here. He'll work with the SPD on the public announcement of her disappearance."

"Good. I have to believe that will help significantly."

"I hope so. That's what the detectives told me."

Just then, the two men saw the police emerge from the house carrying several boxes. Chase jumped from the car to see what they were taking.

"Stand back, Lieutenant," Mr. Stoker warned. "We're just taking a few things to examine at the lab. We'll leave you with a complete list as a receipt so you'll be able to account for everything."

"Okay, that's fair. Please give it to Major White. I've got to run now." If there was no traffic, he could still make it on time—barely. Then it occurred to him the police had also been searching his truck, so he had no transportation.

"When do you think you'll be done with my truck? I need to pick up my in-laws at the airport."

"We just finished going through it. You're free to take it now."

"Great, thanks, Mr. Stoker."

CHAPTER 13

CHASE WAS WAITING FOR HIS in-laws at the baggage claim. He'd been pacing back and forth with worry. When they finally emerged from the security area, he rushed over and threw his arms around them. He was so relieved to be able to share his load with family. Of course, they were just as worried about Addison as he was, and the stress showed on their faces.

"We got here as quickly as we could, Chase," Julia Parkin said as they embraced. She was a youthful fifty-five years old, of average height, and was dressed conservatively in a navy-blue pant suit. Her hair was naturally gray, and she kept it cut short for ease of grooming.

"I know. And there really hasn't been anything you could have done, but I'm glad you're here now. I've been going crazy worrying about Addison."

"At least we can support each other in person now. Just being together will give us strength," Julia responded.

"Any news since we last talked?" Rick Parkin asked. He stood nearly six feet tall and had an athletic build, with most of his brown hair intact. He carried his fifty-seven years well, tried to stay fit, and it showed.

"I did get an update on the case an hour ago, but the news isn't too good."

"What do you mean, son?"

"We need to keep this information strictly between the three of us in order to protect my boss. If the police find out he's keeping me posted, that might end our updates. I know you're both completely trustworthy, but my boss wanted me to stress that with you. Not even other family members can be brought into the loop. If you don't mind, I'd like to grab your bags and save this conversation until we're in the truck. The airport isn't the most private place in the world."

"Yes, of course," Rick responded.

It only took a few minutes before they were out the door. Once they were settled in his truck, Chase got the air conditioner running but left the transmission in park. He didn't want to talk and drive at the same time. He felt like that would diminish the importance of the discussion. Chase turned in his seat to be able to see both Rick, in the front passenger seat, and Julia, who sat in the back seat.

"There aren't many solid leads in Addison's disappearance that I'm aware of, but apparently, the police believe that Addison may have been the victim of a carjacking by a bank robber. They found his car in the same place Addison had parked, and the robbery occurred about the same time as she and her friends were getting ready to leave Riverfront Park to go home."

"Oh my." Julia gasped as she heard the news. "I suddenly felt a bit lightheaded."

"I'm sorry, Julia. I should have been more thoughtful in how I shared the news with you."

Rick reached to the back seat where Julia was sitting and took her hand in his. "She's faced more than her share of tough experiences. I think she'll be fine." Then he looked back at Chase.

"Do they know where the bank robber is or what he's done with Addison?"

"Not yet. The police think they left town and may be in the mountains west of a little village called Cusick. They have a helicopter searching that area right now. It's pretty close to where we conduct survival training, so they've also asked our helicopter crews to keep an eye out for them during training missions."

"Will they let you fly any search missions in the area?"

"No. I've been grounded until this is all resolved. I even volunteered to fly in the back as a spotter, but the boss refused."

"I hate to say it," replied Rick, "but that's probably for the best. I'm sure everyone knows you want to be involved, but someone in your shoes would probably be less effective than another crewman."

Rick was right. It was he who had inspired Chase to take the same career path he'd followed when Chase had been selected for pilot training. Chase really looked up to him and knew Rick had seen plenty of combat during his career. Rick was now moving up the corporate ladder at a major information technology firm. If anyone could help Chase see clearly through the fog of this personal war, it was Rick.

"There's more."

Rick and Julia looked at each other, concerned, and then nodded. "Okay," Rick said. "I think we'd both appreciate knowing what you know. Don't feel like you have to shield us from anything. Go ahead."

"The bank robber doesn't have a prior record of violence, but he shot and killed the bank guard during the robbery."

After a few more minutes in reflective silence, Julia laid her head back on the headrest and closed her eyes. Chase put the truck in gear and headed for home. By the time they had left the airport grounds, Julia was asleep. Chase doubted she or Rick had gotten much sleep lately.

Rick leaned toward Chase and softly said, "If I know you at all, I suspect you are looking to take matters into your own hands since you aren't able to directly participate in the search. Is that right?"

"I don't know, *yet*. I need to think it through. My commander specifically ordered me to stay clear of the investigation. That's my dilemma. I may be able to do more on the ground than I could in the air anyway. Let's get home and get you two settled first. We can talk more about it then. I'm sure as Addison's father, you're having some of the same thoughts."

The phone was ringing as they walked into the house. Chase ran to answer it before the caller hung up. He hoped it was the police with some news, but it was a newspaper reporter calling to conduct a phone interview. Chase answered her questions and agreed to email her a recent photo of Addison in time to make the deadline for the morning paper.

When he hung up, he noticed the message light blinking and hit the play button. It was a reporter from the local TV station wanting to set up an on-camera interview. Chase called her back and agreed to go on the news that evening. While he was busy with the phone, Rick and Julia found the guest bedroom and unpacked.

Chase hung up the phone and stood there for a minute, as motionless as a stone pillar, his thoughts on Addison. He could feel the exhaustion pulling him down.

Julia appeared at the doorway, and she moved forward to put her arm on Chase's shoulder.

"Chase, are you holding up okay?"

Startled, he instinctively jerked away.

"No!" he shouted, slamming his clenched fist through the drywall. "I'm not all right. My wife's been kidnapped, and here I sit, at home, totally helpless!"

Julia immediately stepped into him and pulled him close. She held him tightly as tears streaked down his cheeks, and his body shook as he sobbed. He slowly regained his composure and then gently pulled back from Julia's embrace.

"I'm so sorry, Julia. I didn't mean to snap like that. I hope you'll forgive me."

"You've done nothing that needs to be forgiven. We'll all need to lean on each other if we're going to get through this nightmare. That's why we're here, Chase. At least now that you've put a hole in the wall, neither Rick nor I will have to do it." She smiled.

"That's about the only good news I've heard lately. You and Rick seem so calm. How do you do it?"

"We're just good actors. We look calm on the outside, but I assure you, our insides are tied in knots. Have you told your parents yet?"

"I did yesterday. With them working in Europe, it will take them some time to get here. Not too long, I hope."

Chase was struggling to control his emotions and was grateful for the distraction when the doorbell rang. One of their friends from church had brought dinner. Chase hadn't even thought about dinner. He graciously accepted the meal and thanked them for their thoughtfulness. Julia and Rick joined them, so Chase made the formal introductions and then ushered the good Samaritans out the door. He didn't want to face anyone right now and couldn't stand the thought of having to run through the details of Addison's disappearance yet again.

Julia took the food from Chase and put it in the refrigerator since he had to run downtown for his evening news interview. She and Rick said that while he was gone, they would touch base with their extended family and assured him they wouldn't speak a word of the news Chase had shared with them.

Chase was back home in no time, and Julia reheated the meal. They ate in painful silence punctuated occasionally by awkward small talk. Julia filled Chase in on what was going on in the lives of her siblings, while Rick not so subtly tried to distract Chase with talk of his new fly fishing hobby. Chase started to clear the table when the phone rang again. He grabbed it and pulled it to his ear, turning away from Julia and Rick.

"Chase?" Major White's voice said.

"Yes, sir. Do you have any news?"

"I do. The SPD just notified our Security Forces that they found Addison's car. It's up one of the canyon roads northwest of Cusick. It looks like it was deliberately run over the edge of a small cliff and then camouflaged."

"Any sign of Addison?"

"No, but they are convinced she was there. The aircrew was able to set the chopper down on a nearby road, and their flight engineer hiked down to the car. He got the license plate number and found some flex cuffs and Addison's purse on the floor of the front passenger seat. There was a little blood on the cuffs and the door, which she may have been tied to. Their forensic team is on the way up there now so they can go over the car with a fine-tooth comb. They will run the DNA right away, so the police need you to bring her toothbrush and hairbrush down to the station ASAP so they have a sample for DNA comparison."

"I'll get it down there right away."

"Is there anything else you need or something I can do for you?"

"No, sir. Addison's parents are here now, and one of our friends brought dinner by, so we're okay."

"By the way, you didn't hear this from me, but we may be doing some search pattern training near the car over the next couple of days. I thought you'd want to know."

"Thank you, sir. And tell everyone else thanks for all they are doing."

"I will. You should know we miss you and can't wait to get Addison back. Now, you'd better get down to the police station. Let me know if they give you any more information, and I'll keep you posted on my end as well."

Chase hung up the phone and told Rick and Julia the news. Then he rushed to the bathroom to get his wife's toothbrush and hairbrush for the police. He headed for the door and then stopped short.

"Rick, Julia, there's something else I need to tell you. Although Addison is in very serious danger, I've had a strong feeling that she's alive and that everything will work out. I hope it's not wishful thinking, but it gives me something to hang on to so I can stay positive."

"We've felt the same way, Chase." Julia nodded.

"Would you like some company down at the police station?" Rick offered.

Chase thought for a moment before replying.

"Thanks for the offer, Rick. I would love the company, if you feel up to it."

"I do," he replied. Then, turning to Julia, he asked, "Would you like to come with us, honey, or relax here?"

"I think I'll just stay here and read or watch TV. It's been a long day."

The men walked out the door, glad to be doing something constructive. The ride downtown wasn't long, but it was quiet, as both men were lost in their own thoughts.

Chase reviewed in his mind all the information he'd collected up to that point. Fortunately, the quality and quantity of information had steadily and quickly grown, so he had much more data to work with now than at the same time yesterday. He wanted to get personally involved somehow, and he used the drive to think that through. He also needed to decide if he should arm himself and just how far he'd go to protect Addison. *Vigilantism isn't looked upon well by the police,* he mused wryly.

The hardest part, he knew, still lay ahead. He realized that no plan ever survived the first shot of battle; it was simply a point of departure. Chase had to be agile enough to stay ahead of the investigation and, more importantly, stay ahead of this Eddie Anghelone guy, if he was going to be effective. And he'd have to be smart enough to avoid drawing attention to himself and ticking off the police. No easy task.

And most importantly, if he did come across Eddie and he was holding Addison against her will, would he have the backbone to use deadly force if necessary? It was one thing to serve as a military officer and quite another to actually take a life—especially outside of combat. He hoped he would be equal to whatever task was necessary to get Addison back home safely.

Finally, Rick broke the silence. "Do you mind me asking what you're thinking about?"

"No, I guess not. I've been mulling over what options I have to help find Addison and bring her home safely."

"That's what I thought. Truth be told, I've been thinking the same things."

"We should probably talk that through together when we get home. The police station is just up ahead."

CHAPTER 14

"Hi, I'm Chase Roberts. Is Detective Bateman in?"

"Have a seat, Mr. Roberts, and I'll let him know you're here," the receptionist responded.

It was late in the evening. Chase was impressed that the detectives were still on the job. He guessed they had to work at the pace dictated by the investigation. But he was glad they were still there. He fidgeted while he waited, unable to control his nervous energy. He picked up an ancient *National Geographic* magazine from the chipped end table next to him and thumbed through it. A door opened and in walked Floyd Bateman.

"Lieutenant," he called out as he walked over to meet him. "How are you holding up?"

The two shook hands as if they'd been friends for years.

"I'm doing okay under the circumstances." Then he nodded toward Rick. "This is my father-in-law, Rick Parkin. I hope you don't mind him being here too. We brought you Addison's brush and toothbrush, like you asked."

"Great. Thanks for coming down so quickly. I'll get them over to the crime lab ASAP. Mr. Parkin, I'm sure sorry about Addison. We're working day and night on her case."

"Thank you, Detective. I have no doubt you are."

"While we're here," Chase asked, "do you have time for a quick update? It's hard to be on the outside looking in."

"Sure. Walk with me, and we'll talk on the way. And we can get into details in my office, if need be."

They picked up visitor badges from the receptionist, and then Floyd led them back through the cubicle maze toward the lab.

"I know it can be very frustrating sitting on the sidelines and trusting people you don't even know to find your wife. Believe me, I understand. But it's also important to gather the evidence deliberately so we don't jump to wrong conclusions that end up wasting the precious little time we have to find Addison."

"I understand all that; I'm just anxious to know what's going on."

"I'd feel the same way if our roles were reversed. But I have good news. We've tentatively cleared you as a possible suspect. We still have a few things to run down, but we should wrap those up tomorrow. You're welcome to take the items we confiscated back with you tonight."

"Thanks for clearing me so quickly, but it's been two full days now. I figured there would be at least a few things you could share with me by now."

"While we've been investigating you, we had to be cautious about sharing information with you. Unfortunately, it often takes a long time—perhaps too long—before we can bring family members into the loop. I'm sure you understand."

"I do."

"There are a few things I can tell you, but I don't want to discuss it in the open. Even in the middle of the police station, we have to be careful what we say and wary of who might be listening. Let's drop off Addison's things at the lab and head back to my office, and I'll tell you what I can."

Ten minutes later, they were walking back to Floyd's office when they passed Ted Strickland.

"Hey, Ted. Can you join us in my office when you get a chance?"

"Sure. I'll be there in about five minutes."

Floyd showed them into his office. "Take a seat, gents. Let's give Ted a few minutes to join us, and we can begin."

While they waited, the conversation turned to small talk. Floyd was telling them about his time in the army when Ted walked in. Chase and Rick stood as they introduced themselves to Ted. When everyone was seated, Floyd got right to point. "As you probably saw on the news," he began, "we've put out a couple of press releases asking the public to help us. One for Addison, and the other for the guy that robbed Harvest Bank and killed the guard on duty at the time. We think there may be a connection between them. Namely, that the bank robber, Eddie Anghelone, might have carjacked Addison and headed north."

"Yes, I saw both, but I had no idea they were connected. Frankly, that scares the devil out of me. Can you tell us why you think that's the case?"

"I'll do my best. Since the releases came out, we've gotten literally hundreds of tips. Detective Strickland and I have been running them down with a few uniformed officers who've been assigned to help in both investigations."

"Any of them pan out yet?"

"Yes, but I want to stress that this information is confidential. You can't share it with anyone. Part of our strategy in cases like this is to keep the perpetrator in the dark as much as possible about what we know and don't know. Understood?"

"Agreed, so long as we can share it with Addison's mother, who is waiting for us at home. Her parents flew in today and are staying with me. I don't want to withhold information about their daughter, if that's okay with you. She's as worried as we are."

Rick nodded in agreement.

Floyd and Ted exchanged glances and an almost imperceptible nod. "Fair enough."

"Okay, then. First, and most importantly, we located Addison's car a couple of hours ago about seventy miles north of Spokane. It was off the side of a dirt road up in the mountains and covered up with dirt and tree branches in an apparent attempt to hide it from view. Our chopper crew spotted it from the air. We had eyes on the ground soon afterward, and they confirmed the license and registration and collected some evidence, most notably blood on the passenger side armrest, multiple fingerprints, and Addison's purse. That's why we had Major White ask you to bring down Addison's things—so we can compare DNA."

"How confident are you that your theory is correct?"

Floyd looked over at his partner before answering. "Right now, I'd say better than fifty-fifty. But we really don't like to share things we don't know for certain. We're telling you more than we normally would, because you wear a uniform, like us. We do think the blood is Addison's. It makes sense if the perp who robbed the bank—Eddie Anghelone—did carjack Addison after he dumped his car across from Riverfront Park, presumably in an attempt to throw us off."

Floyd paused a moment, apparently to let Chase and Rick absorb the startling information and process it.

"If I understand you correctly, then you're pretty confident Addison is still with Anghelone, right?" Chase asked, gripping the armrests on his chair tightly. Beads of perspiration formed on his forehead as the news finally sank in. Hearing it straight from the police made this nightmare real.

"Like Detective Bateman just said," Ted jumped in. "We *don't* know for sure, but a lot of circumstantial evidence points to that conclusion."

"Do you think Addison is still alive?" Rick interjected.

"Let's just say we have found zero evidence that she's not," Ted answered. "That's the best we can do right now."

"Are there any leads on where they might be now or if they are on foot?" Rick asked. "I doubt Anghelone could have stolen another vehicle up in the mountains."

"No one has reported a missing vehicle in that area," said Floyd. "And we don't know yet what direction they took off in. There was a pretty severe thunderstorm up there that could have washed away tracks and possibly any scent. We're assuming they weathered the storm, so we have a couple of dogs and handlers from the canine unit on site. So far the results are disappointing. The good news is that wherever they were when the storm ended, they would have left new tracks and fresh scents. We just need to find that spot to zero in on."

"Is anyone else up there searching?" Chase inquired.

"The Pend Oreille County Sheriff and some of his deputies are searching right now," said Ted. "We expect other law enforcement officers from here and nearby cities to begin arriving on site shortly. A manhunt in the mountains will be challenging enough, and if Anghelone still has Addison, we'll have a hostage situation to deal with."

"You should know, Chase, we've asked your air force helicopter unit to join the search," added Floyd. "Having the extra eyes and night capability will give us twenty-four-hour aviation support. We'll be able to cover a lot more ground that way."

"That's fantastic. What about legal ramifications for using the military? I know there are some pretty big barriers to overcome."

"You're spot on. We've coordinated with the U.S. Attorney's Office in Seattle as well as the JAG at the base. Air force personnel won't carry weapons or participate directly in the apprehension. That would definitely cross the line, but we can collaborate in just about any other way."

"That's great news. They will give you everything they can. What are your plans from this point forward?"

"Sorry, Chase, we have to keep that to ourselves. Operational security. Tipping our hand could put our people at risk, and more importantly, it could cost Addison her life."

"I wouldn't want you to put anyone in harm's way needlessly, especially Addison."

"But, if you just happen to be watching the ten o'clock news tonight, you'll see an announcement by the FBI that we're sure you'll be interested in."

"We really appreciate the information you've given us and the fact that you are still here this late working the case. I came in feeling pretty down, but things look much better now knowing the investigation is moving forward aggressively. I can't thank you enough."

They got up from their chairs and walked Chase and Rick back out to the lobby.

Floyd said, "Don't forget to turn on the news when you get home."

"You don't need to worry about that. All three of us will be watching. Thanks again, detectives. My entire family appreciates what you're doing to find Addison and bring her home safely. We're grateful for your time today and for bringing us up to speed."

Chase picked up his personal items from the desk sergeant, and he and Rick left the building. The drive back home only took fifteen minutes. The men were eager to share what they'd learned with Julia.

CHAPTER 15

CHASE AND RICK WALKED INTO the house to the lingering smell of their earlier dinner and the sound of the TV coming from the living room. Julia was sitting on the couch reading the newspaper. Rick joined her on the couch, and Chase sat down next to them in his recliner.

"How did it go at the police station?" Julia asked.

"It went pretty well, I think," Chase offered. "We spoke with both of the detectives handling the case. They confirmed much of what we'd heard from Major White."

"Did they say anything about Addison?"

"She's their most important case, and they're using the best resources they have," Rick responded. "They won't know if the blood they found in the car is hers until they finish running the DNA tests tonight, and the lab is also processing a lot of fingerprints from her car."

Julia sighed. "I'm so glad they are pulling out all the stops to find her. I don't know what we'll do if we don't get her back soon."

Rick opened his mouth to speak, but the sound of the doorbell cut off his comment. Chase frowned. "I wonder who that is. I wasn't expecting anyone."

He excused himself to answer the door. It was Captain Bret Hartman, one of the pilots from Chase's helicopter flight. "Captain Hartman, what are you doing here? Is everything okay?"

"Of course. How are *you* doing, Chase? That's the more important question."

"As well as can be expected. Come on in." Chase ushered him inside and closed the door. "Come into the living room. I'd like to introduce you to Addison's parents."

Julia turned off the TV so they could visit without the background noise. After a few minutes, Bret explained why he was there. "I apologize for coming over so late. Major White sent me to check on you and to see if you'd like to borrow a handheld tactical radio so he can stay in constant communications with you and keep you posted on the search. He said he'll contact you on channel two." Then with a wink, he added, "But if you *accidentally* happened to turn to channel six, our tactical channel, you could listen in on the in-flight communications from our crews while they're searching for Addison. There wouldn't be anything we could do about that."

"Seriously?"

"Seriously."

"He told me you guys might be doing some training southwest of Cusick, but the police told me they'd asked for your help. Is that what's happening?"

He nodded. "Since Addison is family, we agreed immediately. The law enforcement agencies will handle the daylight searches, and we'll mostly search at night since we have FLIRs and night-vision goggles."

"When do you start?"

"Tonight. But you didn't hear that from me. Also, the boss told me to tell you to stay as far away from this as humanly possible. He can't protect you if you do something stupid. You could put Addison or yourself in danger. Understand?"

"You know I do, sir." He smiled. "Thanks for stopping by. Tell the boss how much I appreciate the radio."

"I will. I hope you know we've all got your back. We'll do anything and everything to help find Addison."

"I know. It means a lot to me, to all of us."

"Okay. I'll get out of here. Is there anything else you need from us now?"

"I don't think so. Just glad you guys have joined the fight."

"So are we."

Chase walked the captain to the door and saw him off. He stood there for a few minutes, lost in thought.

"Chase?"

He quickly turned around. "Yes, Julia?"

"Is everything all right?"

"Yes. I was just thinking about what the captain said."

"He seemed like a thoughtful man, and genuinely concerned about you and Addison. You must work with a great group of people."

"I definitely do," he replied as they walked back to the living room.

Chase sat down for a few minutes before he realized what time it was. "We need to watch the news," he said, clicking on the TV. He turned to Julia. "The detectives told us to watch tonight to see an announcement about the FBI."

They didn't have to wait long. It was the lead story. "The search for Addison Roberts is heating up. FBI Special Agent in Charge, Bob Sackett, joins us now from our Seattle affiliate. Special Agent Sackett, what can you tell our viewers about the investigation?"

"Effective tomorrow morning, the FBI will be joining the investigation into Addison's disappearance and potential connections to the perpetrator of the Harvest Bank robbery. We will be leading a joint task force of law enforcement officers from the Spokane Police Department and several surrounding police departments. We will be establishing an on-site presence from which we will operate in the town of Cusick. That's all I can share with you tonight, but we're optimistic we will find Addison soon."

"Wow," Rick exclaimed. "That was a huge announcement. They're bringing in the A-Team. That's a relief."

"I'll say," Julia chimed in. "That really gives me hope Addison will be okay. Don't you agree, Chase?"

"Of course I'm glad the FBI is involved, but we still don't know any more about Addison than we did before the news."

"True," Rick said. "But the odds of finding her just increased exponentially. Julia is right. We have more hope now for a quick and positive outcome."

They visited a few more minutes but were all tired and mostly talked out for the day. Rick and Julia decided to call it a night, so Chase excused himself and went to his office. He desperately wanted to get involved, and his mind was racing with the possibilities. He still felt helpless, like he had turned his back on Addison when she needed him most. But now, with the unexpected arrival of the radio, he suddenly had options not previously available.

He pulled out a notepad and pen and began to sort through his options, first identifying each one and then building a pro-con list. He avoided the most obvious con for now, which was risk. There would be risk with any decision. Risk he'd be shot or captured by Eddie. Risk that he'd get Addison injured or worse. Risk he'd be arrested for obstruction of justice. If he considered risk in his decision, he might as well give up now, since it seemed to be a universal disqualifier.

Chase looked at the clock on his desk, amazed to see nearly thirty minutes had raced by. He heard a soft knock on the door and glanced up as Rick opened it and asked if he would like some company. Chase nodded and motioned him toward the other chair next to his desk.

"Julia's reading in bed, so I thought I'd touch base with you before we turn in. What do you think about the radio your commander sent over? That was very kind of him."

Chase nodded. "He really tries to take care of his people."

"Anything else?"

"What do you mean?"

"You and I both know the radio's capabilities. And if he just wanted to make sure he could reach you, I'm sure your cell phone would do the trick."

Chase looked down, smiling sheepishly. "The captain who dropped it off said if I accidentally turned to channel six, I'd be able to monitor their search activity in real time. But he also sent me a clear message to stay away from the investigation. It does seem like he's sending contradictory messages." Chase was tempted to read between the lines.

"Not necessarily. He might just want you to keep abreast of what's happening, at least on the air force end, while still warning you to keep physically away from the case. And that raises the question I asked earlier: Are you going to stay away?"

Chase was slow to respond as he pondered exactly what to say. "I still haven't decided. You spent twenty-five years in the air force; this isn't your first rodeo. If you were in my position—heck, you are in my position, except as Addison's father—I suspect you'd look for a way to get right in the middle of it rather than sitting on the sidelines doing nothing. Am I right?"

Rick nodded.

"But I know I could be putting Addison in greater danger and could even find myself under arrest and charged with obstruction of justice or interfering with an official investigation if I don't do things just right."

Rick nodded again. "That's the last thing Addison would want, son. If we do take a more proactive approach to finding Addison, we'll have to make sure that doesn't happen. And obviously, we can't put her in greater danger. There won't be any margin for error. Is this still the direction you want to head?"

Chase thought about it for a moment and then resolutely nodded his head. "I just can't sit here and do nothing while my wife's life hangs in the balance. I'm all in."

"That's what I figured. If you hadn't reached that conclusion, I'd have been mighty disappointed in you. A man sometimes has to do whatever it takes to protect his family. Count me in."

Chase looked into his father-in-law's eyes with heightened respect for the man; they had a shared commitment to put Addison's welfare above everything else. It was that unique respect found between brothers and sisters in arms—they knew they had each other's backs.

"I know you've been in here probably thinking of how best to help Addison. What have you come up with?"

"Nothing firm yet. I've been thinking through, evaluating the pros and cons. There are only a couple of approaches we can take that wouldn't get us unwanted police attention. Those would be lower risk but also unlikely to yield much in the way of meaningful results. There are more options if we work overtly, but the risk is significantly greater."

Rick nodded his agreement. "Our main choice seems to be whether to let the police know what we are doing. If we bring them into the loop, they will definitely restrict what we can do and, in all probability, even push back. I think if we're serious about finding Addison, we'll need to go it alone."

"Exactly."

Chase ran through his plan, with Rick interjecting comments. They decided to camp near where Addison's car was found and listen to the tactical radio as well as a police scanner. Between the two radios, they thought they might be able to glean enough intelligence to guide them to Addison or at least to be able to respond quickly if the police found her first.

"Being closer to Cusick and on higher terrain should improve both radio and cell reception," Rick said. "I didn't bring any camping gear along, but I did toss in a portable emergency radio with batteries that can be recharged either by solar cells or a hand crank. It has a USB port, so we can charge our cell phones."

"I have enough camping gear for both of us, and we can grab some extra batteries on the way, just in case. I suppose we can even rotate to a nearby motel when we need to clean up, eat a hot meal, and get a good night's sleep."

"I love it when a plan comes together," Rick said, quoting *The A-Team*. "Wow, it's already after eleven. We'd better get to work so we can get some sleep."

The two divided responsibilities, knowing there was much to be done. More detailed planning and precise execution could mean the difference between success and failure. They wandered back to the living room, surprised to see Julia still awake and waiting for them in her pajamas and bathrobe.

"Well," Julia said as they walked in. "What did you two decide?"

"What do you mean?" Chase asked innocently.

"Chase, I've been married to a military officer for nearly thirty-five years now, and I've learned a thing or two about how they think. I know neither of you is the kind to sit and wait. The military is all about planning and executing, so I know darn well you two have been in there concocting your own plan to find and rescue Addison. Am I wrong?"

Chase looked at Rick, who shrugged and smiled. "What can I say? She knows me too well."

"Then I suppose you're against Rick and me getting involved."

"I am. I don't want to see either of you or Addison getting hurt. I think these things are best left to the professionals . . ."

"But . . ." Rick chimed in. "I know there's a 'but' coming."

"But I also know there's nothing I could say or do to keep you from going after Addison. I know how much both of you love her, and I respect that. I just want you to promise me a few things."

"That's the least we can do," said Chase.

"First, I want you to promise you won't take any chances with Addison's life. None of us could live with ourselves if we inadvertently contributed to her death or serious injury."

"We won't," Rick said. "We agreed we wouldn't put her in greater danger as a result of anything we do. Her safety is paramount."

Julia nodded. "Second, I don't want either of you to break the law in any way. I couldn't bear the thought of either of you ending up in jail or with a record. I don't think Addison would want that either. The police aren't too lenient toward people who take the law into their own hands. Can you live with that?"

The men looked at each other and nodded.

"We just had that same discussion," Chase said. "We want to get as involved as possible in helping to find and rescue Addison, but we won't cross any lines that would expose us to criminal charges. And, we don't want to get into a gun fight with Eddie."

"Fine. Lastly, I want you to keep me informed by checking in by phone every day or a couple of times a day so I know what's happening and that the two of you are safe. I'm not looking forward to being here by myself, wondering what's going on. I need to be able to contact you in case someone calls here for either of you. We don't want to raise any unnecessary suspicion."

"Agreed," Chase said, the men nodding their commitment.

Rick added, "We know how hard this will be on you. We'll do our best to stay connected."

With that, Rick and Chase split up to work on their respective checklists. They wanted to get their gear ready before they hit the sack so they could leave first thing in the morning. Chase had to hand it to Julia. She didn't agree with what they were doing, but she was willing to support them in holding down the home front while they were away. They were modern-day musketeers, just as committed as those of old and every bit as determined to right the wrongs of others.

Chase and Rick packed their gear over the next half hour and loaded it into the back of Chase's truck. They grabbed some freeze-dried food from Chase's food storage and filled two five-gallon water jugs.

When they had everything loaded, Chase and Rick went back into the office. Chase unlocked his gun safe and handed Rick a 12-gauge shotgun and .30-06 scoped deer rifle. He threaded a holster onto his belt and strapped on a 9mm handgun to complete their arsenal.

"Are you sure you want to go up there armed?" Rick asked. "That might be inviting trouble we don't need."

"Eddie's armed. I think we need to be prepared for anything."

"Okay. But maybe we should stow them in the truck until we're sure we'll need them."

"Fair enough."

Before closing the safe, they both grabbed a few boxes of ammunition and then locked up.

Addison, Chase thought, *we're on our way. Stay safe!*

CHAPTER 16

DAY 4

ADDISON WOKE WITH A START. Confused, it took her a moment to remember where she was. It was still dark—her watch told her it was just after midnight. Then the thought hit her hard—*Where's Eddie?* She had no idea. After a full day of walking yesterday, she had been exhausted and had fallen asleep in a copse of trees. She slept soundly, but something had awakened her.

She lay still, trying to control her breathing and quiet her mind. *I'm fine. I'm well hidden. Eddie, if he's even still alive, doesn't know where I am.* The sun wouldn't be up for hours. Should she try and go back to sleep or get up and move?

As she pondered the question, Addison gradually became aware of the sound of voices carried on the night breeze. They were muffled. She couldn't understand what was being said, but she was certain there were people nearby. *Why would they be out this late at night—and in this remote part of the mountains?*

Her curiosity drove the thought of sleep from her mind. She sat up and peeked out through the branches that hid her. The voices were definitely coming from farther down the draw. Addison pulled back the branches to get a better view. In the soft moonlight, she could see that the draw forked about forty yards from where she was sitting.

It was faint, but she thought she could see the flickers of a small campfire down the left side of the fork. She wondered who it could be—maybe a group of campers visiting around the campfire before turning in. The possibility brought a sudden sense of relief until she realized Eddie's camp was supposed to be close by too. Could Eddie be camped there with some of his buddies? Though unlikely since he should be behind her, the mere thought of Eddie being so close, and with others potentially like him, made her sick.

Still, the odds were in her favor. She knew immediately she had to see who it was. If it wasn't Eddie, and she doubted it was—if he was meeting others, she thought he would have mentioned it—she would no longer be alone. Surely, the campers would help her get to safety. And even if Eddie caught up with them, he couldn't possibly be stupid enough to take on a group of people. *Well . . . maybe he could.*

Addison made her decision. She was going to sneak as close to the camp as possible without risking exposure. Once she knew whom she was dealing with, she'd decide whether or not to reveal herself. She stood up, pulled Eddie's backpack on, and stepped out into the open.

Moving quickly yet quietly, she darted back across the draw and into the safety of the trees on the other side. She stood as still as possible, listening carefully for any unusual sounds. First, she decided to climb up the side of the draw to try to look down at the camp. After fifteen minutes of exertion, she realized it was too steep and the footing too loose for a nighttime attempt, so she backtracked down into the draw and walked toward the sound and the flickering light.

Addison's breathing seemed loud to her in the stillness of the night, and her heartbeat pounded in her ears like a base drum. *Settle down, Addison*, she reassured herself. *It might seem loud to you, but no one else can hear it.*

Addison continued in the direction of the voices, taking a few steps and then pausing to listen. She crouched low to shrink her silhouette as she drew closer and moved from tree to tree, pausing frequently to listen and then continuing forward. Soon, the muffled sounds of conversation became more distinct, and she could make out some of the words. She inched closer still, always being careful to step lightly and softly. Her safety, she felt, largely depended on her ability to stay hidden.

Time seemed to slow to match her pace as Addison crept ahead. There was no room for a mistake. She followed the fork in the draw to the left, and the glow of the campfire brightened, lighting up a small clearing not far in front of her. She counted seven people, sitting around it, quietly talking to one another.

Addison dropped to her belly quietly and slithered closer. She paused every few feet to study the scene unfolding before her. She wanted more than anything to run to the campers and plead for their help, but something made her hesitate. She couldn't put her finger on it, but she knew she had to be cautious about exposing herself to strangers. She didn't want to jump from the frying pan into the fire.

So she stopped and listened again, continuing to gather as much information as possible about the group. Her judgment as to whether they were friend or foe could mean the difference between escape and bondage. Life and death. She had to get this right. As she slid even closer, she realized the group was only men, and they were dressed in camouflage. But she knew in an instant that they were not professional military men.

Some were dressed in mismatched camouflage; they each wore different types of boots, and several had long hair and beards. These were not soldiers in the active-duty army. She thought they could be hunters, though she didn't think it would be hunting season until fall. And their weapons, she was startled to realize, were assault rifles, not scoped hunting rifles or shotguns. They must be part of a militia.

She'd learned a little about militias during the welcome social that was hosted by the Family Support Center for new arrivals on base. And Homeland Security was always warning the public about the threat of homegrown terrorism from armed militias. Of course, most militias were peaceful and patriotic and of no threat to society. It made sense to Addison that a militia would be in the mountains—they'd probably want to avoid being seen.

Addison could finally hear most of the conversation from the men facing in her direction, but still couldn't understand much of what the men facing away from her were saying. It sounded like they were planning some kind of military exercise or critiquing one they had just completed. She couldn't be sure. One thing she was sure of, though—these were not men whose company she would normally keep. *But,* she thought, *they are armed and could definitely protect me from Eddie.* On the other hand, what might they do with a woman out here all alone?

Addison dropped her forehead down to rest on her crossed arms. She closed her eyes to better concentrate on what to do. Should she bypass the group out of an abundance of caution, or walk into their camp and ask for help? Why did she feel so conflicted? Addison froze at the unmistakable sound of a gun being cocked behind her. Then she felt the cold hard steel of a barrel press firmly against the back of her head.

"You don't belong here, little lady."

"I don't know who you are, but I mean you no harm."

"Then what are you doing spying on us like that? We don't take too kindly to spies, you know. What part of the government are you from, anyway?"

"I'm not from any part of the government. I was just getting ready to walk around your group and keep hiking down this draw. With your permission, I'll be moving on now."

"I don't think so. Are you part of our exercise tonight?"

"What do you mean?"

"I mean, did Gunner put you here to test us?"

"I don't know anyone named Gunner, and I'm not part of any exercise. I'm just trying to get back home. Can I go now?"

"Not a chance, missy. You're coming with me. Put your hands behind your head and interlock your fingers!"

Addison slowly stood and did as she was told, all the while wondering how this nightmare could get any worse.

The man grabbed her by the back of her collar.

"Now walk toward the fire slowly. Don't try nothin'. I'd hate for this gun to go off accidentally, if you know what I mean."

They walked slowly out of the cover of the trees and into the meadow. The men around the campfire stopped talking and just stared at the two of them.

"Hey, Gunner. Look what I found hiding in the woods, spying on us. Did you plant her there as part of the exercise? I hope I get bonus points for finding her!"

"No, you idiot! Point that gun somewhere else and help her over here. That ain't no way to treat a lady. Show some respect."

"Sorry, ma'am. I thought you was part of the exercise."

Addison walked over to the fire warily but was relieved to know she was no longer being held at gunpoint. She wondered who these men were and if they'd help or harm her.

"What's your name, miss?"

"Addison . . . Addison Roberts."

"What on earth are you doing out here in the mountains by yourself in the middle of the night?"

Addison hesitated as she thought about how much of her situation to share.

"You are alone, aren't you?" asked Gunner.

"Yes, I'm alone. I was kidnapped yesterday by a man named Eddie. I was able to get away yesterday, but I think he's still chasing me. Can you please help me?"

The men just stared at her not knowing what to say or how to respond.

"Are you serious? Where is he now?" asked Gunner.

"Dead serious. He carjacked me after robbing a bank in Spokane and killing the guard. He dumped my car up here in the mountains. We've been wandering around for the past few days trying to find some camp of his where he stashed supplies. I was able to hit him in the head with a rock and escape just before dark two days ago, and I've been running ever since. I don't know for sure where he is right now." Again she asked, "Please, can you help me?"

Gunner looked around the campfire at his crew. They didn't look like much, but to Addison, they could mean the difference between life and death. "Heck yeah, we'll help you. You've stumbled across the perfect rescuers. We like to call ourselves the North Country Rangers, and it would be our honor to protect you until we can get you back to safety. Where are you from?"

"I live on Fairchild Air Force Base near Spokane."

"Then that makes you one of us—at least an honorary member. Most of us done some time in the service ourselves."

Addison smiled for the first time in days. She looked from face to face around the campfire and was comforted to see them each nod agreement in turn. Maybe, just maybe, her hope for a safe return would come to fruition.

"Thank you. You can't imagine how relieved I am."

"Most of my friends call me Gunner." Then, pointing to the others, Gunner said, "This here's Jeremy, Ramon, Cory, Zach, Casey, and that knucklehead over there that brung you in is Greg."

Addison smiled and nodded to the men.

"You look like you've had a rough go of it. Can we get you some water or food before we hike out of here? My cabin ain't far, but you probably ought to put some fuel in your tank before we go."

"Yes, thank you. I'm beyond thirsty. And, I haven't eaten much in the past couple of days. I'd appreciate anything you're willing to share."

Gunner passed her his canteen and a granola bar and then looked at his comrades.

"I guess the first thing to do is to get back to the cabin and secure the perimeter. We'll plan on leaving the cabin at first light and get Miss Addison back home."

"Do you have a phone?" Addison asked. "I'd like to call my husband to let him know I'm alive. And we should contact the police as well."

"We do have cell phones, but there ain't no reception up here in this part of the mountains. And there are a few things we need to clean up at the cabin before we contact the cops. We're a militia, and you can imagine how interested in us the Feds might be if they find out we've been operating around here. I'm sure you understand."

"Of course. As far as I'm concerned, you're the cavalry riding to my rescue. The last thing I'd ever want is to somehow bring harm to you or your group. I will always be grateful for your willingness to help me."

"Tell you what . . . once we cover our tracks at the cabin, we'll head down out of the mountains and call the cops and your husband as soon as we can. No point in waiting 'til dawn, I guess. But I'd ask that you forget you ever heard we was a militia. We don't mean nobody no harm, but we like to train and prepare to protect our individual liberties and constitutional rights in case we ever need to. But, as far as you're concerned, we're just a bunch of friends hanging out at the cabin for the weekend."

"That sounds perfect, Gunner. And you can believe me when I say the existence of your group is absolutely safe with me. As far as anyone will know, I stumbled upon your cabin and you were kind enough to help me." Addison smiled her warmest smile as she reached out and touched Gunner's arm, hoping to forge a bond that wouldn't be broken. She wanted to give them every reason to help her get back home.

Gunner looked in the general direction of his crew. "Okay, fellas, let's put out the fire so the coals are cold to the touch. Then we'll hike back to the cabin. We'll follow our usual patrol method—single file, ten feet between us with point and trail guards watching for the enemy—this Eddie guy chasing Miss Addison. Any questions?"

Silence.

Someone poured water on the fire and stirred the coals to ensure there were no hot spots remaining. The group cleaned up after themselves so no one would know they had been there and were on their way in less than fifteen minutes.

They elected to keep their flashlights off to avoid degrading their night vision or risk giving away their location in case Addison was being followed. The moon was well to the west now and didn't provide much illumination as they walked. This slowed their progress, but it was certainly safer than using their flashlights.

* * *

As he watched from the edge of the clearing, hidden in the darkness of the trees, Eddie frowned at this turn of events. He tried to consider his options, but his head pounded where Addison had hit him, making thinking nearly impossible. At least the bleeding had stopped. That was good. He felt strangely like he was hung over but knew it was worse. Probably a concussion. He couldn't wait to get his hands on that woman; she was going to pay for what she'd done. *At least she's still got my pack and my money . . . for now.*

When Eddie had regained consciousness after being clocked in the head by Addison, she was long gone. He'd managed to get up and start walking down the draw—not because he'd made an actual decision to go that direction; it was just easier walking downhill. He kept going, even after dark. With the police on his tail, he knew he needed to keep moving. He rested frequently but resisted the urge to sleep. There'd be time enough for that later.

He just kept plodding along. That is, until he stumbled on the campfire and that ragtag bunch of militiamen. What a stroke of good fortune! He figured Addison was either already with them or would end up here just like he had. All he needed to do was watch and wait—let Addison come to him. And that she did. But there wasn't much Eddie could do about it yet. He was badly outnumbered and outgunned.

When the militia and Addison left the clearing, Eddie followed them. In the back of his mind, he knew he should just forget about Addison and worry about staying ahead of the police, but he wanted his money. The way his head felt, he couldn't force himself to think things through to their likely conclusion. Instead, he continued to function on impulse alone, pretty much like he had his whole life. And right now, he was so mad at Addison, he only had two things on his mind: revenge and money. It wasn't just business anymore; it had become very personal.

As he trudged along behind the group, even Eddie couldn't help but see his previous plan was unraveling faster than a ball of yarn in a room full of cats. If only he could turn the clock back. He'd made some bad decisions, there was no denying that. But that wasn't all his fault! Addison was to blame for most of it. She'd really made a mess of things.

And now I got her mess to clean up. If he didn't get to her fast, she'd call the cops as soon as she found a phone with reception. He had to stop her, or he'd never get his money back. Heck, he might even kill her. It'd be easier than dragging her along. Her days were numbered.

Eddie kept his distance as he trailed the group. He didn't want to risk getting caught. Besides, they were in a narrow draw, so unless the terrain changed, he knew where they'd be going. That was good, but he'd heard one of the men talking about heading to a cabin. That could complicate things for him. And it would probably put him a little too close to other cabins and more people than he'd like.

Eddie was about out of steam, but he forced himself to keep walking. But he was worn out and didn't think he had the juice in him to keep this up much longer. Suddenly, he heard the unmistakable sound of voices on the trail just in front of him. He skidded to a stop in his beat-up athletic shoes. *What the heck am I doing? I gotta pay more attention.* Addison and the militia boys were right in front of him. He could've been caught or killed.

Fortunately for Eddie, the darkness of the night coupled with the noise the militia was making had protected him. He stepped quickly to the side of the trail and shrunk down into the underbrush. Thank goodness they were taking a break so he could too. *The good Lord must look out for fools and drunks, or I'd be dead for sure.*

CHAPTER 17

THE MILITIA WAS UP AND moving again before Eddie could even catch his breath, but he pushed himself up off the ground and continued following the group through the darkness. Other than heading to a cabin, he had no idea where they were going or just how long it would take. He just hoped he'd be able to grab Addison and reclaim the bank money before she could rat him out to the cops. He wasn't optimistic, but he didn't know what else to do.

His lips were cracking, and his tongue was slightly swollen. His canteen was in the backpack Addison now carried. He was incredibly thirsty. He didn't want to risk getting sick by drinking untreated stream water—that much he remembered from his army days—but now he needed water. But as he thought about it, it wasn't really water he was craving. Even though his mouth was as dry as a dusty cave, and water would be great, Eddie really needed a drink of something stronger.

He pushed that thought from his mind and focused on Addison. Vengeance was the best fuel to keep his fire burning hot. As long as he could concentrate on revenge, he knew he could put his other discomforts behind. In the back of his mind, he wondered if he was being irrational because somehow Addison had come to represent all the wrongs he'd suffered over the course of his life, but at this point, he didn't really care. He just needed to fight back against someone. Anyone. And Addison was a better target than most.

Almost without warning, Eddie saw a light up ahead and halted in his tracks. Distance and trees obscured his view, but they looked like lights from a cabin. He couldn't be sure but figured that must be the group's destination. *Probably nobody else around here's fool enough to be up at this time of night anyway.*

Eddie approached the side of the cabin cautiously, assuming the men Addison was with would be watching for him. Even though his senses were dulled by fatigue and pain, he fully understood that these men were armed. His arsenal, a single revolver with only four remaining bullets, didn't offer him much in the way of firepower. Still, he hoped to assess the situation and figure out a way to grab Addison. *These weekend warriors probably ain't even got bullets for their guns.*

He crept quietly through the woods, avoiding the open terrain. He could see the cabin up ahead and realized he was almost to the edge of the clearing in which it stood. He dropped to the ground and crawled to the wood line, careful not to make a sound.

Eddie stopped behind a small juniper tree that offered cover while giving him a mostly unobstructed view of the cabin. The glare from the lights was not making it easy for him to see. The longer he looked, the greater his loss of night vision.

He really needed to know if there were guards outside the cabin. He raised a hand to his face to shield his eyes from the direct light. As they adjusted, he scanned the base of the house and adjoining meadow for movement. He looked around for any other cabins or signs of life. He spotted a few more cabins in the distance, but all were dark. Nothing else stood out.

After watching quietly for about fifteen minutes, he spotted someone walking around the cabin. As he watched, Eddie could see the man was stopping periodically, probably checking with the other guards that were posted outside the cabin. Eddie watched how the guard patrolled and then checked his watch to time the next couple of rounds. There didn't seem to be a set schedule. That wasn't good.

A couple of other men came and went through the cabin door, loading boxes into the back of a pickup truck parked in front. There were three other cars parked nearby. Only the lights in the front half of the cabin were on. The back half was dark. *I wonder if she's asleep in a back bedroom. Too bad there ain't no back door.*

Once Eddie was satisfied he had this side of the cabin set in his mind, he worked his way around the edge of the meadow until he had an unobstructed view of the other side. There was another guard sitting there. Eddie watched again for a few minutes. Things looked pretty much the same on this side.

While he silently looked on, Eddie noticed a gasoline canister sitting on the ground right next to the cabin, along with a few old paint cans stacked next to it. It made sense to him to keep flammable materials outside, but not that close to the cabin. They just might come in handy, though, if he could figure out what to do with them.

Then, slowly, like a dense fog lifting in the morning light, an idea began to form in Eddie's mind. He wasn't sure if the gas container had anything left in it, but if so, he could use it to smoke out Addison. Maybe even capture her again. Or—he chuckled to himself—put an end to her. But that would also burn up the cash in his backpack. The risk was high, but he couldn't think of another plan. One idea every couple of days was about all Eddie could manage.

He searched his pockets for his cigarette lighter and pulled it out. Now all he had to do was avoid the guards and count on the element of surprise. When the roving guard made his last round, he had to kick the guard closest to the gas can in the boots to wake him up. *I'll bet the bum has gone back to sleep. He ain't moved a lick since I been watching him.*

With a little luck, Eddie thought he could get to the gas can quickly enough to splash it around and light it on fire before anyone spotted him. If he got caught in the process . . . well, that'd just be par for the course. But if he was successful, he may just get his hands on Addison again.

Eddie looked for the best approach path, circling around the clearing toward the front of the cabin. There was a large aspen tree near the front porch with a picnic table under it and a couple of smaller pine trees between the wood line and the aspen. He could use these as cover to hide his approach. Other than that, the meadow where the cabin stood was wide open.

From the aspen tree, the gas can was within twenty feet and nearly the full length of the cabin away from the sleeping guard. *I just might be able to pull this off.* He paused a moment to collect his thoughts. Smoking out Addison seemed to Eddie like his best option. The only other choice was to wait for her to come out, but if that happened, she'd be surrounded by the men protecting her. If she didn't come out, it could be they had called the cops already and were waiting for them to get here. But since they were loading up the truck, they probably planned on leaving soon. *That probably means there ain't no landline in the cabin and they still ain't got a cell phone signal.*

So Eddie decided waiting wasn't really an option. He'd have to smoke her out. If it worked, he'd grab Addison when she came running out the door. The men would probably be trying to put the fire out, and she'd be vulnerable. If it didn't work . . . well, he just wouldn't have to worry about her anymore. Either she'd be dead or he would.

Eddie began his approach from the woods, crawling on his belly. He made his way past the juniper trees and paused under the picnic table, watching the guards. A soft breeze gently touched his face, blowing from the direction of the cabin. *Perfect.* The breeze would muffle the sound of Eddie's approach, and they wouldn't be able to smell him coming either.

Eddie waited patiently for just the right time to pounce. The roving guard was making his rounds again, kicking the feet of the other two guards to make sure they were still awake. Seeming satisfied, the roving guard checked his watch, knocked on the cabin door, and went in. Eddie, who was still under the picnic table, looked up and could see him through the window—almost close enough to touch. He was talking to another man and then stepped to the sink to splash cold water on his face. *I'd give just about anything for some of that water right now!*

The roving guard walked back outside on the porch and headed for the side of the cabin. Eddie again thought it looked as if they were getting ready to leave. He was running out of time and had to act. Just as the roving guard rounded the front corner of the cabin and stepped into the darkness, Eddie streaked out from under the table and struck hard, clubbing him at the base of the neck karate-style and knocking him out cold. As the man collapsed, Eddie caught the man loosely in his arms and then lowered him quietly to the ground.

Eddie stopped momentarily to see if anyone had spotted him. All he heard was soft rhythmic snoring from the guard posted at the back corner of the cabin. He smiled to himself. *I knew I could count on him! Reminds me how much I hated guard duty. I reckon it's the same for everyone.*

Eddie had to move fast now if his plan was going to work. He lunged for the gas canister and lifted it up. He was in luck. It was half full. He unscrewed the cap and poured the gasoline on the side of the cabin and the dry prairie grass growing next to it. He set the can down, pulled out his lighter, and lit the grass on fire. Eddie sprinted back toward the wood line.

In the safety of the trees, he turned around and dropped again to his belly. He'd wait there to grab Addison when she came running out, hoping the men would be distracted by the fire. As far as he could tell, his plan was off to a good start. The fire had taken hold instantly and spread quickly. With a slight gust of breeze, it exploded up the side of the cabin and was already licking at the eaves. Thanks to the dry grass, it also raced along the lower length of the cabin. In another few minutes, he thought the whole cabin would be in flames.

The sleeping guard awoke with a start, jumped to his feet, and began patting the bottom of his trousers, which were on fire. He looked up frantically at the cabin.

"Fire!" he yelled at the top of his lungs, running for the front door.

He tripped over the body of the unconscious guard in the darkness and fell to the ground. He quickly regained his composure and pulled the roving guard to safety before alerting the others.

In no time, the fire consumed the group's entire attention as they scrambled to stop its spread. Some tried to stomp out the grass fire, but it moved faster than they could keep up. Another found a hose and was fumbling in the dark to attach it to an outside faucet.

Eddie watched as the group's leader appeared at the door with two fire extinguishers he'd brought from inside and quickly sized up the situation. "Here, use these!" he yelled at his men, tossing out the extinguishers. "Get the fire stopped! I'll take care of Addison."

So Addison is inside. Come on, girl, run for safety—right out the door and straight to me! The thought of that happening put a smile on Eddie's weary, banged-up face.

* * *

Addison awoke to a chaotic situation but had no idea what was happening. She rubbed the sleep from her eyes and willed herself to get up. She looked at the bedroom window and could see the unmistakable flickering of fire as she heard the men yelling outside. Gunner knocked once and then burst into the room.

"Addison, the cabin's on fire, and we need to get outta here!"

Gunner left the lights off and grabbed Addison by the hand as she sat up on the edge of the bed. Without warning, the bedroom window exploded from the heat. The flames began climbing the inside wall and across the ceiling. Smoke was sucked in through the broken window. Visibility suddenly dropped near to zero.

"Come on! Follow me. We have to hurry!"

"Let me get my shoes!" Addison cried as she picked them up on the way out of the bedroom.

"What are you doing?" she asked. "We need to get outside. Everything's on fire!"

"We can't go out the front door—the porch is on fire, but there's an escape tunnel in the root cellar. I'm pretty sure the guy chasing you set the fire and is waiting for us to burn up or run out the door into his waiting arms. I put this tunnel in last year just in case something like this happened. The Feds are always harassing us. For once, being a prepper is paying off."

Gunner pulled Addison to the kitchen and opened a door in one corner. A set of roughed-in stairs appeared, leading down to an unfinished cellar. He grabbed a flashlight from a rudimentary shelf at the bottom of the stairs and thrust it into Addison's hands. They crawled under the stairs and Gunner pulled open a plywood door that revealed the tunnel.

"Take the flashlight and follow the tunnel out to the woods at the edge of the meadow."

"What about you?"

"I'll be right behind you. Wait for me at the other end."

Addison disappeared into the tunnel just as Gunner ran back upstairs, presumably to check on his men. The front door was nearly burned through. Addison could hear his muffled voice calling for his men, but no one answered. She heard Gunner's footsteps as he hustled back downstairs and into the tunnel. Pulling the plywood door shut behind him, he hesitated momentarily.

He uttered a mild oath and grumbled, "I left my rifle upstairs. Too late now." When he saw Addison only a few yards in front of him, looking over her shoulder at him, he hollered at her. "Move, Addison. This ain't a Sunday walk in the park!"

"But I forgot my backpack!"

"Too late now; we can't go back into the fire. It'd kill us for sure."

His sense of urgency spurred Addison into action. She crawled the length of the tunnel quickly, being careful not to brush against the walls or ceiling for fear of causing a collapse. She thought she had gone about a hundred and fifty feet when the tunnel abruptly ended. She looked up and saw another trapdoor, turned off the flashlight, and carefully pushed the door up. It was much heavier than she expected, and it took all of her upper body strength to get it opened enough to crawl out.

Once outside, she understood why: Gunner had covered it with several inches of dirt. Addison dropped the flashlight back down into the tunnel and then waited for Gunner next to a nearby tree. She thought Gunner was right about Eddie setting the fire and frantically looked around for him in the darkness. She wondered if he was watching her now—a thought that made her skin crawl.

Peering through the trees at the cabin, Addison could see it was now fully engulfed in flames. She couldn't see any of the North Country Rangers anymore and noticed that all the vehicles were gone except for the truck, which must be Gunner's. *I guess they gave up on the cabin and turned tail before Eddie got them. Or maybe they're just going for help. Either way, it looks like Gunner and I are on our own.*

Addison jumped as Gunner climbed out of the tunnel. He followed Addison's gaze toward the burning cabin.

"My aunt is going to kill me," he said. "She lets me use the cabin but didn't expect me to go and get it burned to the ground."

"You won't need to worry about her if Eddie kills us first! I'm sure he set the fire."

"Yup. No way that fire was an accident. We need to get away from here as fast as possible."

"We don't know where Eddie is! I haven't been able to see him, and I sure don't want to accidentally bump into him. Maybe he'll think we died in the fire."

"I sure hope so, but I don't know if he'll hang around long enough to find out. If he does, there's a good chance he'll notice there aren't any bodies in the rubble. He may even stumble across the tunnel and figure out we left."

"You're right, but he can't go through the remains of cabin until the fire burns out. I imagine the Forest Service fire department will get here before that happens, assuming someone reports it soon."

"You're probably right. I know some of the folks up this way live here all year. Hopefully one of them will report it. Anyway, we need as big a head start as we can get." Then Gunner looked toward his truck. "I hate leaving my truck behind. Maybe we can come at it from behind and take it. That's the best escape we can hope for. But, if I was Eddie, I'd plant myself close to the cabin door and the truck so I could grab you when you ran out."

"Me too. Since I escaped from him, my plan was to work my way down toward the Pend Oreille River and the highway to get help, but I don't know the area like you do. I imagine Eddie will think that's still where I'm headed. Maybe we should go a different direction—maybe up into the mountains. What do you think?"

"Seems odd running away from potential help toward somewhere more remote, but I get your point—doing something Eddie doesn't expect. Sounds like a plan to me. I know my way around here pretty good. But more important than direction is to put as much dirt between us and him as fast as we can. When we have some breathing room, we can decide where to go. But for now, let's get out of here. There's a trail out to a dirt road over this way."

"I'll follow you."

They found the trail in the dark, but before leaving, Addison couldn't help but look back at the cabin one last time. There was something about a fire that size that made it nearly impossible to turn away. That's when she heard the last groan of the supporting beams and watched as the cabin's roof collapsed in an eruption of sparks and flames. The sheer force of the fall pushed the flames out in all directions, like a giant bellows.

And standing nearby, staring into the raging fire, was Eddie.

"That's him!" Addison hissed. "That's Eddie, right where you thought he'd be."

"Yeah, I see him. Well, that answers two questions. He did set the fire, and he is still chasing you. Did you tell me he was armed?"

"He was the last time I saw him. He had a chrome revolver of some kind."

"Oh great! I didn't have time to arm up before we ran. Now our only hope is not getting captured. Let's move out."

Gunner quickly scooped some dirt up in his hands and spread it over the trapdoor. He repeated the process twice more to hide from Eddie the evidence of their escape, Addison assumed. That done, he took Addison by the hand to guide her onto the path to the road. Even with his help, she stubbed her toe on a tree root and went down hard.

"Are you okay? Can you get up and walk?"

"I'll try."

Holding Gunner's hand, Addison stood and dusted herself off. "I think I'm fine. Let's keep going. Now's our best chance to dodge Eddie."

CHAPTER 18

IT HAD ALL HAPPENED SO fast. *One minute I was sound asleep in what I thought was a safe location,* Addison thought, *and the next minute I'm crawling through a dark tunnel and running for my life with a man I've only known for less than a day.* She just wanted this to be over with so she could crawl into her own bed and sleep, safe and sound.

By now, Addison was completely and totally exhausted in mind, body, and spirit. The human soul could only take so much abuse, and she knew she was approaching her limit—she was hitting her wall.

Still, she had read of other people's experiences and how they managed to defy the odds under similar or worse circumstances and lived to tell about it. They'd returned home with their heads held high. And the most amazing thing was that they were just ordinary people, like Addison, who managed to be extraordinary in the hour of need. As she reflected on her ordeal, she realized she had already endured more than she ever had before or ever thought she could. *Maybe I have a little more to give.* She didn't plan to stop until she was free and safe from Eddie.

Addison and Gunner made it to the dirt road near the end of the escape tunnel and then turned south and ran as fast as their weary bodies would carry them. They were on Calicoma Road, which loosely connected the few cabins in the Sportsman Pond area. As they jogged, Gunner explained to Addison that Calicoma would lead them to Sicley Road, which was almost due south of the cabin and was one of the most-traveled roads in and out of the area. But the word *traveled* was obviously relative. The road was deeply rutted, and there were no vehicles or cabins in sight.

When they found Sicley Road, they could see it continued south while Calicoma turned to the west. They stayed on Sicley, but less than a quarter of a mile ahead, they came to another junction. They chose the road to their right. This put them on the southwesterly course through the foothills they had decided upon while running from the cabin. Hopefully, that would throw Eddie off.

Even though she had suggested it, Addison was still disappointed in the change of direction. She felt like she was running in circles, almost back to where she and Eddie had left her car. But she knew they needed to keep moving to get away from Eddie, and their feint in this direction might work. They made good speed on the dirt roads, but when this one turned abruptly back to the north, they took a break to decide what to do. They had no map, but at least Gunner had a compass. He'd told her it was still in his uniform pocket from the militia drills last night.

"Addison," Gunner said. "I think it's time to leave this road and head south again through the woods. If Eddie's still following us, this could be another chance to throw him off. The terrain still generally descends, and we should hit another road soon. Up here, most of the roads go east and west to access the mountains from the river valley. If we head south, we can turn east on the next road we hit and pick up on your old plan. What do you think?"

"I like the idea of getting off this road. I know we've been able to move faster, but I feel like we're out in the open. We'll definitely be safer in the woods. How about we stay on the road for another fifteen minutes and then backtrack to here along the grass next to the road before turning south?"

"That's good by me."

"Once we get away from the road a safe distance, let's look for water and find a good place to hole up for the day. The sun will be up soon. I don't know about you, but with two nights of not much sleep and a lot of running, I'm completely spent."

"I ain't run out of gas yet, but my warning light is on." He smiled.

The two stood and walked on the road as it bent to the north, jumped off the road, covered their tracks, and walked back to where they'd stopped before. They took one last look toward the way they'd come to see if they were being followed. Seeing nothing but a small dust devil, they turned south and disappeared into the woods.

"Gunner," Addison said softly when they were a safe distance from the road.

He stopped and turned. "Yes?"

"I just wanted to thank you for suggesting this. Just a few minutes here in the woods has made me feel much better—more secure. Do you know what I mean?"

He smiled. "It'll be much harder for Eddie to find us off the roads. Since we're going to stop and rest, the thicker the woods, the better. If we can find water close by, we'll be doing great."

"Yeah, we'd better keep an eye out for a stream or something. I just wanted to thank you."

"No need for that. The way I see it, we decided together. And, since we're talking, we probably ought to try and walk half a day, at least, before we stop. With the sun almost up, we'll be able to move faster. Have you got the energy to keep walking?"

Addison nodded. "And let's let the terrain, the forest, and water sources dictate when we stop, rather than how long we've been walking."

"I like the way you think."

CHAPTER 19

AFTER THE CABIN ROOF COLLAPSED and most of the militia members had left, Eddie walked slowly around the fire looking for any sign of human remains. He found none. He knew Addison and the militia leader hadn't left through the cabin's only door. There was a good chance the two of them were inside when the roof caved in.

In order to find his twisted form of closure, Eddie wanted—needed, even—to prove to himself that Addison was dead. But time was short, and he figured the cops or firemen would be there soon. He didn't know if anyone had called 911, but house fires were difficult to hide. He figured someone must have reported it, so whatever he was going to do, he needed to do it fast.

Eddie turned away from the fire's captivating flicker and walked quickly toward the truck, the only remaining vehicle at the site. He found this more than a little puzzling. On one hand, the presence of the truck indicated not everyone had made it out of the fire, or at least he hoped that's what it meant. He had seen six people, the militia flunkies, leave in the other vehicles. Addison and the militia leader must have either burned to death or somehow vanished.

On the other hand, with the pungent smell of burning flesh absent, it was possible no one had been caught inside the cabin as it had burned. But that wouldn't explain the truck or the two people who were unaccounted for. Eddie stopped in his tracks.

He'd been hiding in the woods near the truck so he could keep an eye on it and the front door. But maybe Addison and the militia guy hadn't come for the truck, anticipating that Eddie was hanging around. *But how in blazes did they disappear? Maybe they didn't.* His head was killing him just trying to think this through.

Facing more pressing needs, Eddie finished walking to the truck and tried the passenger door. It was unlocked. He opened it, looking for anything that might prove useful, especially the keys. He noticed the tire iron under the seat and grabbed it, thinking it might come in handy as a weapon if he ran out of ammunition for his handgun. He also grabbed a map from the seat, a flashlight, and two water bottles—one he drank immediately, and the other he stuck in his back pocket. *I wonder if that woman got past me and still has my backpack.* He could sure use it now.

Eddie quickly checked the driver's side but didn't find anything useful. Next, he ran his hands under each fender, looking for a magnetic key box. No luck. *I guess I'll have to keep walking.* But before he left, he knelt beside the two rear tires and let the air out just in case its owner was alive and returned. *If I gotta walk, so do they!*

Next, Eddie decided to search the cabin's perimeter for any clues about Addison's whereabouts. He wasn't sure what he was looking for, but he searched anyway. He couldn't imagine how Addison could have escaped, but the thought of her outsmarting him was gnawing at him like a rat on a dead animal.

Eddie knew he was being stupid. He should just make a run for it and worry about getting his hind end out of the area, but he still couldn't do it. He let his emotions, his greed and thirst for vengeance, drive his thoughts. *I'm gonna catch that woman if it's the last thing I do! The cops has to be closing in on me now. I got no wheels, no hostage, no money from the robbery, and I can't even find my dang camp.* As unlikely as it seemed, he thought Addison was still alive and his only way out of this mess. *If I ain't got no hostage, I'm dead or going to jail. And with no money, I got nothing to live on even if I do get away. That woman has gotta pay for crossing me!*

After his first trip around the cabin's perimeter, he came up empty, so Eddie moved to the outside edge of the meadow and began a wider search. He had nearly come full circle when something caught his eye. It blended in with the rest of the forest floor but had an unnatural look to it. It seemed too angular for Mother Nature. He hurried over to investigate. *Well, I'll be a blue-nosed gopher!* He discovered a trapdoor hidden beneath some dirt. He never would have guessed that was how she and that G. I. Joe had gotten away.

Eddie flipped on his flashlight and searched around the trapdoor for footprints that would show him which way they'd gone. He easily spotted two sets of fresh tracks in the soft soil that headed away from the tunnel. He followed them through the trees to the west until they disappeared in the hard, packed dirt of a nearby road.

Eddie scratched his head. This didn't follow Addison's previous behavior of running east and downhill, but now she had help. It looked like she, or they, were changing things up—trying to pull the wool over his eyes. He smiled briefly at the thought of Addison thinking she could trip him up. *It'll take more than this to get away from old Eddie.*

Eddie was startled out of his thoughts by the loud beating sound of a helicopter approaching the cabin. He immediately recognized it as a Huey. No other helicopter in the world made that sound. He shut off his flashlight and, after a few seconds of searching, spotted the helicopter as it approached from the south. Since he was already in the tree line, he didn't think he needed to hide. He was sure they couldn't see him in the dark.

The chopper passed overhead, and when Eddie thought he was in the clear, he continued out onto the dirt road, looking for any sign of Addison or her new partner. There wasn't much. He walked up and down both sides of the road to see if she had left the path, but that proved a complete waste of time. Against his better judgment, he even used the flashlight again in the vain attempt to find their tracks. Nothing. A string of profanity ran through his thoughts as Eddie's frustration mounted. Just when he'd caught a break, he ran into another obstacle.

Growing angry, Eddie killed the light and paced back and forth. *What should I do?* The question hung over him like a dark cloud. With every minute of indecision, he knew Addison was getting farther away, and that only added to his stress. As he pondered his decision, he slowly became aware of the sound of approaching sirens—faint at first, but getting louder by the minute. *Ugh! The first responders will be here any second. I gotta get out of here fast!*

Eddie ran across the road and stopped under the trees. He pulled the map out of his back pocket and clicked the flashlight on again. He wanted to pinpoint his location, but it wasn't necessary. The map's owner had the cabin circled. This had to be Calicoma Road. He looked in both directions, still locked in indecision. Finally, when he could wait no longer, Eddie turned south and started a slow jog down the road. Where to, he had no idea. But he hoped this was the way Addison had gone, since it was downhill and she could move faster.

Plus, he thought, *south and east lead toward more towns where she could find help.*

CHAPTER 20

DAY 5

EDDIE WATCHED THE SKY LIGHTEN as he walked, happy to see daylight coming. Unfortunately, the temperature also rose. An hour and a half had passed since he'd left the cabin site, and he needed a break to rest and cool off. He stopped along the side of the road, darted inside the tree line, and sat down with his back against a tree. He took a few swigs from the water bottle he'd found in the truck. When he finished, he wiped his mouth on his shirtsleeve. Good manners were something he'd never been accused of.

Despite his best efforts and an exhausting couple of days, Eddie had little to show for it. Since heading this way, he'd occasionally spotted small footprints he thought might be Addison's, but nothing definitive. To his untrained eye, they looked like the ones he'd seen at the tunnel's exit, so he'd stayed on the road, but now he wasn't so sure.

At least I'm away from the cabin and the hoard of cops and firefighters. He hadn't seen any vehicles on this road, so he doubted Addison and G. I. Joe got picked up. In the best-case scenario, he thought she might still be ahead of him and running to get away. In the worst case, she might have turned off the road or been hiding in the woods back by the cabin until Eddie left. But his gut still told him she'd gone this way. Either way, she was long gone. He needed to get going again if he was going to have a chance of catching up.

Eddie forced himself to stand up, stretching the kinks out of his tired muscles. He hadn't slept for close to thirty-six hours, and fatigue continued to erode his will to continue. He stumbled back toward the road and then stopped abruptly, listening. It sounded like a truck was coming his way, but he couldn't tell from which direction.

Eddie's first inclination was to hide. He searched the woods frantically, but with nothing substantial to hide behind, he simply froze. He looked back down the road toward the vehicle, hoping it was just a local resident's truck but realized it was a Sheriff's Department Jeep. He reached under his shirt in the small of his back and touched his pistol to reassure himself. Then he put on his best game face in case the Jeep stopped.

As he expected, the Jeep slowed as the distance separating them shrank to zero. He nodded to the two men in front as the Jeep stopped even with him. The passenger window was already down, and a state trooper was sizing him up. His nametag said Hendricks. He was lean, with dark close-cropped hair under his Smokey-the-Bear hat. The sheriff behind the wheel looked to Eddie to be much more seasoned; it showed in his gray hair and rotund midsection. "Morning," Hendricks called out.

Eddie nodded again, wary of saying much of anything.

"Sheriff Mitchell and I are looking for several people last known to be heading in this direction. Have you seen anyone else out here?"

"No, sir. You're the first sign of life I've seen all day. What's this all about, if you don't mind me asking?"

"Just a routine investigation. This is kind of in the middle of nowhere. What exactly are you doing out here?"

"Just taking a walk. I'm staying at my uncle's cabin back yonder. It's such a pretty morning, I decided to head outside and get some exercise. That ain't against the law, is it?"

"No. But you're a long way from any cabin. Where are you heading?"

"Nowhere, really. Like I said, just getting some exercise . . . maybe even see some wildlife. Truth is, I'm pretty much a city boy, and I'm bored to tears hanging out up here." Eddie looked down at his watch. "I hadn't planned on going much farther before turning back."

Eddie was starting to sweat beyond what the sun would normally make him produce. A slow tremor began in his hands as he pondered where this impromptu interrogation might lead. He wouldn't be this jumpy if he had a few drinks in him, but there was no pub around here. And then the question he was dreading landed like a prizefighter's punch to the gut.

"Can I see some identification, please?"

Eddie paused just a little too long trying to think up a response. Sheriff Mitchell opened his door and started to get out. Eddie panicked.

"I got it right here in my wallet. Just hang on."

Instead of reaching for his wallet, he reached for his pistol. He pulled it quickly and shot Hendricks through the window before the trooper could react. The sheriff pulled his weapon and ducked behind the car for cover.

Eddie ducked too, and crouched near the back of the vehicle. He looked under the car and saw the sheriff's feet moving slowly around the front. Eddie repositioned himself behind the car and waited. By the time the sheriff peeked down the passenger side of the car, Eddie had him squarely in his sights, and he fired, hitting the sheriff in the face. He crumpled to the ground.

Eddie didn't spend much time thinking—only reacting to his new situation. First, he dragged the sheriff around the front of the Jeep and into the woods, laying him in the shadows behind a rotting log. Then he returned for the trooper. He pulled him from the vehicle and dumped his body a few feet from the sheriff's.

Good. Can't see neither body from the road.

He didn't think either of the cops had gotten a call off after they'd stopped. That meant he'd have time to sort things out, but right now, the Jeep was a lifesaver. He grabbed both handguns from the dead cops and the state trooper's assault rifle. Eddie checked the back of the Jeep and found a treasure trove of equipment, from flashbang grenades to emergency food. He shut the tailgate, jumped into the front seat, and drove off in a cloud of dust.

For the first time since robbing the bank, Eddie felt like the tide against him was finally turning. The Jeep gave him mobility—at least until the cops realized its original occupants were not responding to radio calls. He had enough firepower for a small army, and most importantly, he had food and water.

CHAPTER 21

"DID YOU HEAR THAT?" CHASE shouted excitedly after listening to the report on the tactical radio. Chase and Rick had been on the road since before dawn. They'd stopped at five-thirty for breakfast at the Usk Grill, just a few miles south of Cusick. After wolfing down their meals, they were back on the road, driving west and up into the mountains. They planned to set up a base camp near there and begin tracking the police activity on their scanner. But before they could even find a good place to stop, the tactical radio paid its first dividend.

"You bet I did," Rick responded.

One of the air force helicopter crews had just called back to their operations center at the base to report a cabin fire near Sportsman Pond. It wasn't far from their current location. But more interesting than the fire was the report that they had spotted two people running away from the cabin to the southwest and a third individual near the road just west of the cabin. That meant two, maybe three people were headed in Chase's and Rick's general direction. Unfortunately, the helicopter was forced to return to the base due to low fuel and couldn't pursue the runners.

"I hope this is the break we've been waiting for," Rick continued. "But let's not get our hopes up until we have something more concrete than a cabin fire to go on."

"My army buddies are fond of saying, 'Hope isn't a course of action.'"

"They're right about that!"

"But innocent people don't normally run away. Those two people could have set the fire and are running from the scene of the crime, or they could be running because someone's chasing them. In any case, they're headed our way."

"No way of knowing for sure, but it is a suspicious coincidence worth checking out. I imagine the handful of folks living up here don't see this kind of action too often."

"Hopefully one of them will pick up the phone and say something."

Chase and Rick drove up the dirt road leading into the mountains for about five miles. Chase handled the driving while Rick navigated using a topographical map Chase had grabbed from work. Rick could see on the map that the road went up over the mountains to the west and down into the town of Chewelah.

"I doubt if Eddie would be this far south from where he dumped Addison's car," Rick said. "How about we set this road as the southern boundary of our search area?"

"Okay. That sounds good for now."

Next, Rick located Sportsman Pond on the map, so he had a pretty good idea of where the cabin fire was. "Since the people running from the cabin headed south and west, Sportsman Pond would make a good northern boundary—at least until we gather more information," he said. "Let's head north as soon as possible so we can get closer to the action. I've also set our eastern boundary as the Pend Oreille River, and the crest of the mountains for the western boundary. I don't think Eddie and Addison could have traveled beyond those boundaries by now on foot. There are a lot of logging roads in the area," continued Rick. "None of which go in a straight line, but I'll steer us toward the center of the search area. I'd like to try and intercept the two people running from the cabin in case one of them is Addison. If she's not one of them, then we can set up a search pattern for the area within these boundaries for the third person."

"Sounds like the start of a good plan."

"We should be coming up on a road heading north in about a mile. Let's turn there."

Chase spotted the turnoff a couple of minutes later and turned north.

"This has to be Winchester Creek Road," Rick said, pointing to the map. "There's no other road heading north marked on the map."

"I think you're right. It looks like it leads to a maze of logging roads, but with a little backtracking, we should be able to get pretty close to the site of the cabin fire. We can set up camp as planned and check out the lay of the land before deciding our next move."

They quickly ate up the distance to the next turn and then reset the odometer again for the next leg. They followed this painstaking process for the next fifty minutes—slower than they would have liked. The farther they traveled from the main road, the worse the road conditions became, but it was nothing the four-wheel drive pickup couldn't handle.

They barely averaged ten miles per hour on the next stretch of road, but the men believed that with every mile they conquered, they were getting closer to Addison. At the moment, that was all that mattered.

By midmorning, they pulled to a stop where Smalle Creek meandered through a narrow meadow. Just a short drive up the ridgeline from there would put them within ten miles of the cabin and very nearly dead center in their search area. The higher ground on the ridge would make for better radio and cell phone reception, along with good visibility, so they decided to set up camp there before resuming the hunt.

They had no time to waste if they were going to intercept the runners. Within fifteen minutes of stopping, they had their tent up and sleeping bags stowed inside; they opted to keep the rest of their gear with them. The men jumped back into the truck and drove down through the next draw and up onto the following ridgeline where the expanse of wooded hills opened up.

They stopped to get their bearings and plan their next move. Rick got out, opened the tailgate, and jumped up into the truck bed for a better view. Chase grabbed his binoculars and joined him. From their vantage point, they could see for miles in nearly every direction.

Instantly, they were struck by the shear vastness of the territory spreading out before them. The only man-made objects they could see were a couple of communications towers on the higher peaks to their west. They knew the main road in the area paralleled the Pend Oreille River in the valley to the east, but at this distance, they could barely make out the river.

"There's the smoke plume from the cabin fire," Rick said, pointing to the northeast.

Chase trained his binoculars on the spot. "I can't see much of the burned cabin, but I can see the fire trucks nearby. It looks like the fire is mostly out." He passed the binoculars to Rick to take a look. "You know, Rick, I fly over this country all the time, but I had no idea just how remote most of it is. Just looking around from here, I can't spot any of the usual signs of human activity. There are a lot of Forest Service and logging roads up here, but I don't see any of the dust clouds you'd expect vehicles to kick up. Talk about searching for a needle in a haystack."

"We have our work cut out for us. How on earth are we going to find Addison in all of this? Or the people running from the fire? If we miss them, I'll bet no one else will see them either."

For perhaps the first time since Addison was kidnapped, the reality of the task before them loomed large. Maybe too large. Sobered, but not defeated, Chase rose to the challenge. "I don't know, but we can't ever give up." He smiled at Rick and slapped him on the back. "One thing we do know for certain is we won't find Addison or the runners just standing here. Let's take a look at the map and decide on our next move."

The two knelt down and began studying the map. Chase grabbed his old Boy Scout compass and oriented the map to true north. They glanced up periodically to look for prominent geographical landmarks and match them to the map.

Chase pointed to the map. "We know we're here, and I'll bet the two runners will keep heading our way, for a couple of reasons. First, they're obviously in a hurry, so they'll probably stick to the roads where they can make better time—at least initially. And second, the terrain will factor in since it gradually descends in the direction they're running. If I'm reading the map right, both the roads and terrain south of the cabin will likely funnel them to right about here." He again pointed to the map. "Just like water flowing down a draw after a good rain."

"And speaking of water," Rick offered, "they'll have to find a water source before too long. That will also affect their route once the heat of the day sets in."

The two men stood looking at the map, still thinking through the many variables. "Let's assume Addison is one of the runners," Rick proposed. "Depending on who she's with, I see two main courses of action."

"Good. I hadn't thought about that. Go on."

"If she's with her kidnapper, then he'll probably want to avoid the roads and head deeper into the mountains. If she's with someone else, they're probably running for their lives and making snap decisions. I think most people would take the fastest and easiest route available."

"Based on what we heard from the aircrew, my gut tells me the two people are Addison and someone trying to help her—maybe the owner of that cabin. If she had escaped from Eddie and gone to the cabin for help, that would explain the two runners—Addison and the cabin occupant. Eddie just might be the third person. This is all speculation, but I doubt if there are many people up here running around the woods in the middle of the night. We might as well check them out."

"I like your reasoning, but playing devil's advocate, the third person could be the cabin owner standing a safe distance away, waiting for the fire department to show up. Or a neighbor, for that matter. If he left the site of the cabin fire before the fire trucks arrived, then he might be hunting the other two, who could be arsonists."

"True, but that would suggest a lot of coincidences. Since we don't have any other leads, let's just suppose it's Addison and someone else running from Anghelone. And let's hope he's not much of a tracker."

"I doubt he is, but if he finds their footprints heading to the south, he could pour on the speed to catch up with them," Chase said grimly.

"And, in theory, he'll be funneled in the same direction by the roads and terrain as Addison. Even if he's a lousy tracker, he may just blunder his way to her. We've got to get to her before he does."

"Fine," said Chase. "Let's head to the bottom of the natural funnel we marked on the map and see what happens. We'll listen to the radios, look for anything out of the ordinary, and adjust as needed."

"You mentioned being ready for Eddie in case he pops up. Do you think we should load the weapons and go in armed?"

"Most definitely. Eddie probably still has the handgun he shot the guard with, unless he dumped it. I think we should plan for the worst case, don't you?"

"I do. If you don't mind, I'll take the shotgun. You can use your handgun and the rifle."

"I'm fine with that. Let's decide where we'll sit and watch from."

They pored over the map again, this time with a greater sense of urgency.

"The logging roads end short of where the terrain would funnel them, so if the runners stay on course, they'll have to leave the road and cut their own trail. The descending terrain would lead them into this valley around here"—Rick indicated a spot on the map—"just about four miles north of us.

"From there," he continued, "they could choose a couple of different routes, but still moving generally south and probably downhill. Either way, they'd connect with the logging roads that wind through those draws. Both look like good places to stake out. And both eventually lead down to Sicley Road, here."

"If they're looking for speed rather than cover, they would probably pick up one of those roads and continue heading south. But, if cover is more important to them, they may avoid the roads and stay hidden in the woods. That would slow them down and really complicate matters for us and the police."

"There's no rational course of action for us to follow in that case," Rick said. "I think we should assume they've opted for speed in the belief the kidnapper is looking for them east of the cabin. That would probably push them to one of the two roads and increase the odds of them flagging down a vehicle for help or stumbling across another cabin or maybe campers."

"Okay. Let's split up and cover both roads. I'm thinking here and here," Chase said, marking the two points on the map.

"It looks like we can drive there, although it's a roundabout series of logging roads. Do you think we can get there before them in the truck or should we go in a straight line on foot?"

"Hmm . . . it's about six miles by road and four miles as the crow flies, so we should drive. It'll take us twenty minutes. I'll drop you here where the two roads fork, and we'll split up. One of the two stakeout spots should pay off. Let's stay in touch via cell, assuming we still have reception there."

Rick nodded. "If not, then if I find them, I'll walk them toward you. If you find them, you can just drive back to pick me up. I'll hear you coming. How about we set a time limit—say three hours, and then we'll regroup and figure out plan B. In the interim, I'll call you every thirty minutes if we have cell coverage, just to check in."

"Let's do it."

The drive to the stakeout locations took longer than expected. The terrain was hilly, and the roads were in terrible shape. When they found the road junction they were looking for, Chase turned to the right and drove about fifty yards before stopping to let Rick out. There was nowhere to turn around, so he backed his truck to the junction and drove up to his stakeout location.

Chase turned onto his road and then pulled over close to the intersection, thinking it best to watch both roads for any activity. He parked just off the road, where he could make his truck a little less obvious. Then he hopped out and set up a lawn chair and settled into it with his scanner and binoculars nearby. Since the air force choppers only flew at night, he wouldn't need the tactical radio— just an earbud plugged in to the police scanner. That would allow him to listen to police activity in one ear and still hear an approaching vehicle or hiker with his other ear, without the radio giving away his location.

Now I know why I'm not a police officer, thought Chase. Just sitting, watching, and listening in the hot sun was harder than he'd imagined—and incredibly boring. He wouldn't have lasted through his first stakeout at the police academy. Every few minutes, he stood and stretched and then popped out his earbud to walk around and get the kinks out. Then he was back to his chair.

I'm not sure how much more of this I can take, he thought in a moment of weakness as tears clouded his eyes. He was so worried about Addison, and it felt like he wasn't doing enough to find her. But he had to suck it up. Getting emotional wouldn't help him or Rick find Addison any faster. Absent the information the police had, this was their best shot at finding Addison, so he and Rick would do whatever they had to. Even if they didn't spot the runners, they were still right in the middle of their planned search area. He just had to trust in the plan and do his best. He was sure Rick would do the same.

CHAPTER 22

CHASE, SETTLED INTO HIS STAKEOUT location, began scanning the area with his binoculars for anyone or anything that moved. He watched as the sun passed its zenith and moved lazily toward the mountain peaks. The heat peaked in midafternoon, and the temperature began to drop as the cooler air in the mountains flowed down the canyons. He downed a bottle of water and ate a granola bar to satisfy his more primal needs. Chase struggled at times to stay alert, but the police chatter from the scanner helped.

He perked up immediately when he heard a familiar voice. It was one of the detectives he'd spoken with earlier—Detective Strickland he thought. He was describing the cabin fire first reported by the air force chopper crew. The on-scene fire inspector was already calling it arson, but fortunately, no bodies were found inside. That gave him a little more hope that Addison could be one of the two people on the run, even though there was no evidence that was the case.

A few minutes later, a canine team from the SPD arrived at the scene and checked in with Ted over the radio. *That's great news*, Chase thought. Now they could track the people seen running from the cabin.

Just then, Chase heard a vehicle approaching. He pulled the earbud from his ear and jumped up. It was a Pend Oreille County Sheriff's Department Jeep. Chase waved to get the driver's attention, but he didn't stop. That really surprised Chase, since he figured the sheriff would have wanted to question him. After all, Chase was right in the middle of the search area and one of very few people out and about. The more he thought about it, the more it bothered him.

At first, Chase rationalized that the sheriff might not have seen him or his truck, but that just didn't seem possible. The truck was pretty obvious, and Chase was certain he had made eye contact with the driver, even if momentarily. There was no rational explanation for not stopping—at least not one he could think of. He pulled out his cell phone and tried calling his father-in-law, but the call didn't go through.

Chase checked his signal strength. No bars. He needed to get to higher ground or just drive back over to Rick's location. He chose the latter and tossed his gear in the truck. As he pulled back onto the road, he deliberately crawled along slowly to avoid raising a dust cloud. He still didn't want to draw attention to himself and Rick.

He worked his way down the dirt road to where he had previously dropped Rick. He figured his father-in-law was concealed and hoped he'd emerge when he recognized Chase's truck. He constantly swept the road from side to side as well as behind him. Nearly to the end, he caught movement out of the corner of his eye and hit the brakes. Rick stepped out of the brush onto the road.

"I noticed we had no cell phone reception, so I'm glad you're back," Rick said. "See or hear anything?"

"The police and fire marshal have been up at the site of the cabin fire for a while, and a canine team just arrived. The fire marshal has already determined it's arson with no fatalities. They should be out with the dogs soon, presumably tracking the people seen running away."

"What about the third person the chopper crew reported? Any sign of him?"

"None that I picked up on the scanner chatter. He hasn't been mentioned at all, so it probably wasn't an occupant or a neighbor. Can't imagine either of them not waiting for the fire department. I'm assuming the third person was Eddie."

"And?" Rick asked. He must have sensed something else was bothering Chase.

"I'm not sure if it's anything important or not, but I decided we ought to talk it over since it could change our plans. That's the main reason I drove over here."

"What happened?"

"About ten minutes ago, a sheriff's Jeep drove by, moving pretty fast. I tried to flag it down because I wanted to see what the sheriff was doing and how the search was going. I also expected him to question me about what I was doing there and if I'd seen anyone or anything unusual."

"Go on."

"Nothing happened. He didn't wave back and, in fact, tried to pretend he didn't see me, but I looked him right in the eye. I thought that was pretty strange."

"You're sure he saw you?"

"Positive. I thought about going after him but figured if it wasn't the sheriff, that might not be the smartest move."

"How long ago did you say this happened?"

"Not more than ten minutes."

"He could simply be racing to check out a tip."

"He could have been, but I didn't hear anything on the police scanner, so if he got orders from the task force or another law enforcement agency, they didn't come over the radio. I would have heard it."

"That is strange. I think we should follow him and see what happens. But we need to avoid being seen in case he's not with the sheriff's department. We'll have to be smart about where and when we confront him. If we confront him at all."

"Okay, hop in."

Once again, Chase backed out to the intersection with Sicley Road and then pulled to a stop and put the truck in park.

"Let's check to see if we can tell which direction he turned. There ought to be some visible tracks."

The two men split up and meticulously scoured the intersection in opposite directions. Moments later, Rick gave a low whistle to get Chase's attention and motioned him over. Chase watched where he stepped to avoid disturbing any fresh tracks and hustled over.

"It looks to me like he turned this way," Rick said. "There aren't any tracks on the hard, dry portions of the road, but look here in the softer soil near the shoulder. You can make out tire tracks, and they look fresh."

"That's good enough for me. Let's go."

* * *

As he drove down the road, Eddie pulled together the first elements of a plan. He needed to close the gap between himself and where he thought Addison would be. Thankfully, the Jeep was helping him do that. Next, he needed to find a place to dump it. One where he could conceal it. It wouldn't take long for the Jeep to become a major liability. Lastly, he needed to find a place to hole up for the night. He didn't figure there'd be much daylight left by the time he accomplished his first two tasks.

Eddie continued driving south on Calicoma Road. After just a few minutes, the road forked. He pulled over and looked at the map again. Calicoma continued to the left, generally southward. Turning right would loop him back toward the cabin. He opted to veer left and stay on Calicoma.

Three miles farther down Calicoma, Eddie came to an intersection with a road joining from the west and turned onto it. He paused to check the map and found the road cut a southwesterly course, eventually intersecting with Sicley

Road. Near the bottom edge of the map, he spotted two ponds along the eastern side of Sicley.

That's the direction he took, thinking Addison would opt for the main south-bound roads. And he thought he might be able to ditch the Jeep in one of those ponds where it would sink out of sight. He planned to camp near there and keep a lookout for Addison or the cops. That is, if he wasn't sound asleep.

As Eddie rounded a bend, he saw a gray Dodge pickup truck off to the side of the road. This was the only vehicle he'd seen other than the one he was driving. The other driver waved his hand as though trying to get Eddie's attention, but Eddie pretended not to see him and drove on. He wasn't wearing a cop uniform and definitely wasn't in a talking mood.

It was midafternoon by the time he found Sicley Road and turned to follow it. He was at Conger Pond, the larger of the two lakes, in another fifteen minutes. Eddie pulled over next to the pond and stopped. He got out and looked around for other people. He didn't see a soul, nor did he see any smoke, road dust, or other indications that he might not be completely alone. *This oughta make a great hideout since I can't seem to find my own dang camp. What a fool!*

Eddie retraced his steps back to the Jeep, climbed in, and positioned it so it would run downhill into the pond. He put it in park and then unloaded the weapons, gear, and food he'd need later. He found a solid stick he could wedge between the gas pedal and the seat. He broke open a first-aid kit for the surgical tape and crudely attached one end of the stick to the gas pedal. Then he wedged the other end into the front of the seat. With the engine screaming like a banshee, he leaned in, put the gearshift into drive, and jumped out as the Jeep lurched forward, gathering speed as it raced toward the water. It plunged into the pond with a big splash but slowed quickly. *Ha-ha! That's twice now I got to do that. I'm getting pretty good at it.*

The engine raced for another minute until the Jeep sank into the pond deep enough to choke off the air supply. The Jeep settled, listing about twenty degrees to the left with six inches of the top remaining above the waterline. Eddie cursed. *The pond's too shallow.* Eddie hadn't planned on that but hoped it would be hidden enough to slow the cops down. There was nothing he could do about it now.

Back on the road, he loaded the food and water into one of the sheriff's back-packs, along with flashbang grenades and spare ammunition clips, and tied it shut. Before leaving, he looked around him to make sure he wasn't leaving anything behind. Eddie hoisted the pack onto his shoulders and struck out for the small lake north of Conger Pond that he'd passed on the way there. It was only about half a mile away at its nearest point, but it extended to the north another quarter of a mile. He could set up camp in the woods bordering the lake and monitor the roads in and out of the area.

If Addison, or the cops for that matter, were coming his way, he would be able to see or hear them early enough to respond appropriately. Eddie didn't feel invincible, but he was comfortable staying here for the night without risking capture. He desperately needed sleep. *If I don't find Addison in the next twenty-four hours, I'm done with her and the bank money. I'll make a run for Canada and lie low up there.*

After a small meal of jerky and dried fruit, Eddie made himself a bed of pine boughs and used his pack as a pillow. He lay back to relax, hoping to grab a short nap. Too stressed to sleep, he began replaying the day's events in his mind. He thought about how far he'd come and where Addison might be. Then he sat up suddenly and grabbed the map.

He hadn't really had time to study it in detail before. But now he concentrated on the terrain and network of logging roads and tried to picture where Addison could be. It looked like at least three valleys or draws merged right here by the ponds, each with a road following streams or streambeds. A larger valley continued south along the stream emptying into and then out of Conger Pond.

The spot he'd stumbled upon for his camp actually put him in the perfect position to watch and wait. The valleys and roads would naturally funnel travelers right past Eddie. It was a choke point of sorts, and keeping an eye on it could pay big dividends. Eddie lay back down on his pack and soon dozed off as fatigue and the warmth of the late afternoon sun overcame him.

CHAPTER 23

NOT MORE THAN AN HOUR later, Eddie woke to the sound of a vehicle coming his way. He looked at his watch—6:45. *Can't a guy get a little shut-eye around here?* Eddie slapped his face a couple of times to try and wake up and then rolled over onto his stomach and crawled to where he had a good view of the road. *Sounds like a truck or SUV.*

Eddie watched as a pickup truck rounded the nearest bend very slowly and crept down the road in his direction. *Hey, wait just a minute! I know that truck.* It was the one he had passed back up the road a bit—the one whose owner had waved to him. *I wonder what he's doing here and why he's driving so slow.*

The truck crept past Eddie. That was the truck and driver he remembered, but there was another guy in the passenger seat he hadn't seen before. Both of them were looking right and left for something. *Could be why they're moving like a turtle.* And then the lightbulb in his head lit up, and he wondered if they were looking for him. *But they don't look like no cops I ever seen.*

When the truck was well past him, Eddie got to his feet and walked to the edge of the woods by the pond. He watched the truck slowly drive down toward Conger Pond. *Well, they're gonna see the dang Jeep any second.* Sure enough, almost on command, the brake lights lit up and then went out again as the truck drove on. *Maybe it's my lucky day. They might not care about the Jeep at all.*

No sooner had the thought crossed his mind than the truck pulled to a stop again. The doors opened, and the two men climbed out and walked over to the shore of the pond. It was too far away for Eddie to see much, but he could tell they were just staring at the Jeep. Then they turned and looked up to the top of the hill across the road from the pond. *Don't do it. Don't you do it!*

They did it. They headed across the road and plunged into the woods, probably to climb the hill. *There could only be two reasons they'd do that,* Eddie thought. And he didn't like either of them. They either wanted to see a bigger chunk of land or they were fixing to use their cell phones to report the Jeep.

CHAPTER 24

IT HADN'T TAKEN ADDISON AND Gunner long to realize how much slower they were forced to go once they'd left the road and began cutting their own trail. It didn't matter to her though. She felt safe for the first time in days. They stayed in the draw after leaving the road, keeping a slow but steady pace. They'd decided to bear left whenever it made sense, knowing with each labored step they'd be closer to civilization and rescue. The late-afternoon sun angled through the trees, and a light breeze stirred the branches. They'd been on the run most of the day.

"How are you holding up, Addison?"

"I'm bone tired. You?"

"Pretty much the same. It won't be dark for another couple of hours, but we might want to stop for the night soon. What do you think?"

"We don't have many options. We need to find food and water, which will be easier if it's still light. And if we don't get some sleep soon, we'll both collapse."

"You're right about that. We ain't worth a plug nickel right now. Let's find water first. The food can wait if it has to, but it would give us some much-needed energy, come morning."

"Yeah, my mouth is as dry as the Sahara Desert. I'm not an expert, but I think I can find us something to eat once we locate water. Let's pick a spot to camp before we look around," Addison said.

"I didn't have you pegged for the outdoor type. Where'd you learn all that?"

"You're partially right. I like camping in regular campgrounds, but I can live without wilderness camping like this. I've been through a short survival orientation course put on for families of the military members assigned to the Air Force Survival School. I remember most of what I learned. I just didn't think I'd ever need it. We'll see if it pays off."

"The time I spent in the army taught me a few things about survival too. Between the two of us, we ought to be able to take care of ourselves until we find our way out of this predicament."

"How long did you serve?"

"Oh, just a couple years. It weren't for me. But I'm glad I done it."

"If you didn't like it, how come you started your militia group?"

"Well, if I were the boss, then I could keep what I liked and get rid of what I didn't like. It weren't too tough a decision."

"What parts did you like, then?"

"Well, I liked the sense of belonging to something bigger than myself, and I liked the tight bonds of friendship that form when you go into combat with your platoon buddies."

"So, you saw combat?"

"I saw my share in Afghanistan. It's something that never leaves you once you seen it. It's always a part of you, no matter where you go or what you do."

"I can only imagine. Are you still close to anyone you fought with?"

"Not so much. Only a couple of 'em live around here, but they ain't in my militia. But I hope to recruit 'em one of these days. I've bumped into a couple of old drinking buddies from the army who live here in the northwest. Let's see . . . there's Steve Grogan and Craig Plattenburg and another couple of guys. But they don't want to move to Spokane. What about you? I know you're married and that your husband is in the air force, but that's about it."

"There's not that much to tell—I'm only twenty-one—but I'll try. I grew up as an air force brat. I was born in Germany and lived in Japan, South Carolina, and Ohio until my dad retired in Maryland. I played field hockey and softball in high school—"

"Wait a minute. What's field hockey? I only know the kind that's played on ice."

Addison laughed. "It's mostly played back east, but it's an Olympic sport for women and men. It's about three centuries old and came from the English. In many ways it's like ice hockey, but it's played on grass with a shorter stick. We run instead of skate and use a hard ball instead of a puck."

"If you say so."

"And, I might add, unlike those big soft ice hockey players who have to wear pads, we small but tough women don't need no stinking pads. We only wear helmets and gloves."

They both laughed out loud.

"What did you do after high school, go to college?"

She nodded. "I went to Brigham Young University in Provo, Utah. My mother graduated from there, so I wanted to keep the tradition alive. During spring break, I flew to Wisconsin to help my parents clean out my grandparents' house after they passed away and get it ready to go on the market. Then my mother and I got into a serious accident. She was helicoptered to the medical center for surgery, and I rode in the ambulance. That's when I met my future husband, who just happened to be the paramedic on duty that night. We got married when he graduated from pilot training, and we moved here."

"What's your husband's name?"

"Chase Roberts."

"Well, he's a lucky man. I hope to meet him when all of this is over with."

"I'd like you to meet him." She pointed. "Hey, is that a road up ahead?"

"Hmm, I think you're right, Miss Addison. Let's be careful about it, just in case."

They approached the road carefully, not knowing what to expect. They only caught glimpses of it through the trees until they were at the road's edge. Gunner leaned out from behind a tree and looked up and down the road.

"I don't see anything. No buildings or vehicles—and it doesn't look like it's been traveled much. It isn't in too good of shape. Probably one of those roads cut through the trees by lumber companies. Nobody keeps them up once they get the logs out."

Addison stepped out to look for herself. "You're probably right, Gunner. It seems to follow that draw up on the other side of the ridge we've been following, and it looks like it winds down toward a widening valley. That could be good news, don't you think?"

"Don't rightly know. But I reckon we can walk along the side of it, keeping in the trees, if you like. There may be some cabins down where the valley opens up. And where there's cabins, there's usually people and telephones."

They'd only been paralleling the road for a few minutes when they stumbled on another lumber road cutting in from the left, right across their path, and joining the road they were walking along. Even better, there was a small stream running on the far side of the road in front of them.

"Well, that solves one problem," Gunner said. "Let's drink up while we have the chance."

"I hate to drink the water unfiltered. All we need is giardia. But, right now, I don't see that we have a choice."

"The army taught us to take a couple of small sips first, wait an hour to see if there is any reaction, and then repeat that a couple of times. I know we're both thirsty, but that might be the thing to do."

"I agree."

Gunner stood watch while Addison laid down next to the stream and drank a few swallows. She could tell how much her body was craving the cool liquid but forced herself to stop before she drank too much. They reversed positions, and Gunner did the same while Addison stood watch.

When Gunner finished up, they decided to backtrack down the road about twenty-five yards and walk into the woods to a spot between both roads. From that vantage point, they could watch for any vehicular or human traffic passing on either road while staying hidden.

"Let's grab some pine boughs to spread around us so we won't be so obvious," Addison suggested. "Until we know exactly where Eddie is, I'd rather risk not being found by a Good Samaritan than expose ourselves to that monster."

"Great idea."

They spent the next half hour setting up their makeshift camp. Hungry, both began to search their immediate surroundings for anything edible. Addison spotted some sego lilies and dug up the bulbs, collecting them in a small pile. Gunner recognized the thin green shoots sprouting from wild onions nearby and pulled two handfuls. They pooled their collections.

"Where'd you learn about the lilies? I didn't even know you could eat them."

"My Dad taught my siblings and me. Whenever we went camping or hiking, he was always teaching us how to navigate, find food, what to do if we're lost, stuff like that. He even taught us how to snare small animals. I'm no expert, but I did learn a few good things and got to practice some of them. What kind of gear do you have with you, Gunner?"

"What do you mean?"

"You know, what do you have in your pockets that we could use right now?"

Gunner patted down the pockets of his old camouflage uniform and pulled out some nylon cord he'd used for militia training the previous day, a crumpled pack of cigarettes, a lighter, his compass, and he remembered his Leatherman multi-tool on his belt.

"That's all I have. Do you have anything?"

"No. Eddie made sure of that when we began this little adventure. There were a couple of his things in the backpack I had before the fire, but they're gone now. But your stash is perfect. I noticed the cigarettes. I haven't seen you smoke at all today."

"Yeah, I been trying to quit. Mostly have. I guess I carry the pack around just in case I might need one. Kind of like a pacifier."

"Well, good for you! I know it's tough to quit, but your body will thank you." She paused a moment before continuing. "I'd like to set a couple of snares and see if we can catch something more filling. We might even catch our breakfast while we sleep."

She decided not to tell Gunner about the sharpened bone she had in her pocket. It wasn't much, but it was better than nothing, and she wanted to keep that fact to herself. Gunner seemed like a great guy, but she didn't want to unnecessarily put herself at risk.

Gunner handed her the nylon cord and his Leatherman, and then watched as Addison got to work. Setting snares was a new experience for him. Even the army didn't teach it, except to special forces and aviators.

First, Addison scanned the area around them for signs of a small animal trail. Finding several, she cut a few lengths of nylon cord and began to fashion a miniature noose in the first one.

Next, she propped the noose up in a narrow section of one of the trails between some small bushes so that an animal running along the trail in the dark would get caught in the noose. Then she anchored the other end of the cord so her catch couldn't get away once snared.

She repeated the process on another trail and tied off the loose end as the full weight of the past two days settled heavily upon her. She was too tired to do anything else but crawl back to camp. Leaning against a tree and closing her eyes, she tried to catch her breath and will herself to finish their campsite preparations.

After a few minutes, Addison forced herself to get up. She and Gunner took the sego lily bulbs and wild onions to the stream to clean them off before their makeshift dinner.

"How do you feel?" Addison asked. "Any side effects from the water we drank earlier?"

Gunner thought about it for a few seconds.

"No, not that I can tell. How about you?"

"Nope. Let's wash the bulbs off in the stream and drink a little more before we head back to camp and eat up."

They sat down in their pine bough fortress and used their last few ounces of energy to eat. Even chewing seemed difficult, but both knew they needed the energy only food can provide for whatever the next day would bring.

Addison glanced at her watch—6:20.

"It won't be dark for another two hours, but I think we should call it a day. I'll take the first watch," Addison said.

"Do you really think that's necessary?"

"It is with Eddie. He comes across like a broken-down drunk, but somehow, he keeps showing up when I least expect it—like back at the cabin. We can't afford to be surprised by him again."

"Fair enough, but let me take the first watch. Like you said earlier, you're working on a lot less sleep than I am."

"Thanks, Gunner. I hope you know how much I appreciate your help."

"Well, I gotta admit I never figured we'd be on our own like this, running from a murderer, or I might have thought twice about it. Just the same, it's been kind of exciting to be back in the fight again, so to speak."

"It's exciting all right, but I can think of a lot better ways to find excitement in my life. This little adventure could still result in the loss of our lives."

Gunner stood up and stretched as Addison settled down into the pine boughs for the night. Before Gunner could even step away, Addison was lost to the world.

***

He'd found a place to sit nearby, and as he kept a lookout, Gunner couldn't help but review the incredible series of events over the past twenty hours that had led him to this point. He shook his head and smiled at the absurdity.

He tried to picture what Eddie might look like in case their paths crossed, but he came up blank. He'd served in the army with a guy named Eddie but couldn't remember his last name or what he looked like. His reminiscing ended with the sobering thought that they were still running from a known killer. That wiped the smile off his face and refocused his immediate attention on his job as a watchman.

Gunner lowered himself to the ground, leaning back against the log he'd been sitting on. Dusk was settling on the forest as the daylight gathered in the west. He looked all around, taking in the beauty of the mountains. He took in a deep breath and let it out slowly. The rich aroma of the pines teased his senses. This was Gunner's favorite time of day, when all the stress and worries of the day seemed to melt away with the setting sun.

I could really enjoy this if I wasn't running for my life or trying to protect Miss Addison! The mountains had always been his refuge, but not tonight. He wasn't too excited about this Eddie person running around loose trying to track Miss Addison down. Not one bit.

CHAPTER 25

WHILE CHASE CONTINUED SCANNING THE horizon with his binoculars, Rick laid the map out on the ground and was orienting it with the terrain. Chase knew he would have their location pinpointed quickly since the peak they were on and the two ponds below would be easy to find. In the distance, he could hear a helicopter, and as Rick stood up, Chase searched for the source of the sound. In seconds, he spotted it three or four miles north of them, circling just above the trees.

"I wonder what's got their attention," Rick said.

Chase focused his binoculars on the helicopter.

"It's a police chopper. I can't see what they're doing, but there are flashing lights on the road below them."

Just then, the police scanner Chase was carrying came to life.

"JTF ops, this is Chopper One."

"Roger, Chopper One."

"We are reporting two delta on Calicoma Road one point four miles south of Four Dog Lane. Do you copy?"

"Roger, we copy. We'll get the coroner, forensics, and a patrol car there ASAP."

"Roger. The SPD canine unit is at the scene and will secure the area pending their arrival."

Chase and Rick stared at each other, worried looks on their faces. Both understood the implications of the word *delta*. It represented the letter *D* in the phonetic alphabet and was used to indicate the deceased to avoid specific references to death over the open airwaves. Chase could feel his pulse quicken and his neck muscles contract. *Please, please, please don't let that be my Addison!* Chase, trying to keep his voice from shaking, said, "We just drove by there a few minutes ago and didn't see anything."

The radio crackled again. "Ops, be aware the two delta are lima echo. Do you copy?"

"Roger, Chopper One, lima echo."

Chase gave a big sigh of relief. Lima echo represented the letters *L* and *E* and stood for law enforcement. The two bodies discovered were police officers.

"I hate to hear that," Rick said.

"Me too, but at least we know it's not Addison."

"They probably gave their lives trying to find her."

"I know. How can we ever repay them or their families?"

"By finding Addison and capturing the kidnapper!"

The radio crackled again. "Ops, also be advised their vehicle is missing."

"Roger, Chopper One. Request you begin an immediate search."

The same thought popped into both men's minds simultaneously. "I'll bet that's the sheriff's Jeep they're looking for," Rick said. "We'd better call it in."

"We can't use a cell phone; they'll be able to tie it to us instantly. It shouldn't take the chopper crew long to spot the Jeep in Conger Pond. Maybe we should just let this play out a while and see what happens. We can always report it later if we have to."

"All right. I think I'll call Julia, anyway, to check in like we promised. Who knows when we'll have cell coverage again?"

While Rick placed the call, Chase turned his attention back to the hunt. He moved to the western side of the hill and climbed onto a rocky shelf that overlooked the ponds below. He began slowly searching the area due west of them, following the same pattern as before. As he swept the area near the other pond, Chase caught a glint through his binoculars. That seemed strange since, as far as he could tell, no one else was near them.

Suddenly, a three-round burst of bullets hit the rocks in front of Chase before the sound reached his ears. Chase dove for the ground; Rick followed a split second later.

"Was that what I think it was?" Rick asked.

"It most definitely was. I guess we're getting close. Must be poking the right tiger in the eye."

"This tiger is using an assault weapon on three-round automatic. And we're unarmed." Rick suddenly realized he still had Julia on the phone. "Hey, I can't talk right now. I'll call you back."

Rick hung up and turned back to Chase. "Did you see where the shots came from?"

"I caught a reflection off the rifle scope just before the shots were fired. They came from this side of the road right next to that other pond we passed."

"And to think, we just drove by and didn't see a thing. We've been close to this guy twice already today but didn't notice anything out of the ordinary."

"He sure noticed us, and clearly he wants us to stop whatever he thinks we're doing," Chase said.

"He's probably gathered we climbed up here for cell reception to report the Jeep. You'd think he'd know shooting at us would encourage us to call," Rick said.

"Unless he just wants to scare us off this hill before we can get a call off. He may be smarter than we're giving him credit for."

"Well, I'm convinced—we definitely need to get off this hill, fast. But we left our weapons in the truck. We're sitting ducks."

"Not if we aren't caught sitting. We need to move, but where to? If Eddie is on his way up here now, we can run down the back side of the hill and get to the truck before he makes it to the top. But if he's watching the truck hoping to catch us when we return, we could be running right into a trap. Come on! Let's at least get off the hill and hide in the trees near the truck until he shows his hand. It'll be dark soon, so I think hiding is our best option."

Chase took off running with Rick only a few steps behind him. They found a draw that angled down toward the truck and followed it, pulling up short of the road. They hunkered down behind a stand of pines to look and listen. Chase could see his truck, but everything seemed quiet in that direction. Rick watched the hill behind them to see if the shooter was following them. Nothing yet.

Rick leaned over and whispered to Chase, "With the body count Eddie is racking up, us getting caught isn't an option!"

"I'll say! I feel a little exposed right here. It wouldn't take a rocket scientist to figure out which way we ran to get to the truck. Whether the shooter followed us or not, he probably has a pretty good idea of where we'd end up. I'd feel better if we climbed back up the hill partway and over to that next ridgeline south of us."

"Sounds good. We can still wait and watch from there without being quite so easy to find."

Chase jumped up and darted toward the ridge. Rick was right on his tail. When they settled in and hid themselves as well as possible, they turned all of their attention to spotting the shooter.

CHAPTER 26

THE DARKNESS GATHERED AROUND THEM, squeezing the last drops of sunlight from the day. Visibility dropped from yards to feet. Chase and Rick remained motionless as they strained to see their stalker. Hiding was a wise decision when they had first scrambled from the hilltop, but it was passive—something neither of them relished. Both were men of action, and just hiding in the dark was taking a toll on them. Chase leaned over to Rick and whispered softly, "I've been thinking while we've been lying here, and I have an idea."

"I'm all ears."

"Since we're unarmed, it seems to me that we have two choices. We can stay here and hide in the dark, hoping the shooter doesn't find us, or we can try to even the odds by sneaking back to the truck for a weapon. If we hide, we turn our fates over to him—either he finds us or he doesn't. But if we can arm ourselves, then we can take control of our own fate. I don't know about you, but I prefer the latter."

Rick nodded but apparently wasn't in any hurry to answer. After a few minutes, he responded. "I hate just sitting here as much as you do, but there are risks with either path you've proposed. While it's true hiding puts us on the defensive, the growing darkness works in our favor. It helps us stay hidden, and it discourages the shooter from hanging around until daylight. With the police tracking him, it would be too risky. If we try to get to your truck and arm ourselves, we will likely give away our position and invite an attack. To me that increases our own risk . . . unless we succeed. If we *can* arm ourselves, then the momentum swings in our favor."

"Well . . . I've never been one for sitting around. Since it's nearly dark, now, I think my chances are pretty good that I can get to the truck and grab a gun before he can respond. If that is Eddie, I don't want to lose because we hid all night," Chase said.

Instinct took over, and the two men headed toward the truck. Halfway down the hill, they turned south and planned to loop around the base of the hill back to the road where the truck was parked. They moved as fast as the terrain and visibility would allow. They didn't know where the shooter was or where he'd be when they got to the truck, but they didn't want to give him any extra time to find them.

* * *

Eddie was making his way up the hill, hoping to find and eliminate this new threat. With three murders under his belt, he didn't even hesitate at the prospect of adding one or two more. If he pulled this off, he might just prevent a call to the cops while eliminating two more of the posse chasing him.

By the time Eddie scrambled to the top of the hill, he had to stop to catch his breath and cursed the cigarettes he'd smoked most of his life for the damage they had done to his lungs. He could tell the two men had been here, and he easily followed their trail off the top—even in the dark.

* * *

"Hang on, Chase," Rick said. "Let's use the truck for bait."

"What do you mean, bait?"

"Let's just lie low about fifty feet south of the truck to see if the shooter shows himself. He'll either be watching the truck, hoping we'll return or chasing us up the hill and then back down this way. I think the latter is more likely. If he's following us, we'll either hear him coming down the hill or see him when he pops out of the woods. If he stayed put and is watching the truck, then we'll still be safe. Rather than let him use the truck to bait us, let's turn the tables on him."

"Unless he's executing Plan C and running away while we stay hunkered down. We may miss our chance to get him. Remember, one of the deciding factors in going for the truck was the increased probability we might catch him."

"If he's running away, how does getting to the truck increase our odds of capturing him?"

"We can arm ourselves, and the truck gives us greater mobility."

"True, but I just don't think he'll run. He has to know we're outgunned, so why wouldn't he attack while he has a strong advantage? Plus, if he's waiting for us near the truck, like you said, we could be walking into a trap."

"I see what you mean, but I still don't like sitting here unarmed."

"Let's just give it a few minutes and see if he shows himself. Then we can look at getting to our weapons."

"All right."

The two of them hid in the wooded area above the road and just south of the truck as Rick suggested. They sat quietly, listening and watching for any sign of Eddie. The delay was killing Chase, but deep inside, he knew Rick was right. And the wait paid off. Before long, they heard Eddie start down from the top of the hill in their direction. Stealth wasn't one of his strengths, apparently.

"How about if I make a run for the truck and grab us some protection before he gets here?" Chase asked. "I'll stay on the downhill side of the truck so it'll shield me if he starts shooting. If he doesn't, I'll be back here before you know it, and we'll both feel better."

"Okay. Go now! Watch your front; I've got your six," he said.

Chase hugged the trees alongside the road and then broke left and around the front of the truck at the last second. When he opened the passenger door, the interior light popped on like a beacon, signaling his presence. He chastised himself—he'd forgotten about that. He frantically searched for a weapon so he could shut off the light.

The glass shattered at the same time he heard the shot fired. Eddie blew a hole in the driver's side window. The round crashed through the glass at a downward angle and embedded itself in the console between the seats while showering Chase with glass shards.

He reached under the seat and felt around for his handgun. Grabbing it, he crouched down low, slamming the door shut to kill the light. He ducked behind the right rear wheel and crawled underneath so he was shielded by the left rear wheel. This gave him a pretty good view of the hill without exposing himself. There was no doubt now that Eddie was closing in.

Chase could barely see Rick in the darkness. He was pointing up the hill toward Eddie and signaling that he was going up there. Chase tried to signal his opposition, but Rick was already on the move. So, he waited . . . again. The silence was deafening. No one else moved, and no one fired a weapon. Even the birds stopped chirping. This was turning into a potentially deadly game of chicken.

In the deepening shadows, Chase was having a tough time spotting Eddie, even though he heard him lumbering down the hill. Then he caught a glimpse as Eddie darted from tree to tree. No chance for a clear shot. Chase wondered if Eddie knew he was under the truck. If so, Eddie could use the truck to his advantage and trap him beneath it. But if Chase moved, he might also give himself away.

Chase made a split-second decision and quickly pushed himself back out from underneath the truck. Keeping low to the ground, he moved to a hiding spot at the edge of the pond. The reeds there were thick and offered a halfway decent hideaway. From his new location, he would be able to see Eddie clearly when he circled the truck looking for him. Now the advantage moved to Chase.

Chase didn't know where Rick was but didn't plan on him being of much help since he was unarmed. He also knew there was a chance he could mistake him for the shooter in the darkness. But he felt like Rick understood the danger and would take the right precautions to avoid any friendly fire risk.

Chase's choice proved to be a sound one. He spotted Eddie dashing across the road to the far side of the truck and then creeping around the front. Chase hunkered down in the brush and stayed perfectly still. He could only see Eddie out of the corner of his eye—he had stopped in his tracks and looked around. He tilted his head to one side as if he was listening. Suddenly, Chase caught some movement near Eddie.

He was shocked to see that Rick matched Eddie step for step from the bottom of the hill to the truck but remained a good twenty feet or so behind him and hidden from view. By moving when Eddie moved, any noise Rick may have made would be covered by noise from Eddie's own footsteps. *Nice job, Rick, but be careful.* From his actions, it was obvious Eddie never heard a thing and never considered a threat coming from his rear.

Eddie sprinted around to the passenger side of the truck, clearly expecting to confront his prey, but no one was there. Chase watched silently as Rick knelt right where Eddie had been before crossing the road. He lost sight of him when he ran to the driver's side of the truck but knew he was still there. For a few moments, no one moved. No one made a sound.

Chase remained motionless, head down, listening for Eddie's approach. Two minutes passed, then five. It seemed like each minute stretched into an hour. Eddie was far slower to react than Chase expected. The only noise that broke the stillness was the croak of a lonely bullfrog somewhere across the pond. And then Chase heard him move but kept his head down to reduce his profile.

It sounded like the rustling of dry leaves about ten feet to his right front. Goosebumps formed up and down his arms, and the hair on his neck stood straight up, warning him of imminent danger. Chase's hand gripped his weapon even tighter, and every one of his senses was focused on Eddie's movement. Chase could barely make out the sounds of Eddie's footsteps as he closed the gap between them.

Adrenaline surged through his body as Chase struggled to restrain himself. Then he slowly turned his head until he spotted Eddie through the slits of his eyes. Like a well-trained bird dog, Eddie silently worked the deep grass and cattails along the pond's edge, probably hoping to flush Chase out.

He moved at a snail's pace, his head on a swivel. In the stillness of the night, Chase could hear Eddie's breathing—even smell his body odor. He could almost make out the rapid beating of Eddie's heart but knew that was just his imagination.

Chase's own heartbeat pounded louder with every step Eddie took. Sweat dripped down the side of his face. He clenched and relaxed the grip on his handgun, wondering when he should act. Eddie took another step and jumped at the sudden flapping of wings as two spooked ducks flew out of the cattails. Immediately, he turned toward the sound and snapped off a couple of rounds into the edge of the pond.

Chase capitalized on the distraction and jumped up not three feet away from Eddie, gun pointed directly at him. Eddie turned and started to raise his gun in Chase's direction.

"I wouldn't do that if I were you!" Chase said.

Eddie looked alarmed, but then he smiled at Chase. "I don't think you got the guts to pull that trigger, boy."

When he started to raise the assault rifle in Chase's direction, Chase charged him. He hit him like an NFL linebacker, lifting Eddie off his feet and driving him hard to the ground.

The hit caused the rifle to fly from Eddie's hand, landing harmlessly in the water at the edge of the pond. But Eddie was able to grab Chase's shirt as he fell and pulled him down with him in a tangled heap.

Both men scrambled to their feet. Eddie, who was still holding the front of Chase's shirt, pulled sharply, yanking Chase into him. He quickly grabbed Chase's head and pushed it down sharply to meet his rapidly rising knee. The impact stunned Chase, and he staggered backward. His vision blurred instantly. In the far reaches of his mind, he knew his nose was broken and blood was streaming into his open mouth, causing him to gag. He tried to shake off the pain.

Eddie reached behind his own head and pulled a tire iron out from the pack he was wearing. It may not have been as powerful a weapon as the assault rifle, but Chase knew it could be equally deadly in a close-quarters fight. Raising it above his head, Eddie cocked his arm and charged Chase. He swung hard, like a lumberjack splitting wood, aiming for Chase's head. At the last second, Chase raised his left arm to block the blow as he spun to his right. His quick response mitigated the full force of the blow and likely saved his life. But the tire iron smashed Chase's exposed wrist. The crack of the bone from the blow seemed to echo across the pond, followed by a loud grunt. Chase quickly recovered and stepped into Eddie with a strong thrust of his right fist into his midsection.

Out of nowhere, Rick ran full speed into Eddie, and the two of them tumbled into the water. Eddie managed to twist on the way down, landing more or less on top of Rick. Rick struggled to stand, but Eddie pushed him deeper into the water, rolling him onto his back.

Pinning him to the bottom, Eddie pushed his knee into Rick's stomach. He used his weight to hold Rick underwater as he struggled to break free. Chase knew Rick could be dead in less than a minute.

Chase scrambled to find his handgun in the grass. He grabbed it and fired off two quick shots which hit the water a few feet from Eddie. He was about to squeeze the trigger again but hesitated, fearing he might hit Rick.

 Eddie let go of Rick, and his limp body floated partly to the surface as Eddie pushed off for the far shore underwater. Chase could barely see a ripple on the water's surface, but fired another shot blindly into the water where he thought Eddie would be. Then he plunged into the water after Rick. Feeling around for Rick's body, Chase grabbed his shirt collar and dragged him out of the water using his good arm.

Eddie had made it to the opposite shore and climbed out, and Chase heard him shout, "You'll never catch me! You're too weak and too stupid! Just go back home and leave me alone, or I'll put you in a grave too!" Then he turned and was gone into the night.

Rick lay unconscious on the shore with his legs still in the water while Chase frantically worked to revive him. He turned Rick's face to the side and with all his might, thrust his one good hand up and into Rick's diaphragm just below the rib cage. This forced murky pond water out of Rick's lungs and mouth. Chase repeated the procedure two more times with diminishing results. Panicked, he pulled Rick's head back, his chin up and out, to clear the air passage and blew several hard puffs of air into Rick's lungs. Chase checked for a pulse. Finding none, he began CPR. "Come on, Rick, breathe! Don't let that lowlife win! Not this way! Not now!" He compressed Rick's chest about fifteen times and then gave him two sharp breaths before returning to the chest compressions. No matter how hard he pushed, the one-handed compressions seemed to have only a marginal effect. He needed to try something else while he still had the chance.

Instead of using his good hand, Chase laid his elbow on the lower end of the sternum and pumped his weight through his elbow to compress Rick's chest. It was awkward but seemed to be more effective.

Chase kept working with a laser focus while praying silently for providential intervention. After a few minutes without results, he checked his watch and then checked his cell phone—no bars. No chance to phone for help. He was on his own. Rick's life was in his hands. He went back to work on Rick, silently vowing to continue until help arrived or he collapsed from fatigue.

Every few minutes, Chase stopped to check for a pulse and to see if Rick was breathing at all on his own. In the darkness, it was hard to tell if his diaphragm was moving. He leaned in close to Rick's mouth and listened. He thought he could hear shallow, raspy breaths, but wondered if his mind was playing tricks on him. Still, the thought gave him enough hope to press on. He really didn't have a choice.

Chase continued the chest compressions, periodically switching elbows in a futile effort to find relief. He ventured beyond the edge of his endurance and then on some more. His mind began to wander. He thought about Addison and wondered where she was and how she was doing. He remembered some of his more challenging saves as a paramedic. He tried to think of anything that would keep him from facing the possibility of losing Rick. And then an almost imperceptible but comforting thought settled into his consciousness, like a fall leaf fluttering to the earth.

It was a James Russell Lowell quote he had memorized in college but hadn't thought of since—until now. Why it had come to mind was a mystery, but it was just what he needed. "It is by presence of mind in untried emergencies that the native metal of a man is tested." This untried emergency was certainly testing Chase's metal, and this was a test he could not—would not—fail.

CHAPTER 27

ADDISON WOKE WITH A JOLT and looked around. It was completely dark, and she sensed she was alone. *Were those gunshots that woke me, or just a bad dream?* she wondered. Her heart was pounding in her chest. She checked her watch. It was just after ten P.M. She tried to stay alert as she listened for more shots, but the need for sleep was too powerful. Overwhelmed with hunger, thirst, and fatigue, she drifted back to sleep in seconds.

Addison jumped awake again as another gunshot echoed through the hills. She was wide awake now. Another shot followed a minute later. It was close, not more than a mile away, she thought, but it was hard to tell in the mountains. She sat up and looked around and then ducked back down on her stomach as she heard movement in the brush.

"Gunner, is that you?" she called in a loud whisper.

No reply.

"Gunner!"

"Yeah, it's me! Keep your voice down."

"Did you hear those gunshots?"

"I did. I got back here as fast as I could."

"Where have you been? You were supposed to be standing watch."

"I was watching, but I had to get up and walk around to stay awake."

"Okay, never mind that. We've got to move. Those gunshots were way too close. We can't follow the road south like we planned since it will take us toward the gunfire. Let's head back up the road toward higher ground. Grab your gear, and let's go!"

Addison took off to the west, the opposite direction from which she'd heard the gunshots. That meant following, at least for now, Sicley Road back to the northwest. She didn't like the change in plans, but she felt like she had no choice. Gunner followed.

Addison had gotten a couple of hours of sleep, which had given her a small reserve of energy. They walked fast, keeping to the shadows as usual. Neither spoke, but both were contemplating this turn of events. Despite their planning efforts, things just kept happening to force them to take different directions.

As she walked, another thought popped into her head—something she had heard Chase say. "Adapt and overcome." It was one of his favorite sayings and one he frequently used. In truth, Addison had also grown to like it since it came to represent a no-quit attitude, especially when things didn't go her way. *I guess we'll adapt and overcome tonight and see what the morning hands us.*

Twenty minutes later, Addison stopped and headed back into the woods. Gunner followed.

"Boy, am I glad you stopped, Addison. I'm not in as good a shape as you."

"I could use a break too. Mostly, I want to hide and watch what happens. We may not be the only ones running from that gunfire. We need to make sure we aren't surprised from behind."

"If no one comes up the road, I guess this is as good a place as any to wait out the night. We might even get some sleep if we're not careful." Gunner smiled.

"I'm not worried about sleep right now, but if things stay quiet, we might as well try. I got a few of hours already. Why don't you try to get some rest while I stand watch. I'll wake you in two hours if nothing happens."

"You sure?"

"I'm sure. You probably ought to walk back into the woods another twenty or thirty yards in case you snore. Hopefully that will keep the sound from making it to the road. I'll stay here where I can see if anyone comes or goes."

Addison watched as Gunner dutifully walked farther into the woods and laid down. Then she looked around for a better observation point. She worked her way behind a fallen tree, sat down, and leaned against a small pine. Only her head was exposed. She could clearly see both near and far sides of the road and perhaps fifty feet in each direction.

Cognizant of her light complexion and blonde hair, she spit into her palm, mixed in some dirt, and then rubbed the dark paste onto her face. Then she pulled her hair back and tucked the long strands into her shirt collar. It wasn't much, but it would have to do.

As she sat alone in the dark, the forest seemed to come alive around her. She had never spent much time in the mountains except for at campgrounds and was amazed at the variety of sounds she heard. *I thought most animals slept at night, but it sure doesn't sound like it.* With a little practice, she thought she was able to recognize different animals and distinguish between the sounds they made in contrast to the kind a person would make. Addison realized the darkness, once something she feared, could be quite comforting.

Alone with her thoughts, she reflected on everything that had happened in the past few days. She missed Chase and her family so much right now and couldn't wait to get back home. Tears formed in her eyes. But, it wasn't over yet. She knew she'd been strong so far, but she'd have to stay strong to the end. As terrible as this ordeal was, she knew it would prove to be life-changing in the end. She could already see how she was changing and how her self-confidence and determination had grown. When she got back to Chase, she wouldn't be the same person he married, but she hoped he'd appreciate and love the person she was becoming. Addison paused for a moment to offer a prayer of thanks. *No matter what happens over the next day or two, I'll know I did my best.*

Her two-hour watch came and went without Addison even realizing it. She squinted at her watch. It was nearly one o'clock in the morning. She looked around one last time and then got up to find Gunner. As she approached him, she softly called his name. His snoring continued. She called out again while softly touching his arm. He sprang upright, ready to fight. When he realized it was Addison waking him for his next shift, he breathed out a long sigh, rubbed the sleep from his eyes, and quietly traded places with her.

Addison kept an eye on him to see if he could stay awake. He picked a log to sit on—something that wasn't too comfortable by the look of it. He needed to stay awake and alert, especially if Addison was going to feel safe going back to sleep. It had been more than three hours since the gunshots, and nothing else had happened. She hadn't seen anyone in either direction on the road behind them.

Gunner seemed to be reminiscing about something. She noticed a frown on his unshaved face when he looked in her direction. *He's probably doing what I've been doing–running through everything that's happened lately. That would make anyone frown.* She chuckled to herself. She was just getting ready to lie down and try to sleep when she heard what sounded like plastic being crinkled up.

She sat back up and looked at Gunner, realizing he must have taken a cigarette out and lit up. She was instantly angry with him but quickly calmed down. It was the first cigarette he'd had all day. If it helped him stay awake and deal with the stress, Addison decided she wouldn't say anything. *What harm could it possibly do?*

CHAPTER 28

CHASE WAS STARTING TO FADE. He'd been performing CPR on Rick for more than an hour, and his resolve was starting to crumble. Abruptly, Rick coughed up more pond water, and Chase quickly turned Rick's head to the side to avoid aspiration. He coughed some more and then seemed to slip back into unconsciousness.

Chase put his fingers to Rick's neck and felt for a pulse at the carotid artery. It was faint but definitely there. He laid his hand on Rick's chest and thought it was moving ever so slightly up and down. As he leaned in toward Rick's face, he confirmed shallow but regular breathing. Chase closed his eyes and said a quick prayer. *Thank you, Father, for finishing what I couldn't do alone.*

He slumped back against the truck and breathed in deeply, trying to relax and recover. But his rest didn't last long. He still needed to tend to Rick, who was undoubtedly in shock. Chase stood up slowly, leaning on his truck's running boards for support and grabbing the mirror to pull himself to his feet. He opened the truck and began rifling through the gear.

He quickly found his first-aid kit and tossed it onto the ground by Rick. Then he grabbed his and Rick's jackets and their small cooler. Chase backed out of the truck and knelt down next to Rick. He fashioned a pillow with one of the jackets and laid the other over Rick's torso. Then he dragged the cooler down by Rick's feet and hoisted them up onto the cooler to ensure Rick's blood supply remained near his brain and vital organs. *That should treat the shock symptoms and help him rest more comfortably.* Finally, he used the first aid kit to clean and bandage Rick's face and hands.

Satisfied with his work, he leaned back against the truck. He was nearly spent. As he sat there thinking about the bind they were in, his mind began to drift. Before he knew it, his head dropped and his chin rested gently on his chest. He tried to fight it, but defeat at the hands of fatigue was certain, and he succumbed.

Chase transitioned swiftly through the stages of sleep to that place where dreams dance freely about on the open stage of the mind. He saw himself resting peacefully, completely relaxed, before being disturbed by a nearby conversation. He looked around him but couldn't see anyone. He got to his feet and searched the area. The conversation seemed to grow louder the longer he looked, but he still couldn't locate the source.

Then his eyes snapped open, and he sat up and looked around. He fully expected to see a group of people, but Rick was the only other person with him, and he wasn't talking. Then, almost like a bullhorn, the police scanner came to life. Chase could hear it clearly through the shattered window of his truck. That must have been the conversation he'd been dreaming about.

"Juliet 21, how do you copy?"

"Loud and clear, Control. You got something for us?"

"Affirmative. You ready to copy?"

"Roger, Control, go ahead."

"Are you at the crime scene yet?"

"Affirmative, Bateman and I arrived about fifteen minutes ago. We're here with the canine team."

"Good. I need you two and the canine team to get the dogs back on the scent of the subjects seen running from that cabin fire as soon as you can. We received an anonymous tip from a male who said he was at the cabin when the fire broke out. He stated that the perp started the fire and that Addison was inside the cabin at the time. She was with a guy named Gunner, who was protecting her. He thinks they may have escaped the fire through a tunnel and are running from the perp."

"Roger. The canine team was assigned to secure the crime scene here. You don't want us to leave it unprotected, do you?"

"Negative. A unit of uniforms is ten minutes out. They'll relieve the canine team so the four of you can get the dogs back on scent."

"Roger. We'll let you know when we're on the move."

If Chase had the energy, he would have pumped his fist in the air. But he was relieved, even excited, that help was on the way. He knew they wouldn't pick up Eddie's scent south of where he'd killed the police officers, but they had to believe Eddie took their Jeep and was still heading south. *With any luck, that will lead them to Rick and me. They're about our only hope to get Rick to a hospital since I can't reach anyone on my cell phone.*

Chase slid over to Rick, clenched his hand, and spoke softly to him. "Rick, if you can hear me, help is on the way. Addison is still alive and escaped the cabin fire. She's with a man who's helping her, and they're on the move. Everything's going to be fine. I just need you to stay strong and hang in there until help arrives."

Chase blew out a sigh of relief. Maybe their ordeal would end soon. But he and Rick still had to rely on blind luck for help to find them anytime soon. At least the search teams would be heading in this direction. That gave him reason to hope.

To his surprise, he could hear one of the air force helicopters approaching the area. He was surprised more by the timing than the arrival, since he knew they were supporting the nighttime search. Then it hit him: the tactical radio. He finally had a communication link. He scrambled back into the truck and grabbed the radio.

"Save helicopter, this is Lieutenant Roberts; do you copy?"

"Roger, Lieutenant. This is a surprise, especially at this time of night."

"I'm on the ground along your current flight path and in need of immediate assistance. My father-in-law is critically injured, and I have no other communication. He needs to get to a medical center ASAP; I think it's a life-or-death situation."

"Roger, sorry to hear that. We need to call it in to ops for approval, so stand by."

"Will do. When you call ops, have them notify the joint law enforcement task force that the sheriff's Jeep is in Conger Pond, where I am, and the perpetrator was here less than ninety minutes ago. I'll explain later."

"Roger that, I can see the Jeep from here."

Well, there goes my career, but Rick and Addison's safety are far more important. He just hoped Major White and the police were understanding.

Chase listened as the aircrew passed along the request to ops for air evacuation. He was very familiar with the process. Ops would contact Major White and the Air Force Rescue Coordination Center for permission. Rescues like this required life-or-death situations and the absence of civilian helicopter rescue capability. They could check off both requirements, but the final decision would rest with the AFRCC.

Maybe the Major would make a decision on the spot and avoid the bureaucracy in the interest of time. That would be great, but he'd be putting his own career on the line. Chase definitely didn't want him to do that. But for now, he'd done all he could; it was in their hands.

Chase watched as the helicopter orbited south of him while its occupants awaited a response. He checked again on Rick and found his condition unchanged.

"Rick, one of our air force helicopters is waiting for permission to pick you up. It shouldn't be much longer. Then we can get you the medical care you need. Once you're airborne, I'll call Julia and let her know so she can meet you when the chopper lands."

"Lieutenant Roberts, Save 60."

Chase grabbed the tactical radio. "Roger, go ahead."

"We have permission to perform the evacuation. Is there a landing area close to you?"

"Affirmative. I'm about three miles from you, just east of Conger Pond. My truck is parked there, so it should be easy to spot. You can land nearby on the road. I'll turn on my parking lights so you can pick them up on your night-vision goggles. Let me know if you need me to shut them off."

"Sounds good. Any surface winds?"

"Negative. Your best approach is probably over the pond to the dirt road behind my truck."

"Thanks. We'll be there in a minute."

Chase reached in through the driver's window and switched on the parking lights. He knew they'd light up brightly in the night-vision goggles, but sometimes they could be too bright and blot out everything else, shutting down the goggles in a sense. He waited there just in case the aircrew wanted them off.

"Okay, Lieutenant, we have you in sight. You can kill the lights. If you haven't done so already, please secure anything loose and make sure the survivor is protected from the rotor wash."

"Roger. We will be ready by the time you're on final."

While the helicopter crew assessed the winds and landing zone, Chase knelt beside Rick and held the jacket over his face and upper torso so the jacket wouldn't blow away and so it protected him from the sand and rocks kicked up by the powerful winds generated by the rotors. Chase would just close his eyes and look away when the rotor wash hit.

The helicopter circled once overhead and then began its descent into the landing zone. The trees were far enough away from the road to make the approach pretty straightforward. When the chopper was about forty feet in the air, it slowed to a hover and gradually descended as the dirt from the road cleared. They were on the ground moments later.

The cabin door slid open and the flight engineer jumped to the ground. He walked out to the edge of the rotor path, and then hustled over to Chase. "Lieutenant, can your father-in-law walk?"

"He's unconscious. We'll have to carry him, unless you have a stretcher on the helicopter."

"Sorry, sir. We don't. Let's carry him to the edge of the rotor path where I can connect to the aircraft's intercom system. Then the pilots can clear us in."

Chase nodded.

"Will you be coming with us?"

"No, I need to drive my truck out of here. Are you taking him to the medical center in Spokane?"

"Yes, sir."

"Okay. I'll drive where I can get cell phone reception and call his wife, who's at my house on base. She can meet you at the hospital."

"All right, sir. Let's get moving."

Chase quickly tied the jacket that was covering Rick's face around the back of his neck, then picked him up under his arms. The flight engineer grabbed his legs, and they hustled him over to the edge of the rotor path. They set him down gently while the engineer reconnected his communications line and got clearance to load Rick. Without a litter, they had to hoist his limp body onto the cabin floor and push him all the way inside. The engineer wrapped a strap around his waist and secured him to the floor for flight and then untied the jacket covering his face and folded it under Rick's head as a makeshift pillow. The med-tech onboard was already checking Rick's vital signs and condition.

Once Rick was settled, Chase tapped on the pilot's window and gave a thumbs-up sign, requesting permission to exit out from under the rotors, which the pilot gave. Chase bent over at the waist and hurried out from under the swirling blades and jogged back over to his truck. He waited as the crew wound the engines back up to full power and lifted off for Spokane.

Once the helicopter disappeared from sight, Chase gathered their belongings and tossed them into the truck bed, and cleared the broken glass from the front of the truck. Before he left, he climbed back up the hill to where he knew he had cell reception and gave Julia a call.

"Hello. Chase?"

"It's me."

"Is everything all right?" she asked fearfully.

"No. Rick is on his way to the medical center in Spokane on one of our air force helicopters."

She gasped. In a frantic voice, she said, "Is he all right?"

"I think he will be, but he was unconscious when we loaded him onto the helicopter.

"Oh, heavens."

"I'm so sorry, Julia. I suggest you get ready to go to the medical center downtown, and I'll call someone from my unit to pick you up at the house as soon as possible. They will stay with you at the hospital and help you with anything you need. You should be there for Rick."

"Please ask whoever you call to hurry. And thank you, Chase."

"I will. It won't be long."

After ending that call, Chase contacted his unit's operations desk and asked the airman to find someone from his unit to take Julia to the hospital and wait with her until Rick was stable. Chase also asked the airman to instruct the driver to text him Rick's status as soon as possible. That's what he loved about the military. People were available around the clock and more than willing to help one of their own. Now, with Rick and Julia taken care of, he was going after Addison with everything he had.

CHAPTER 29

DAY 6

IT DIDN'T REALLY MATTER THAT Addison was lying on the hard, uneven ground with nothing to cover her. She fell asleep the second her head touched the ground. She was powerless to resist the deep fatigue that now controlled her body and spirit. Even with a couple hours of sleep, her deficit eclipsed any reserves she might still have. And sleep, she knew, was not just a matter of personal comfort; it was essential to survival.

Even in a deep sleep, though, her subconscious remained awake and enlivened—almost as if it were standing watch over her. Addison wasn't aware of it, and it didn't inhibit her rest, but if needed, her subconscious was prepared.

The first hour passed uneventfully. And the next thirty minutes. But then Addison gradually awakened, with a sense of foreboding. She looked at her watch. She still had thirty minutes of sleep time on Gunner's watch. Then why was she awake . . . and feeling uneasy? She remained still except for her head, which she moved slightly back and forth as she studied her surroundings. Nothing seemed unusual. *Wait . . . where's Gunner? He's not where he was when I lay down.*

She lifted her head off the ground and searched for him around their makeshift camp. Nothing. *Where could he be?* As she lifted herself up on one elbow, she heard voices. They were coming from out by the road. She strained to listen.

"Kneel down! Good. Now, what's your name?"

Oh no! That sounds like Eddie!

"Folks call me Gunner on account of my time in the army."

"I don't care what folks call you. I said, 'What's your name?!'"

"Reginald Archibald."

"What outfit was you in?"

"First Battalion, Sixteenth Infantry Regiment. I was a machine gunner until they ran me out of the army."

"You see any combat?"

"Yeah, I did my time in the sandbox."

"You kill anyone over there?"

"Just the Taliban, if that's what you're asking."

"Well, Reginald Archibald, I killed me a few Iraqis back in the Gulf War. And, more important to you right now, I done killed three people in the last week. And maybe one more."

"Are you Eddie?"

"It don't matter who I am."

"How'd you find us?"

"Your cigarettes, you dang fool. Don't you remember nothing from the army? I seen you light up your first one and got halfway to you before you finished up. I lost you again in the dark, but my patience paid off. When you lit up again, I snuck right up on you."

"My old lady always told me cigarettes would kill me."

"Well, she may be right, but not today. It's your lucky day. I like vets—and since you're a vet, you get to live. I got no beef with you, so I'm gonna turn you loose on the condition you leave the area by the fastest means possible and don't talk to no cops."

"Okay. I agree."

"Now, Reginald, me and you is brothers in arms, and when we make a deal, it can't be broke. If it is, you'll pay dearly. I know who you is, and I promise I'll hunt you down like a dog and put a bullet in your head. Got it?"

"I got it. I would never rat out another vet. I got your back, brother."

"One last thing. You need to follow this road up yonder to the north. It'll take you right back to the cabin you was holed up in, or what's left of it. The firemen and cops should be gone from there by now. Get your truck, if it's still there, and get back home. When the cops find you, and they will, keep your mouth shut about me. Got it?"

"Yes, sir, I got it."

"Now get outta here."

"Thank you. You'll never see or hear from me again. I promise you that."

I can't believe Gunner just sold me out! If Eddie still had his gun, maybe Gunner didn't have a choice, but he sure hadn't put up much of a fight. But then, he'd helped Addison so far. She really shouldn't doubt his loyalty now. She hoped he would call the police when he got away—he had to! *Make it fast, Gunner!*

Addison only had a split second to decide what to do. She quickly reached behind her and grabbed the sharpened animal bone from her back pocket. It wasn't much, but she knew she could inflict some serious damage with it if and when the chance came. Then she lay back down and pretended to be asleep, hoping the element of surprise would give her an advantage.

Once Gunner relented and left, it didn't take Eddie long to find Addison. He crept up on her slowly, but Addison knew exactly where he was. She could hear him coming. It took all of her willpower to remain motionless and calm. In seconds, he was right next to her, kneeling down at her side. Addison focused on her breathing—slow and deep.

Eddie reached down and rubbed the back of his hand against her cheek. Addison just about freaked out at his touch. But she held it together, not really knowing how she did. She could smell his body odor and feel the wisp of his breath on her neck. She couldn't stand it a second longer.

Like a bolt of lightning, she struck instantly and powerfully. Addison swung her right arm with all her might and sank the sharpened animal bone deep into the side of Eddie's neck.

"Hey!" he yelled as he reeled back in pain and then punched her hard in the face. He grabbed at the bone and steeled himself as he yanked it out of his neck and threw it away from him. Addison screamed and rolled to her left, away from Eddie, but not fast enough. He lunged at her, pinning her to the ground on her back, just like before.

In a rage, Eddie thrust his hands around Addison's neck and started choking her. Addison pushed up with her hips and tried to roll from side to side, but he wouldn't budge. She grabbed at his hands, unable to pry them loose. Desperate for a breath, she gasped for air but found no relief. She could feel herself getting faint. Her pulse pounded in her ears. Blood from Eddie's neck wound dripped onto her face.

Addison frantically scratched at Eddie's face, digging her nails into his flesh as hard as she could. He pulled back slightly but still held on, choking the life out of her. She grabbed for his face again, but instead of scratching him, she punched him hard in his right eye, causing immediate swelling and discoloration. He yelled and reflexively turned away, grabbing his eye. This gave Addison the opening she needed to escape. She forced him off of her and scrambled to her feet.

"You worthless animal! You will never control me. If you don't leave me alone, you'll lose more than your eye!"

Eddie seemed too stunned to respond, though he did get off a string of expletives while holding his hand over his blackened eye.

Addison looked down at the pathetic man in front of her, sucked in a deep breath, and turned and ran.

CHAPTER 30

CHASE RACED BACK DOWN THE hill toward his pickup but stopped in his tracks when someone yelled, "Stop! Police. Keep your hands where I can see them." Chase complied immediately, but his frustration was near the boiling point. The only thing he cared about was finding Addison before Eddie did. A man stepped out from behind his truck. Chase squinted in the glare of the policeman's flashlight but otherwise stood still, with his hands in the air.

"Is that you, Roberts?"

"Detective Bateman?"

"Yes. I can't believe what I'm seeing after we told you in the strongest terms to keep away!"

"Yes, sir, I know. It's a long story, and I'll tell you the whole thing when we have time. Right now, we need to get after Eddie. He was here not more than two hours ago. He attacked my father-in-law and me."

Detective Strickland walked up from the bend in the road, followed by two canine officers and their dogs. Floyd looked back at them, pointing to Chase.

"Look what I found."

Ted just shook his head as he and the others joined Floyd. Then he introduced his colleagues. "Chase, this is Mitch Mathews and Becka Rigby. Becka runs our canine unit, and Mitch is a trainer and handler. The bloodhound here is named Pebbles. She's our best tracker. The German shepherd is Angus, and you can probably tell he's our attack dog. Mitch and Becka, this is Chase Roberts, the husband of the woman we're searching for."

The group nodded to each other.

"Where's your father-in-law?" Floyd asked.

"He just got evacuated by one of the air force helicopters. He's on his way to the medical center downtown."

"That explains the chopper we saw landing and taking off not long ago. We'll deal with you later, but right now, tell us what you know about Anghelone."

Chase rehearsed the events of the last couple of hours as the four law enforcement officers listened, interjecting questions from time to time. When Chase finished up, Ted took charge.

"Thanks, Roberts. That helps us a lot. Mitch, can you pull your rig up here by Chase's truck? Becka, I want to get Pebbles over on the other side of the pond and see if you can pick up Eddie's trail. I want to get moving as soon as she finds his scent."

Then he turned to Chase. "Roberts, I have half a mind to handcuff you and leave you in your truck. Under the circumstances, I won't, but you need to head home right now. We'll find Addison."

"Sorry, Detective. I won't get in the way, but I plan to stay up here close. I can't sit at home. You can arrest me now if you have to, but I'm here to stay."

"Fine. But if you get in the way, I will arrest you. Make no mistake."

"I know."

Mitch pulled the canine SUV up to the group and got out with a first-aid kit. "Let me have a look at your wrist, Chase." Chase walked over and Mitch took a look, pulled out a temporary splint, and wrapped it around Chase's wrist with an Ace bandage.

"There. It's not perfect, but it will provide some protection until you can get to the doctor. Here's a couple of Ibuprofen. Take these now for the pain and inflammation."

"Thanks, Mitch. This should help a lot."

Becka whistled from the other side of the pond and motioned for the team to join her.

"Let's move out," Ted barked. He and Floyd led the way, and Mitch followed behind in the vehicle with Angus in his kennel in the back.

Chase watched as the team faded into the darkness with Pebbles leading the way. He sat down next to the truck, exhausted and dejected. He put his face in his hands and tried to relax but knew he couldn't until Addison was back with him. He replayed in his mind the battle with Eddie, trying to figure out what he could have done differently that may have kept Rick out of harm's way. There seemed to have been only one alternative—shoot Eddie instead of charging him. If he hadn't hesitated, Rick would be fine and Eddie would be dead or wounded.

Chase realized if he continued sitting there he would sink deeper into despair. The best antidote for that, he knew, was action. His mind began to race as he thought about his next move. Of course, he knew he should drive back home like Detective Strickland had told him, but he just couldn't. He had to do something to help find Addison and bring her home.

After a few minutes of deep thought, Chase made a decision. He climbed into the truck and started it. He didn't know exactly where to go, but he would move up into the mountain a ways for higher ground where he could watch and wait.

Before pulling out, a thought hit him. If the police search dogs were following Eddie back up Sicley Road, that meant they would be pushing him, and maybe Addison, in that same general direction. He pulled out his map and turned on the cab light. He quickly found Sicley Road and scanned the immediate area.

His memory served him well. He confirmed that Sicley turned back to the north and rejoined Calicoma to form a loose circle. If he headed around that loop in the opposite direction, he could get out in front of them and maybe cut Eddie off. But he had to hurry. Chase tossed the map onto the passenger seat, clicked off the light, and hit the gas.

It didn't take him long to find the perfect spot. He followed Sicley Road back the way he and Rick had initially come. Passing the site where the sheriff was ambushed, he could see the crime scene unit working the site. Chase soon passed the charred remains of the cabin. After another twenty-five minutes of bouncing along the road, he pulled to a stop and grabbed the map.

He was parked on relatively high ground, overlooking another small lake a few miles west of the cabin site and adjacent to the only intersection between himself and the police. He checked his cell phone; it had two bars. *Perfect!* He needed to call Julia and check up on Rick.

He pulled the truck onto the side road to make its presence less obvious. Then he found a concealed observation point where he could see for a few hundred yards down Sicley Road in the direction of the police. He figured they would be pushing Eddie toward him as they advanced.

Chase looked at his watch—5:05 A.M. Dawn wasn't far off. He pulled his lawn chair from the truck bed and set it up and then set up the scanner and the tactical radio. This time, he brought his gun out with him. He couldn't afford to cross paths with Eddie again. Finally, he took a deep breath and called Julia's cell phone.

"Oh, Chase, it's you! Is everything all right? Any news on Addison?"

"Hi, Julia. I'm doing fine. I've learned Addison is still alive. She escaped from her abductor and is on the run. Eddie is after her, but I don't know how close he is. The police have their canine unit on Eddie's trail and are closing in on both of them. Things are going pretty well under the circumstances."

"Oh my. That's encouraging. I'm so worried about Addison, I can hardly think straight."

"How's Rick doing?"

"He's being examined by the ER team still, but one of the nurses has kept me informed."

"Is he conscious?" Chase asked.

"Not yet, and it sounds like they may keep him in an induced coma. He's on IV antibiotics so he doesn't contract pneumonia from the pond water, and they are running a bunch of diagnostic tests. His condition has been upgraded to stable."

"What a relief!"

"Where are you now? Are you really fine?"

"I'm still up in the mountains. I just can't leave with Addison so close. I do have a broken wrist, but one of the police officers applied a temporary splint, and I'm pretty sure my nose is busted. Right now, I'm watching up a road from the police to see if they flush out Eddie or maybe even Addison. I have a feeling it will all come to a head later today."

"I just keep praying she's okay. I can't stop thinking about how scared she must be."

"Well, you've raised a remarkable woman. I'm sure she's giving Eddie a run for his money."

"I wish you'd come back home—let the police handle it."

"I know, but I'm going to see this through, no matter what happens. I told the police I was staying up here but wouldn't interfere."

"Are they okay with that?"

"No. But they aren't trying to stop me either. I'll be fine."

"Oh, I hope so. This family has already suffered too much. I don't want you to be next."

"I won't be. This will all be over in a few hours. Give Rick my best."

"I will. Be safe, Chase."

Chase clicked off the call, grabbed his binoculars, and carefully studied the darkened terrain. He couldn't see very clearly yet, but he was heartened by the predawn glow of the eastern sky. Within minutes, the light improved, and Chase could see farther down Sicley Road.

Using a scan cycle, he looked up both sides of the road as far as he could see, working his way back toward his position, similar to his scanning up on the hill before Eddie had opened fire. He knew this kind of methodical searching was required. Otherwise, his eyes would follow much more random patterns, leaving significant chunks of the search area unseen.

He set down the binoculars and rubbed his eyes. The lack of sleep and crushing stress were really taking a toll on him. Chase splashed a handful of canteen water on his face to help him stay awake and then picked up the binoculars and started over again.

Suddenly, a lone figure appeared on the road, walking toward Chase. As he watched the person approach, questions flooded his mind. *Who is this guy? Why would he be out in the middle of nowhere at this hour? Is he armed? Could it be Eddie?* Chase felt around for his weapon while keeping the guy in sight. Any thought of fatigue quickly vanished. He senses were on full alert.

He didn't look like Eddie, and he was wearing an old pair of camos. That's not how Eddie had been dressed when he attacked Chase and Rick. He also seemed to be empty-handed. The man was walking fast, though, like he was in a hurry. *I wonder if this is the guy who was with Addison.* He hoped not, because she obviously wasn't with him now.

Chase really didn't know what to think, but he was about to get some answers out of this guy, whoever he was.

CHAPTER 31

ADDISON RAN WITH RECKLESS ABANDON. In the darkness of the trees, she had no idea which direction she was going, but she was determined to get away. She knew she had hurt Eddie badly and was scared of what he would do to her if he caught her again. She was certain he was charging after her like a wounded bear chasing its hunter. So she ran ahead with every ounce of her being.

When she stopped to catch her breath, she could hear him running behind her, cursing her and vowing to kill her after first making her pay for what she'd done. She took him at his word, sprinting away, changing directions frequently and hoping she would throw him off her trail or somehow find help soon. With the brightening sky, she realized hiding from Eddie would be nearly impossible before long.

Almost before she knew it, the sun had crested the horizon. Now she knew she was running north. The terrain was steepening to the right in front of her, so she adjusted to the left to minimize the slope.

Thirty minutes later, she could make out the crest of a steep ridgeline in the distance that might block her path. It looked to be about a mile and a half away. Addison stopped to rest for a few minutes and collect her thoughts. She'd never felt so alone in her life, but there was no time to feel sorry for herself. She had to think. She hadn't crossed any roads or seen any buildings or other signs of life, so there was no obvious direction to go from here. But she also didn't want to just run aimlessly. Her best bet was to get to some high ground for a better view. If there were people around here, that was the best way to find them. She might even be able to see where Eddie was and stay at least a step ahead of him.

Addison looked around and spotted a nearby hill that would give her the view she needed. She put her head down and started toward the summit as fast as her tired legs would carry her. With every step she took, she became more resolute in her determination to survive. Eddie was damaged in more ways than one, and she had no doubt she would win the day. *I'm stronger and smarter than Eddie will ever be. Today belongs to me!*

Addison stopped just below the summit after a short ten-minute climb. She didn't want to silhouette herself in case Eddie was close behind her. She paused long enough to take in the view from every direction. *There has to be somebody around here!*

She didn't see anyone else but did see a good-sized lake just north of her at the base of the steep ridgeline she'd seen earlier. She needed water and, more importantly, lakes this size usually meant there were people nearby—campers, anglers, even birdwatchers. Surely someone was there who could help her.

She spotted a small stream that emptied into the lake and flowed past her just a few hundred yards from where she stood. Her thought was to use the stream to hide her tracks and make following her that much harder for Eddie.

She was there in less than fifteen minutes. Rather than just following the stream, she decided to throw Eddie off by crossing the stream and climbing the opposite bank. She stopped under a large pine tree, where the fallen needles hid her tracks. Then she carefully walked backward, stepping in the same footprints until she hit the stream.

From there she followed the stream northward toward the lake. It wasn't much, but she was desperate to try anything that might save her life. The icy water felt good on her banged-up feet. *If only I could stop and soak them for a while.*

It took twenty minutes for Addison to get to the shoreline. She looked up and down the lake shore in both directions. There was no one in sight. Which way should she go? Time wasn't on her side, so she darted to the right, opting for the higher ground. Eddie had to be getting tired, and an uphill climb would definitely favor her. And with any luck, she might be able to spot Eddie coming her way—if he was still following her. She still hoped to spot other people who might be around. *Come on, Addison. You can do it! You can make it back home to Chase. No rest until the summit.*

* * *

Eddie struggled to keep up, let alone catch up. Addison's sudden attack had left him severely injured. His right eye was swollen shut, and it hurt to move it. Addison had not only blinded him in that eye but also inflicted a searing wound. All he could do was hold his hand over that eye as he struggled on.

He had managed to pull the bone from his neck though. Fortunately, it had missed the arteries, and the bleeding had stopped quickly. It hurt, too, but that was more of a distraction than an inhibitor. Hate continued to propel him forward.

It was all he needed to fuel his attack. Eddie could think of nothing else now but recovering his money and killing Addison. He didn't care if the cops caught him afterward. He had already decided he wasn't going to jail. But he couldn't let it end until he made Addison suffer and die.

"Addison, I know where you is!" he screamed, his voice now hoarse from shouting. "When I catch you, and I'm gonna catch you, you'll beg me to kill you! But I ain't gonna—at least not right away. I'm gonna stretch that out as long as I can! And you dang sure better have my money."

Eddie had no idea if Addison could even hear him, but he wanted her to fear him—to fear what he was capable of doing to her. So he kept up his threats until his mouth and throat ached from dryness and overuse. Then he just tried to keep moving forward. He *had* to catch that good-for-nothing woman. He had to put her down, just like he would any wild animal.

* * *

Addison was running uphill near the east end of the lake. She stopped abruptly and listened. It was Eddie. It had to be Eddie. Who else would be yelling out here? She strained to catch what he was saying but could only understand a few words. Still, it was enough to confirm that he was closer than she wanted.

Fortunately, she had been able to put some distance between herself and Eddie. All those early morning runs with Chase were paying off. *I just need to stay ahead of him.*

Eddie yelled again. This time, Addison was able to tell where the sound was coming from. He was moving toward the lake, while she had turned more eastward. *So he isn't tracking me—just following generally.* She could turn back toward the southeast and completely throw him off.

She did just that and started running down the hill she'd just been on. Just then, a helicopter zoomed extremely low over the lake before pulling up over the woods to the south. It hovered there momentarily and then kept flying. It looked like a police chopper. If it came back this way, she needed to run to a clearing or down to the lake to signal it. She just hoped she wouldn't be giving herself up to Eddie when she did.

CHAPTER 32

CHASE WATCHED CLOSELY THROUGH HIS binoculars as the figure approached. He could see the lone man was wearing old camouflage fatigues from the 1990s but with nonstandard boots and no hat. His hair was long, and he was unshaved, confirming Chase's initial impression that he wasn't on active duty and was probably not in the National Guard or reserves. As the man drew closer, Chase confirmed he was empty-handed and probably unarmed. He seemed to know where he was going and was clearly hurrying to get there.

Chase left his lookout spot and walked down the side road toward Sicley, timing his arrival just ahead of the stranger's. The man looked to be in pretty bad shape—his clothes were dirty, his hair was oily and uncombed, and his face was haggard. Chase stepped out onto the road to confront him.

"Hold it right there," he said, pointing his gun at the man. "Keep your hands where I can see them."

"Are you a cop?" the man asked after raising his arms.

"No, but I'm working with them."

"You chasing that bank robber, uh . . . Eddie something or other? 'Cause if you are, I know where he's at."

"Yes, I'm chasing him, but more importantly, I'm trying to find the woman he kidnapped. Have you seen her?"

"Addison? Yeah, we've been running from Eddie, but I'm sorry to say he's got her now."

Chase was stunned. "How do you know? If you were there, why'd you abandon her?!"

"Hold on now. I've been helping Addison the past couple of days. She showed up where me and some buddies were camping. Eddie was chasing her, but we got her back to my cabin safe and sound. Then Eddie burned it to the ground. At least, I think it was Eddie. Addison and I got away and have been on the run 'til about two hours ago."

"What happened then?"

"Addison was sleeping, and I was standing watch, but Eddie got the jump on me. He sent me running up this road. He said he didn't want to shoot another veteran, so he gave me the chance to get away if I promised not to talk to the cops. I hated to leave Addison, but Eddie told me outright he'd kill me if I didn't leave or if I came back. And if I talked, he said he'd hunt me down and kill me. His threats don't mean nothing to me. I decided to go get help. Mister, you're the first person I've seen."

"How's Addison?"

"She's a tough one, that girl. She's smarter and tougher than me—a real fighter. She's hungry and tired but ain't gonna give up anytime soon. You her husband?"

"Yeah, I am."

"She talked about you, how you were in the air force."

"The police are closing in on Eddie, and I came up here just in case I could help out. Where was Addison the last time you saw her?"

"A couple miles back down this road. She was sound asleep back in the woods a little way. Eddie was hopping mad. He blames her for his predicament. I'm scared of what he might do to your wife now that he's got her again."

"He wouldn't have her again if you'd just manned up!" Chase yelled. "This time, it's on you!"

"No, sir! It's all on Eddie. I did my best and what I thought was right. I'm sorry he's got her again."

Chase breathed deeply to calm down—the man seemed sincere. "What's your name?"

"Gunner is what most folks call me. Gunner Archibald."

"I'm sorry I jumped all over you, Gunner. Thanks for helping Addison out when she needed it and for filling me in. When this is all over, I'll make sure the cops and the press know what you did for her. I suggest you keep moving until you can get home."

Chase lowered his gun after Gunner was down the road. No telling who he could trust these days. If what he said was true, then Eddie had Addison again. And Gunner sounded worried Eddie would be more inclined to hurt her this time around. As he watched Gunner disappear around the bend, he heard the distinctive staccato sound of an air force helicopter. His unit was back on the hunt but this time during the day. *They must be doing some search training in the area again.*

He turned on the tactical radio and stuck the earbud in his ear. He also fired up the scanner. Chase was anxious to report what he'd just learned from

Gunner. Morning was upon them, and it looked like a perfect day for hunting. Eddie couldn't keep running much longer.

"Save aircraft, this is Roberts."

"Chase! Are you still up here searching?"

"Yes, and I just found out where Anghelone and Addison are. I need you to pass it along to the police since I can't communicate with them."

"No problem. Go ahead. We're ready to copy and will pass it along ASAP."

Chase repeated what Gunner had told him and added that Addison was now in extreme danger. Then he thanked them and returned to monitoring the scanner. He needed to know what was happening so he could find a way to help.

Addison, just hold on a little longer. We're almost there!

CHAPTER 33

Not even five minutes later, Chase spotted the police chopper approaching from the east. This was clearly a coordinated rendezvous. The FBI must want to concentrate every resource they have on Eddie. Maybe that meant they were close. With the two birds in the air plus the detectives and canine unit on the ground, both radios began chirping right away.

It became immediately clear that the police chopper was acting as an airborne command and control platform, with an FBI special agent onboard; the air force chopper would assist in the search and be available as a rescue platform, if needed. The police chopper contacted the ground team as soon as it arrived over the search area.

"Juliet 21, this is SPD One, do you copy?"

SPD One must be the police chopper, since Juliet 21 was the ground team.

"Roger, SPD One, we read you loud and clear, over."

"What's your status?"

"Dogs are on-scent now. We're working our way north from Sicley Road."

"Roger that, Juliet 21. We just received a tip from the cabin owner that the perp might have recaptured the victim. He has to be close. Request you pick up your speed to close the distance. We've got backup on the way with an ETA of one hour."

"Roger, we're on it."

Chase was perched up on the top of the steep ridgeline overlooking a clear mountain lake. He glanced up at the choppers circling overhead. Once he heard the ground team's location, he trained his binoculars in that direction. The trees were too thick to see them now, but he hoped they'd break into the open. That had to be the center of the search activity. He should be able to see some of the ground action from here, and he was close enough to get into the fray if he needed to.

Chase was on pins and needles now. His adrenal glands pumped adrenaline into his system like they'd never stop. He was too jittery to sit, so he jumped to his feet as he watched the scene below him. He watched as the rescue helicopter from his unit, Save 42, performed a standard search pattern, while the police chopper orbited five hundred feet above it. That must mean they're close to Eddie or Addison, or both of them. He'd better be ready.

Suddenly, his eyes were drawn to movement along the south shore of the lake. A person was almost in the water, waving frantically at the helicopters. He grabbed his binoculars but couldn't tell if it was Addison. But it had to be! Eddie wouldn't be waving at them. He hoped they'd get to her before Eddie did.

Before Chase could grab his tactical radio, the rescue aircrew was talking. "SPD One, we have the survivor in sight along the south shore of the lake. We're preparing to recover her now. The trees are too close to the water, so we'll have to use the hoist. Do you know where the perp is?"

"Negative, Save 42. As you begin your approach, we'll drop down to provide covering fire for you if needed. We have a sniper with a long rifle and an agent with an automatic assault weapon aboard."

Save 42 flew directly over Addison and rocked back and forth to let her know they had seen her. Then the flight engineer tossed out a red smoke grenade to mark her location and to get a reading on wind strength and direction. Chase gripped his binoculars tightly, relieved they'd found Addison.

"This is Save 42. We've spotted who we think is the perp on the FLIR maybe one hundred yards due south of the survivor and closing in. Once we pull into a hover, he'll know exactly where she is. Do you know if he's armed?"

"Affirmative, treat him as armed and dangerous. Break, break. SPD, move with all haste north of your location and form a loose line abreast. I want you to pin the perp against the lake so he'll have limited escape routes. Save 42, do you think you can get her hoisted up before the perp gets there?"

"We'll do our best. Anything you can do to slow him down would be appreciated. We're turning onto final approach now for the recovery. We'll be at our most vulnerable in the hover."

"Roger, we're descending to the treetop level between you and the perp. If we spot him, we'll try to hold him at bay. We'll stay south of you, but call in the clear when you pull out of the hover so we can stay out of your way."

Chase was alarmed at what he was hearing and decided he had to act now or risk losing Addison. He ran for the truck and spun his wheels cutting a sharp right onto Sicley, racing toward the western edge of the lake. He didn't know how close the ground unit was to Addison but figured he could get there before they could. At least he was going to try.

Moments later, he caught glimpses of the lake through the trees. It was no more than thirty yards from the road. Chase looked frantically for a break in the tree line through which he could drive the truck. Seeing one, he slammed on the breaks and skidded into the small opening. He could only get about twenty feet off the road, but that was still twenty feet closer to Addison.

His handgun was holstered to his belt, and he grabbed his shotgun as he flew out of the truck. The tactical radio was clipped to his belt and the earbud still in his ear. He was determined to get to Addison before Eddie did. Chase was only about a quarter of a mile away and sprinted through the trees, throwing caution to the wind. The noise of the two helicopters was intense and made it hard to hear the radio. He would be operating largely in the blind.

"Save 42, be advised there is another person approaching on foot from the west. He's running from a gray or black pickup truck parked next to the road at the west end of the lake. We don't have a good visual on him; he's in and out of the trees."

"Roger, SPD One, we're looking."

"This is Juliet 21," Ted shouted into the radio. "That's probably the victim's husband. He's been up in this area and has a dark-gray pickup. He'll likely be armed and focused only on getting to the victim ahead of the perp."

As he ran, Chase saw Save 42 approaching from the east into the wind to maximize its lift and stability. The chopper slowly decelerated and settled into a forty-foot hover over the trees at the edge of the lake. The hoist side of the helicopter was over the water near where Addison was standing.

Though he couldn't see what was happening inside the helicopter, Chase rehearsed in his mind what he knew from experience. A med-tech would be strapping himself into the harness of the forest penetrator, a bullet-shaped piece of heavy steel with three pull-down seats used to rescue people through trees. It also had an orange flotation collar around it for water rescues. Although aircrews trained to use the device without assistance, a paramedic or med-tech was always used in civilian rescues, since the survivor would be unfamiliar with its operation.

The med-tech would be seated near the open door. He'd grab the forest penetrator, pull two seats down, and shimmy himself up onto one of them. Next, he'd remove the one-inch nylon straps above both seats and loop one around his back and under his arms. The other would secure Addison on the way back up. He would slide out the cabin door as the flight engineer rotated the hoist arm perpendicular to the helicopter.

Chase glanced up and saw the med-tech dangling out past the landing skid high above Addison. The med-tech gave the flight engineer a quick thumbs-up signal, and the engineer began lowering him to the ground. The hoist was very capable but not especially fast. When hovering that high, it seemed to take forever, especially now.

Chase was now only about two hundred yards from Addison and tried to pick up his pace. He could see she was concentrating on the helicopter rescue, her back toward Chase. She hadn't noticed him running along the shoreline. But he could tell she kept looking back into the woods, probably expecting Eddie to show up any second. He silently pled for the rescue team to hurry. The med-tech was halfway down when the chopper jerked up and to the left; Addison crouched down and covered her head. Chase looked up and could see that the copilot's Plexiglas window was shattered. Eddie must have shot it out. Addison was in serious trouble now!

CHAPTER 34

CHASE'S WORST FEARS WERE CONFIRMED moments later over the radio. With the helicopter gone, he could hear the tactical radio clearly again. "This is Save 42. We just took a small arms round through the copilot's window. We have one wounded. We're pulling back to assess the situation. The survivor is still at the edge of the lake."

"Roger that," SPD One responded. "We'll try to protect her."

Chase watched as Save 42 pulled up and away to the north side of the lake, climbing up above the ridgeline. Chase knew the drill well. They would need to find a wide spot to land—probably on Sicley Road. He figured the copilot's wound would be minor or the chopper would have flown immediately to the nearest hospital. Since that didn't happen, he expected the med-tech would treat the wound quickly so the crew could return to rescue Addison. While the med-tech worked on the copilot, the flight engineer would inspect the exterior of the helicopter for any other damage while they were on the ground. If he found none and the copilot was treatable, they'd quickly return to the action.

As if on cue, Chase could hear the engines when they spun back up to full throttle and the chopper lifted off from its nearby landing place. Chase heard the pilot again on the radio. "Save 42 climbing back to altitude for another pass at the survivor."

SPD One responded, "Roger. Juliet 21 is closing fast and should be able to help protect the victim."

While the air force chopper climbed to altitude, they orbited on the western end of the lake. Chase thought that was odd but figured the police must be trying to clear the area for another rescue attempt. Sure enough, he watched as the police helicopter came in low over Addison, clearly looking for Eddie. Then he heard the unmistakable sound of an automatic weapon as the police chopper spewed out dozens of rounds per second in short bursts. *They must have Eddie in sight.* Chase looked around, heart pounding. *There!* He could see Eddie at the tree line.

It didn't take long for Eddie to respond. Chase watched as Eddie, clearly panicked, fired at the chopper as it was pulling away. The pilot banked the helicopter so the agents in the back had a clear line of fire. They caught Eddie running through the trees and cut loose with a full clip. Eddie dove to the ground, hands over his head. When the firing stopped, Chase saw Eddie jump up and hustle to find better cover. They must not have hit him. *That jerk must have nine lives!*

Chase was closing in fast on Addison, who was hunkered down behind some rocks along the shoreline. He was almost there—less than a minute separated the two of them. He couldn't watch Addison and Eddie at the same time. As a consequence, he lost sight of Eddie. He hoped the police gunfire would keep him pinned down. If not, Addison and Chase would be totally exposed, but he didn't have any choice.

Up ahead, Chase saw someone lean out from the tree line toward the lake and quickly look up and down the shoreline. When he spotted Chase running full-speed toward him, he ducked back into the woods. *Eddie!* Chase knew Eddie was looking for Addison. He'd love to take him on, but the police were tracking him. Chase had to get between Eddie and Addison.

Chase focused intensely on getting to Addison, ignoring Eddie. Suddenly, Chase's right leg buckled under him, an intense burning sensation searing through his calf. He crashed hard to the ground, shotgun flying out to his side as he thrust his arms forward to break the fall. He gritted his teeth to keep from yelling and looked down at his right leg. His jeans were torn at the calf, blood spilling on the ground. *I've been hit!* Eddie must have stayed put to ambush him.

He glanced up in Addison's direction. Eddie didn't have her yet, but he could see a look of shock on her face. He gave her a quick thumbs up signal, thinking he didn't want to stand and give Eddie a bigger target.

Chase stayed low and reached for his holster. He didn't know where the shot had come from but understood immediately it had to have been fired from the woods. Chase crawled as fast as he could for the trees. He was totally exposed on the shore and knew he needed cover if he were going to survive—if he and Addison were going to survive.

He spotted a thicket of low-lying brush just ahead and to his right. Scooting into the middle of the brush, he pulled branches around himself to hide. He held his handgun in his right hand, pointing it awkwardly out in front of him. He slowly looked around for any sign of Eddie. Nothing.

Chase listened for Eddie moving in through the trees. He figured Eddie would be coming for him, but any noise Eddie might be making was easily drowned out by his own rapid breathing and the police helicopter hovering overhead. What he could hear was the rustle of dry leaves underneath and around him. Whenever he adjusted his position, it sounded like a class full of school kids wadding up their homework papers before tossing them in the trash. His leg wound burned like he'd been hit with a red-hot poker, but it would have to wait.

He lay as still as he could and watched and listened for Eddie. *This feels familiar,* he thought wryly. A minute passed. Then another. Ten minutes later, Chase decided he could stand it no more. He slowly got to his knees and paused to look around and listen. Addison was still on shoreline, looking up as the air force helicopter was approaching. The noise from the helicopter quickly drowned out any other sound.

Chase slowly got to his feet and stole another quick look at Addison. She was frantically pointing behind him. Instantly, he knew she was signaling he was in danger. He started to turn, but Eddie hit him full force, and his world went dark.

CHAPTER 35

CHASE SLOWLY OPENED HIS EYES and looked around. His head was killing him. He struggled to remember where he was and what had happened. Then his eyes settled on a stranger—a scraggly, filthy man who was holding a gun on him. He looked vaguely familiar. Then it hit him—Eddie.

"Eddie?" he said, slowly sitting up. "I should've killed you when I had the chance!"

"Boy, nothing gets by you, does it? What you shoulda done was stay in bed this morning and nothing woulda happened to you. Too bad you had to be a hero."

"I'm hardly a hero. Had I rescued my wife, you might have an argument there, but I obviously failed."

"That ain't the half of it. Not only did you fail to rescue her but now you're gonna help me get her back."

"Why do you care so much about capturing Addison? She's of no use to you. You have me as a hostage now. Why not just forget about her?"

"If I knowed a couple of days ago what I know now, I would've gladly given her away. But now it's downright personal. She stole my money and fought me every step of the way. She ruined what shoulda been an easy getaway. Now I'm gonna get caught or killed for sure."

"If you know that, then why not just give up and stop the running and the killing?"

"Maybe I would if that stupid bank guard hadn't got himself killed. But now he's dead, and I killed two cops because of it yesterday, so what do you think my chances of getting out of this alive are? Even if I do, I ain't gonna rot away on death row not knowing when I'll die. I'd rather die on my own terms!"

"But why not use me as a hostage to help you make a deal with the cops? I still don't understand why you are so hung up on Addison."

"She's the reason I'm in this mess now. She's gotta pay for that. I don't plan on getting outta this alive, but I'll promise you this—I'm taking her down with me!"

"Exactly how is she responsible for you being in this mess? She didn't ask you to kidnap her. You wouldn't be in this situation were it not for your own bad choices. What did you expect would happen if you robbed a bank and shot the security guard? Addison had nothing to do with any of that."

In a split second, Eddie swung his pistol, smashing Chase in the side of the head and slashing him across the face. Blood erupted from his broken nose again and flowed freely from his cheek and lips. He fell backward, stunned at Eddie's sudden viciousness. Eddie was obviously over the edge and very close to the breaking point.

"I think you said enough! Now just shut up and do what I say or your family will be burying the both of you!"

Chase wasn't in a position to argue; he didn't want to provoke another attack, so he kept quiet. If he was going to stay alive and save Addison, he had to stay as healthy and strong as possible. He also needed to keep his wits about him. Another blow to the head wouldn't help. For now, he decided to go along with Eddie while banking on the probability he could gain the upper hand in time.

The tactical radio came alive, and Chase automatically reached for it on his belt, only it wasn't there. Eddie had it, but he didn't have the ear bud. It must have come loose when Chase went down. He grimaced at the sound. Now Eddie would know what law enforcement and the air force crew were planning. They both listened as an FBI agent spoke from the police chopper.

"Save 42, are you ready to reengage?"

"Roger. We're orbiting to the west and can be over the target within a couple of minutes. Have you cleared out the perp yet?"

"Negative. We see Juliet 21 closing in, and we expect to engage shortly. I need you to be ready to go but flexible. Depending on how this goes down, I may need you to pick up the victim or law enforcement officers if there are casualties."

"You know what they say, 'flexibility is the key to air power.'"

"Good. The perp has your guy Roberts captive now, so we'll have to deal with a hostage situation, but at least it's not the victim."

"Roger. Do you have a clear visual on Roberts?"

"Affirmative. The two of them are at the edge of the woods. The perp is likely planning to use your guy."

"Where's your ground team?"

"They're due south of the perp, concealed in the trees. They have dogs and a sniper in position."

"Roger that. Call us when you need us. We're ready to go."

"Will do."

"Well, Roberts," Eddie sneered. "It's awfully nice of you to bring me that radio so I know what the cops is fixing to do."

"It's the least I could do," Chase responded sarcastically.

"Not really. I need you to bandage up my bad eye that your wife gave me. I had a first-aid kit in the backpack your wife stole, but that won't do me no good now. Tear off a long chunk of your shirt and make a pad to cover my eye. You can use the rest to tie it around my head so it don't move."

Chase took his shirt off and ripped it as Eddie had instructed. He applied the dressing to Eddie's eye and started to walk behind him to wrap it in place.

"Don't try it. Do you think I'm so stupid I'd let you get the drop on me? You can tie it just fine from the front, where I can keep my gun in your gut." Chase cinched the wrap down and took a step back.

"That's about the best I can do with what I had to work with," he said, bending over to grab his shirt. He'd only needed to rip upside of his shirttail, so he pulled the rest of the shirt on and buttoned it up.

"It'll be fine. Now turn around. I'm gonna hold this gun right in your back while we walk out to fetch Addison. Don't try nothing stupid. I'll get off one round into you before you could make much of a move."

Eddie picked up a duffle bag, his gun trained on Chase. He kept Chase in front of him, while he walked closely behind. He obviously wanted to discourage an attack from above.

"Don't worry about them cops in the helicopter up there, Roberts. They can't do nothing for you. Just keep walking. I seen the rescue chopper hovering up ahead, so that's got to be where Addison's hiding. Me and you is going to go find her. Then I'm gonna have me some fun! Whether you live or die depends on us finding your woman. You help me find her, you get to live. If you don't, you die, and then I'll find her anyway and kill her too. It's all up to you."

The two emerged from the trees and walked along the shoreline until Eddie stopped. He dropped his duffel bag and held Chase in a loose chokehold from the back. This allowed Eddie to move him around as he looked for Addison. It didn't take long for him to find her footprints in the sand.

"Looks like she's disappeared again, Roberts." Then Chase heard Eddie's warped laugh as he said, "Call her name, Roberts. Tell her to come out."

"I can't do that, Eddie. She's my wife, for heaven's sake. I'll be your hostage. You can kill me once you're free."

Eddie smashed the revolver into the back of Chase's head again, not hard enough to knock him out but hard enough to show his impatience. At least

Eddie knew Chase was of no use to him if he were unconscious. "Call her name, I said!"

"No. I'm not going to help you murder my wife no matter what you do to me! Besides, she's probably already left the area. There's no way she'd hang around here if she has a chance to escape."

"No, I know she's here, and she knows I got you. You'd be surprised at how close we became. I can read her better than you can, Roberts. Now call her name!"

Eddie cocked his arm back to strike again but stopped at the sound of Addison's voice. "No! Stop it, Eddie! Don't keep hitting him. I'm the one you want, so let him go." Eddie laughed out loud. His delight in winning this small victory was more than evident.

"Now, that's more like it. I can see Addison's a lot smarter than you, Roberts."

"And that's why you'll never outsmart her, Eddie."

"We'll just see about that, now, won't we?"

CHAPTER 36

"THERE'S MY SWEET LITTLE ADDISON," Eddie called out. "I figured I'd find you, but I didn't think it would be this easy. You're one tough little mother, but I never thought you'd give yourself up like this. I reckon we know now who wears the pants in the family! Roberts, I'd be embarrassed if I was you. Ha! This must be my lucky day. Now get over here, Addison."

"Don't do it, Addison," shouted Chase.

"Shut up, Roberts! Addison, if you don't want me to kill your lover boy right now, you'd better get moving. Time is one thing I ain't got much of."

"Take it easy, Eddie. There's no rush. We need to do this right. I'm willing to give myself up, but only after Chase is free. I'm sure you can appreciate the fact that I don't trust you."

"Can't do that, girl. There's cops in that chopper with me in their gun sights, and I know there's more cops on the ground nearby. If I'm left standing alone, even for a second, I'm a dead man."

"Okay. How about if we all just walk back into the woods so we're out of sight? Then you can let Chase go, and I'll surrender."

Addison started sliding to her left toward the woods, never taking her eyes off Eddie. She was determined not to cede control of the situation to him, even if he had the only weapon. She was a good thirty yards away, far enough to be relatively safe from someone wielding a handgun.

She slowly melted into the woods and then peered around a tree as Eddie and Chase continued toward her. Once they closed the gap a bit, she began backing away again, matching Eddie step for step to maintain separation. When she saw Eddie and Chase slip from the sunlight into the shade of the forest, she called out to Eddie, "Okay, Eddie. I think that's far enough for now. The police in the helicopter can't see you anymore. Let Chase go now. When he's out of sight, I'll know he's safe, and I'll come to you."

"How do I know you'll keep your word and not turn and run again? You ain't been much for following orders so far."

"Orders from you, no I haven't, but when I give my word, you can count on it. Here's how this is going to play out, Eddie. While Chase is walking away, I'll walk half the distance to you and stand out in the open so you will have a clear shot if I try to run. Once I know he's safe, I'll walk the rest of the way to you. You can use me to negotiate with the police if you want. You have my word."

"Okay. I guess that's a deal!"

"Addison, he's determined to kill you. Don't do this," Chase pleaded.

"Get moving, Roberts. Head that direction." Eddie pointed to the south. "I don't want you nowhere near Addison."

Eddie gave Chase a hard shove to get him moving in the right direction. Chase paused for a minute, looking at Addison, and she felt their connection. He suddenly looked unsure of himself or what he should do.

"It'll be all right, Chase. Do what Eddie says. I know what I'm doing."

He clearly hated the position he was in, but Addison hoped he would trust her judgment. She had spent the most time with Eddie and understood him better than anyone else present.

Finally, Chase said, "I'll be out of sight, but I won't be far away. I trust you completely. And remember . . . no matter what happens, I love you, and I'm so proud of you for never giving up."

"Ain't that just the sweetest thing I ever heard? Now shut up, Roberts, and get out of here before I change my mind or clock you upside the head again! And if you show up back here, I won't think twice about putting a bullet in you."

"I love you, too, Chase. Let my parents know I love them."

Chase nodded once and then slowly walked directly south, looking back occasionally.

Addison watched as Chase limped slowly away. It was obvious he was taking his time in hopes the police would intervene before more blood was shed. When he disappeared down a small draw, she turned and walked toward Eddie. He watched her every move as she approached, looking her over from head to toe. His smile turned more sinister when she stopped right in front of him.

Eddie pointed his gun at her head, placing the barrel up against her skin. Addison stared him down. He seemed surprised—maybe even a little impressed—that she didn't flinch. He suddenly reached out and grabbed the back of her neck and pulled her close to him. He tried to force her to kiss him, but she kept her lips tightly sealed. He tried again, this time more forcefully and making it more intimate. Addison bit down hard on his tongue and pushed him away in revulsion.

"You little witch! That hurt!" He erupted with anger. He viciously charged her, smashing his fist into her face and knocking her to the ground. Addison rolled away. She was now in a small clearing and could see and hear the helicopter hovering above her. When Eddie came at her again, someone in the chopper cut loose with a full clip of ammo that kicked up the dirt next to Eddie's feet.

He dove for the trees and then pointed his gun at Addison. "Get over here, now, Addison! If I go down, you go down with me. Your only hope of survival is if I survive, so you'd better quit fighting me every step of the way." Addison looked up at the police chopper and then at Eddie.

"Fine, Eddie, but don't ever try to take advantage of me again!"

CHAPTER 37

"ROBERTS! DON'T LOOK AT US. Just keep walking, but angle over this way slowly. Walk down the draw in front of you until you're out of sight and then circle back to us," Detective Ted Strickland called out softly.

Chase recognized the voice and followed the instructions perfectly, relieved that help had arrived at last. He made sure Eddie didn't suspect a thing. As soon as he had dropped below Eddie's line of sight, he crouched and hurried back toward the voice. He was thankful to see the two detectives he'd worked with before, plus Becka, holding Angus the attack dog close to her side. Chase's spirits brightened immediately at the thought of Angus with his teeth sunk deep into Eddie's leg or arm.

"Chase," Floyd said. "You remember Becka Rigby, one of our canine officers, and her dog Angus. Angus just may get to see some action here shortly. We have Mitch as backup in their SUV down on the road. He's got Pebbles with him."

Chase nodded toward Becka. "I'm sure glad to see you all again. I hope I get to see Angus in action! I'd love to watch him tear into Eddie."

"We'll see if he gets the chance," she responded.

"What can you tell us about Eddie and Addison?" Ted probed.

"Eddie has a .38 caliber revolver along with my 9mm semiautomatic, which he took after he shot me. He has a duffle bag with him, but I'm not sure what's inside. It has the Sheriff's Department logo on it. He's very much on the edge and believes he won't make it out of this situation alive. He's determined to kill Addison—he blames her for his predicament—but probably won't until he runs out of options. I'm not sure if negotiations will help at all, since he claims he'd rather die than spend the rest of his miserable life in jail."

"And Addison?"

"She stepped out from her hiding place and insisted I leave as Eddie demanded. I'm not sure she realizes just how much Eddie wants her dead."

"She's very brave, given Eddie's string of murders," Becka said. "She sounds like an incredible woman."

"She is. She's as brave as they come," Chase acknowledged. "Whatever we do next, we'd better do it quickly. Eddie's running out of patience and options fast. The choppers are wearing on him, and he knows your ground team is closing in."

"We do have to move quickly, but not until we agree on a plan," said Ted. "While watching the situation unfold, I've considered several options. Here's what I propose we do."

Ted presented his idea on taking down Eddie and rescuing Addison. He asked for suggestions to improve the plan. They brainstormed back and forth for a few minutes, wrestling with the variables and risks they faced. As much as they wanted Eddie, Addison's safe return was paramount. If they had to, they could catch up with him later, as long as they rescued Addison. They agreed on their plan of attack.

"Let's go over the rules of engagement one more time, and then we'll execute," Ted said. "We must preserve Addison's life at all costs, even if Eddie gets away. We know Eddie has nothing to lose, so we'll shoot to kill if he threatens Addison or us. That possibility appears very likely, so be prepared. Any kill shot will likely come from you, Floyd, as our sniper."

Floyd nodded. He was already lying down next to the group and had Eddie in his sights.

Ted continued. "We'll give Eddie one chance to do the right thing and release Addison. After that, all bets are off. Becka, feel free to use Angus if the situation begins to deteriorate. It will be your call, so don't hesitate. Does everyone understand?"

Ted looked into each person's eyes and saw their agreement and commitment. Even so, Chase was nervous. Going into a fight where taking a life was probable could never be easy—no matter how many times one has done it before.

"I do have one question," Chase said. "Since I'm playing an integral role in what's about to unfold, is there any way I can borrow a weapon? I'll be fully exposed, and I'll feel naked without one. Eddie won't expect me to be armed. But I'll use it only in self-defense."

Ted and Floyd looked at each other. An almost imperceptible nod passed between. Floyd reached down for his backup weapon in an ankle holster and handed it to Chase.

"I want that back when this is over." He smiled. "My dad gave it to me, and it's gotten me out of a few tight spots."

"Anything else?" Ted asked. Silence. "All right then, let's make this happen. Floyd, anything happening with Eddie and Addison?"

"I think they've been arguing, but now Addison is walking over to him. He'll have physical control of her any second. We need to go now."

Ted gave Chase the go-ahead to circle back toward Eddie from the left. Ted and Becka would spread out to the right and approach Eddie and Addison using the cover of the woods while ensuring Floyd had a clear field of fire. Even Angus seemed to know what was happening and seemed anxious to engage the perp.

CHAPTER 38

CHASE LIMPED SLOWLY BUT DELIBERATELY toward Eddie and Addison. He saw them standing face to face and could hear their heated voices. He was careful not to look toward Ted or Becka until they were in place. He couldn't afford to tip his hand. For this operation to work, Eddie had to believe Chase was alone.

As the team took their places, Chase stopped behind a large tree, which he would use for cover. Ted and Becka were positioned about forty-five feet to Addison's rear, with about twenty feet between the two of them. Becka removed Angus's muzzle and stroked his fur to keep him calm and quiet. Chase couldn't see Floyd but knew he remained in his prone sniper position with Eddie's head in his crosshairs.

Ted began the countdown using hand signals. Becka un-holstered her weapon and then unleashed Angus but kept him at her side. Chase saw him bare his teeth and pace back and forth, but Becka seemed unfazed. Angus was apparently well-trained and would follow her commands.

Ted's countdown was almost finished. Three . . . two . . . one . . . go! Chase stepped out partway from behind the tree and called out to Eddie. Startled, Eddie spun toward the sound of Chase's voice, grabbing Addison around the neck with his arm and pulling her in front of him. While Chase was distracting Eddie, Ted and Becka moved close enough to engage him at a moment's notice.

"I told you not to show your face again, Roberts!"

"Eddie, I know I wasn't supposed to come back, but I thought of a way to help you escape. No one has to die today, not even you."

"You have no idea how ticked off I am!"

"I know, and I'm sorry. But calm down a minute. I think I have a solution we can all live with."

"I'm listening. But it better be good, or you just may have got yourself and your wife killed."

"Don't do anything rash; just hear me out. If you don't like it, I'll just leave again. No harm done."

"Like I said, I'm listening."

"My truck is on the road at the other end of the lake—about a quarter mile away. I'll lead you there, and you can tie me in the passenger seat. I won't be a threat to you, and I'll be your hostage if the cops try to stop you. But Addison gets to go free in exchange. In the meantime, you get wheels, a hostage, a little food and water, and a pretty good chance to escape."

Eddie pondered the offer for a few moments before responding.

"Get out from behind that tree so we can talk face to face, like men. It makes me sick watching you hide like a scared dog, tail between your legs and all."

Chase stepped out and raised his arms in an act of submission. Even with Floyd's pistol tucked into the small of his back, he was completely vulnerable.

"What you can't seem to get through that thick skull of yours, Roberts, is that I don't care anymore if I get out of this alive. I ain't going to jail, and I'm tired of running. I just found out from Addison my bank money burned up in a cabin fire. My life ain't worth a bucket of warm spit right now. I gave it my best shot, and it didn't work out. So what? Your offer don't mean nothing to me. This will end the way it ends, and it's about to end for you right now—just like I promised."

"Wait, Eddie!" Chase said. "You must have something worth living for—family, friends, something that means more to you than just giving up today. Do you have any children?"

"Yeah, I got a couple, but I can't spend no time with them. My old lady don't want me anywhere near 'em. I'm a bad influence on them, she says."

"Do you want them to remember you like this? Going out in a hail of bullets after robbing a bank and killing three or four people? You may not like prison, but at least it gives you a shot at redemption. A shot at paying your debt to society and maybe even earning forgiveness from the families of the people you killed. Don't throw all that away today. Make the most of whatever time you have left."

"It's too stinking late, Roberts. Like I told you, I got nothing to live for, so just shut up. Now, I told you, if you came back, you'd forfeit your life. Time's up!"

Eddie still had Addison in a chokehold, using her body to shield his. He raised his gun toward Chase, but before he could act, he was startled by Angus's sudden appearance and his low but thundering growl. The attack dog stood to Eddie's left, not more than seven or eight feet away. The hair on Angus's neck was standing at full attention, complementing his yellow, bared teeth. It would be hard to imagine a more frightening sight.

Out of nowhere, a shout grabbed everyone's attention. It came from behind Eddie and Addison, near the shoreline. "Hold it right there, Eddie!" It was Gunner and two other men in camouflage. "I told Miss Addison I'd protect her, and I aim to do just that." All three men pointed AR-15 assault rifles at Eddie. "Now, drop your weapon, and let Addison go!"

Eddie looked around him. Chase could see Eddie knew he was surrounded—Chase in front of him, cops and the police dog to his left, Gunner's ragtag group behind him, and the police chopper overhead. He was sweating profusely, and his body began to shake. Everyone watching him seemed to know he would either collapse or explode. It was the latter.

Eddie tightened his grip around Addison's neck; she was fighting to breathe. "Everyone just get back!" he yelled as he started backing away from the group. "I swear I'll kill her if you don't back off!" No one moved but Eddie and Addison.

Then Becka suddenly shouted, "Angus, attack!"

Angus charged Eddie at full speed. At the same time, Ted pulled the fuse on a flashbang grenade and tossed it about ten feet behind Eddie, but not before Eddie got off a lucky shot that caught Angus in the shoulder. He yelped as his front left leg collapsed, causing him to hit the ground at full speed and roll. He lay where he came to rest, softly whimpering from the pain.

The concussion from the grenade stunned Eddie and nearly knocked him off his feet. He loosened his grip on Addison to catch his balance and then grabbed for his ears as if he'd suddenly lost his hearing and was disoriented. Addison also threw her hands over her ears but took her chance to roll to her right and out of Eddie's grasp. Eddie grabbed her hair before she got completely away and yanked hard, pulling her backward into a sitting position as he dropped to his knee behind Addison, keeping her in front of him as a shield. He held her tightly enough that their heads touched, making a head shot too risky.

Incensed, Chase charged from his position. Any thought of the pain in Chase's lower leg was swallowed up in a new surge of adrenaline. Eddie turned toward Chase and raised his handgun. Addison grabbed his shooting arm, pulling it toward her just as it went off. Then she thrust her left elbow into his solar plexus with all the strength she could muster, knocking the wind out of him.

That caused Eddie to squeeze off another round involuntarily. The bullet slammed into the dirt just in front of his own feet. Addison swung her fist down hard into Eddie's groin then rapidly back upward into his face. At that point, Chase saw her twist away from Eddie, breaking his grip at last.

Eddie shot wildly, hitting Chase in the gut from close range, dropping him in his tracks. Just as Ted and Becka charged toward Eddie, a shot rang out from behind them. The scene before Chase seemed to unfold in slow motion, one frame at a time.

Before the sound reached Chase's ears, the bullet hit Eddie in the side of his head. The expression of shock froze on Eddie's face as he collapsed in a heap right where he'd been standing.

Addison hit the ground to avoid the line of fire and rolled farther away from Eddie. She buried her face in the ground and covered her head with her arms for protection. The echo from the rifle shot faded in the distance, replaced momentarily by the distant rhythmic sound of the helicopters high overhead. Then the flow of time quickly returned to normal. Chase saw Addison rocket to her feet, frantically searching for him.

When she spotted him on the other side of Eddie, she hurled herself at him, covering him with her body. Chase reached his arm around her and rolled her to his side, away from Eddie. Even wounded, his first instinct was to protect her. Knowing that Eddie was down for good, he whispered softly into Addison's ear, "It's okay now; you're finally safe. Eddie can't hurt you anymore. He can't ever hurt anyone again."

Still in shock, Addison just lay there for a moment; she seemed too stunned to move or speak. Chase could feel her heart pounding, and she was breathing rapidly.

Then she shook her head. "Did you get hit? You're all bloody."

Chase pulled up his shirt. He'd been hit in the side of his midsection, but the bullet had gone all the way through, and the bleeding was almost stopped. "I'll be fine," he said. "It's just a flesh wound."

Ted called out the "all clear," and the police team rushed to Addison and Chase.

Becka pulled out the first-aid kit from her pack. "Are you okay, Roberts?" she asked.

"I will be. It was just a through and through. A few stitches, and I'll be fine."

"Wait a minute," Addison exclaimed. "Where's Gunner?" Then louder, she called, "Gunner?"

Everyone stopped to look around them.

"He's over here," one of his men yelled. "And he's hurt bad! He must have been hit by one of those stray rounds."

Addison jumped up and ran to Gunner's side. Chase pulled himself up with a grunt and followed her, one hand on his side. Addison took Gunner's hand in hers. Someone in the background called for one of the choppers to land so they could get Gunner onboard. Becka knelt beside Gunner, tore open his shirt, and examined the chest wound. She fashioned a large compress out of the available gauze in her kit and then taped it in place over the wound and applied direct pressure to stop the bleeding.

"He's lost a lot of blood, and his lung has collapsed. We don't have what we need here to keep him alive. We've got to get him to a hospital immediately. I can slow the blood loss at the wound, but he's probably bleeding inside as well."

"Gunner, can you hear me?" Addison whispered in his ear. His eyes fluttered open, and Chase could see he recognized his wife. "Stay with me, Gunner," Addison encouraged. "We're going to get you loaded in a helicopter and to a hospital." His eyes closed. "Gunner!" she yelled. "Stay awake! Look into my eyes." Gunner again opened his eyes. "You saved me! I'm alive because of you. You're a hero!"

Chase thought he saw a quick smile before Gunner's eyes fluttered shut again.

"Gunner! Stay awake! Don't you die on me!"

"The air force helicopter is on the way," Ted said. "They'll hover low over the edge of the lake. We should be able to load Gunner onboard, but we'll get our feet wet. Four of you men get ready to lift Gunner."

"I'll talk them in to the hover and get them as close to the shore as I can," Chase yelled as he ran toward the beach, ignoring the burning in his calf and his side.

He could see Save 42 hovering across the lake toward them, twenty feet above the water. The chopper settled into a standard four-foot hover and crept closer to Chase. He used normal marshaling signals to let the pilot know how close he could get. The flight engineer was also looking out the open cabin door and talking to the pilot. Between the two of them, they positioned the helicopter within two feet of dry land, with the rotor blades as close to the trees as they could get without hitting them.

As soon as the pilot set the closest skid down lightly onto the lake bed, Chase and the flight engineer motioned for the men to bring Gunner in. The six of them loaded him onto the floor. The flight engineer hopped aboard and strapped Gunner down before taking his position at the door. The others ran out from under the rotors and watched as the helicopter slowly lifted up and moved out over the water before taking off for Spokane.

When Save 42 disappeared over the ridgeline, Addison buried her face in Chase's chest. It didn't take long for the deep sobs to come. He held her tightly in his arms as all the stress of the last five days drained from her. When she regained her composure, she pulled away slightly and wiped the tears from her eyes and cheeks.

Addison looked into the tired faces of those around her. She took Chase by the hand, and, one by one, she hugged and thanked everyone for helping with her rescue. The canine officers were the last two she approached. They were huddling over Angus, bandaging up his wound and giving him a sedative. Pebbles the bloodhound lay next to him, muzzle to muzzle, whimpering softly. The officers stood when they finished up. Addison quickly hugged both.

"I'm so sorry about your dog." She struggled to get her words out without crying. "I'm touched that he risked his life to protect mine and Chase's. Do you think he'll be all right?"

Becka replied, "We think so. We've already been in touch with the department veterinarian. She helped us stabilize him, and we'll get him to the animal hospital as soon as we can. But even if he recovers, he probably won't be able to continue serving on the force. We may have to retire him."

"You won't have him put down, will you?" Chase asked.

"Oh no. We'll find him a good home where he'll have a loving family and can assume the duties of watchdog, in peace."

"Thank goodness." Addison sighed.

"How about I patch you up now, Chase?" Becka offered. "I'd better clean out the entry and exit wounds with disinfectant and bandage you up until you can get to a doctor."

"I guess you're right." When she was finished, Chase said, "Thank you. That should hold me until I can get the wounds stitched shut."

"Listen up, everyone," Ted bellowed. The group turned toward him and gathered closely to hear what he had to say. "I've got some good news and some bad news. First, the good news. We'll have a couple of fifteen-passenger vans here in fifteen minutes to take us to the JTF trailer. Becka, you and Mitch take your vehicle and the dogs and get Angus to the vet as fast as you can. Check in with dispatch when you get out of the mountains. They've already got a surgical team prepping and will tell you where to head."

"Got it," Becka called as she and Mitch headed for their truck. Mitch was carrying Angus, and Becka had Pebbles on a lead.

"Floyd," Ted continued. "Would you please cordon off Eddie's body and collect all the weapons that were fired? We'll leave them with the uniforms coming up with the vans—they'll guard the scene."

"Sure," Floyd responded. "What's the bad news?"

"I was just coming to that. I'm very sorry to say I just received word that Gunner died before the air force helicopter could get him to the hospital. He did pass peacefully, never regaining consciousness. The ER doctor at the hospital

pronounced him dead shortly after the helicopter touched down, which was"—
Ted looked at his watch—"about ten minutes ago. If you're so inclined, why
don't we pause for a moment of silence to remember him."

Ted surveyed the group as they thought about their loss. There weren't
any dry eyes to be found. Chase and Addison were crying softly, overcome by
Gunner's selfless sacrifice. Gunner's men shuffled back and forth while staring
down at their boots. Even the veteran police officers teared up. Chase felt that
everyone who had ever gone into harm's way, or loved someone who had, knew
how sacred and hallowed the sacrifice of one's life was.

After a full two minutes, Ted turned to Gunner's buddies. "I need your
full names, and contact info from both of you, and then you're free to go.
Thanks for coming back for Addison. That took a lot of guts, but you kept
your word to protect her."

Then he turned to everyone. "Okay, folks, let's get moving so we're ready
to leave when the transportation arrives."

While the group got busy, Chase pulled Addison to the side where they
could talk privately. "Are you going to be okay?" he asked.

"I think so—in time. Gunner and I got pretty close while we were running
from Eddie. I can't believe he's gone. He was such a humble man and immediately
willing to help me when I needed it most. I want to do something for his family."

"I think that's a great idea, but we'll need to put it on hold for a little while.
I expect the police will want our full statements, and we need to see a doctor.
Once those things are done, we can decide who best to thank for all Gunner has
done for us."

"Thank you, Chase. In a very real way, I owe him my life, and I want to
honor his. But, right now, let's find a quiet place to sit and wait for our ride. I
don't know about you, but I can use some quiet right about now."

Chase took her hand and led her to a nearby log, away from the rest of the
group, where they sat down. He pulled her close and leaned in to give her a
kiss, relieved to know it was all over.

CHAPTER 39

TRUE TO TED'S WORD, THE vans soon pulled up. Several police officers bounded out, along with two forensic scientists from the crime scene unit. The coroner would be up shortly. Ted and Floyd spent a few minutes orienting the new arrivals while Chase and Addison loaded into the vans with the others. Ted and Floyd joined them a few minutes later, and they were on their way.

A tidal wave of exhaustion seemed to crash over the group. Despite the bumps and turns on the road out, everyone aboard the vans, except the drivers, fell asleep almost immediately. Nothing short of World War III was likely to wake them until they arrived in Cusick. They were met by Bob Sackett, the FBI special agent in charge of the JTF and the one aboard SPD One who had directed the final operation. Floyd introduced him to Addison and Chase.

"Welcome home," he said as he shook their hands. "It's really good to meet you both under the circumstances. And you are a sight for sore eyes, literally." He raised his eyebrows at their assorted wounds, broken bones, and bruises.

"Thank you, I think." Chase chuckled. "I guess we are a little banged up. But, seriously, thank you and the JTF for your hard work in rescuing Addison. I suppose you need to interview both of us to fill in the blanks and close out the case."

"That's true," Sackett replied. "But it can wait until you've been seen by the doctor. Ensuring your well-being is by far the most important item on the checklist."

"We're okay," Addison said. "Can't we just do our interviews and go home?"

"It won't take long to get medical treatment, and documenting your injuries is part of the investigation. I'll walk you over to the paramedics next to that ambulance," he said, pointing toward the flashing lights. "They will take you to the nearest clinic in Deer Park so you can be examined and treated by a physician. Even though you both look remarkably well to me, given the circumstances, let's let the doctor decide that."

Reluctantly, the two agreed. The three of them walked to the waiting ambulance, and Addison and Chase climbed in. They sat next to each other on the gurney, holding hands. Special Agent Sackett closed the rear doors, and they heard him pound twice on the side of the ambulance to let the driver know they were ready.

* * *

At the clinic, Addison and Chase were determined to stay together through the battery of exams and subsequent treatment. Their recent separation had been more than enough, and they both wanted—needed—to understand the sacrifices each other had made. Chase sat in the spare examination room chair while Addison was examined. While the doctor looked her over, his nurse started an IV to treat for dehydration and to facilitate injections of both antibiotics and pain medicine. Addison's wounds were physically superficial, mostly the two black eyes and other bruising around her face, but the trauma had undoubtedly taken a deep emotional toll on her.

"Well, Addison," the doctor said. "You've been through a lot over the past week, but you are in remarkably good condition. I've asked my nurse to clean up and bandage your scrapes, but other than that, I'll just prescribe an anti-inflammatory and a healthy dose of rest to recuperate. I do want our psychiatrist to visit with you and recommend any follow-on counseling, given the trauma you've endured. I know you just want to shake it off, but the trauma can cause you lingering issues for months to come if not addressed up front."

"I think I'll be fine, Doctor, but I guess it couldn't hurt. Thank you very much."

Following X-rays and an exam, the doctor confirmed Chase had fractured both his wrist and nose. Then he cleaned out his bullet wounds and stitched them up, along with the gash in his scalp from Eddie's handgun. Physically, Chase had taken the brunt of Eddie's anger, but he would heal up just fine over the coming weeks.

"The stitches might leave a scar once they heal, but given their locations, they shouldn't be too noticeable. We can set and bandage your nose, which I'd suggest, but some people choose not to. If we don't, you'll need to work a little harder to protect it and get used to its new shape. Your choice."

"I'd better get it fixed, Doc. I don't want to give Addison any excuses to trade me in," he chuckled.

"Okay. We'll also put a cast on your wrist before you leave that will need to stay in place for six weeks. Everything else will take just about the same amount of time to heal up. Just take it easy until then."

"I will, Doc. Thanks for taking good care of Addison and me."

"Well, you've both been through the wringer, but you should bounce back pretty fast. Glad we could help."

When the medical staff finished with Chase and Addison, they called Special Agent Sackett for a ride back to Cusick for the couple. While they waited, Addison called her mother.

"Hi, Mom. We're back, safe and sound."

"Oh, Addison, I've been so worried about you! We all have. I can't tell you how good it is to hear your voice. I'm so glad you and Chase are back together. An FBI agent called me a couple of hours ago with the good news. I've been so anxious to talk to you. Thank you for calling."

Chase had filled Addison in on her dad's situation. "How's Dad doing?"

"Much better than expected. They put him into a medically induced coma until they could assess his condition and treat him. They've done all of that and are slowly bringing him back out of the coma now. He should wake up soon, and I know the first thing he will ask about is you. I'm sitting right next to him, do you want to say anything to him? I'll hold the phone up to his ear."

"Yes, I'd like that." Addison paused for a moment to give her mom time to hold the phone to her dad's ear. "Hello, Dad. It's me—Addison. I'm safe now, thanks to you and Chase. Now it's your turn to get better so we can bring you home safe. I love you very much. Now, heal up quickly. Bye."

In another minute or so, her mom came back on the line. "Addison? Thanks for doing that. They say people in comas can often hear what's going on around them. I'm sure your voice will put him at peace and help him wake up."

"I'm glad you suggested it."

"When do you think you'll be home?"

"I'm not sure, but probably in a couple of hours. We have to give the police our formal statements, and then I think we'll be free to go."

"Okay. I'd like to see you as soon as possible."

"I can't wait to see you and Dad either. I'll call you when we get home. I love you very much, Mama. Thanks for all you and Dad have done for Chase and me."

They ended the call just as the police cruiser pulled up to take Chase and Addison back to Cusick. They sat together in the back seat, holding hands and talking quietly during the twenty-minute drive.

"I know there's no rush to talk about all that's happened, but I'm wondering how you're doing—really doing," Chase gently said.

Addison thought about it for a few minutes. This was really the first time she'd had an opportunity to process her experience in a safe environment.

"I'm not really sure yet. So much has happened. It seems like it's been a lifetime, even though it's only been a few days. It really frightens me to think that when Eddie carjacked me, I could have had only six days to live. My life could have been over before it's really even begun."

"Instead, it was Eddie that only had six days to live. He got what he deserved, given the bad choices he made. You, on the other hand, made consistently good choices and came through it all alive and doing pretty well. I don't think that was just an accident."

"I'll have to think it through on my own over the next few days. Maybe even longer. What I do know is that I love you, and I'm so grateful you and Dad came after me. In the back of my mind, I always knew you would, but it was incredible to see you in person up at the lake."

"Not really my finest hour." He laughed. "I didn't expect Eddie to shoot me in the leg and capture me before I could ride in on my white stallion to rescue you."

"It was amazingly brave, and I can't put into words how much it means to me that you were so willing to risk your life to save mine." Tears began to roll down her cheeks freely as she tried to express her feelings.

"I wasn't the brave one. You were. I can't imagine what it must have been like to be held captive by an armed murderer for nearly a week. You were the hero—especially when you willingly went to him so I could go free. I'm so proud of you for fighting Eddie all the way—he really hated you for it."

"I'm sure he did." Addison paused for a few seconds and then continued. "This sounds a little cheesy, I know, but I told myself at the very beginning I'd return with honor—just like the Survival School motto says. And I think I have. It will take me time to sort some things out or even to discuss them, but I know I'll never be the same person again. I'm stronger, much stronger. I'm a survivor. And I know I didn't do it by myself. Heavenly Father was with me the whole time. And I knew you were too."

Chase put his arm around Addison's shoulders and pulled her close to him. She looked up to see they were almost to Cusick. When they hit the edge of town, many of the residents lined the highway, waving yellow ribbons or American flags and cheering for them. Addison couldn't believe what she was seeing. Obviously, the police officer driving them had called ahead.

Cusick was a small town, but as Addison learned, it had become intimately entwined in the police investigation and her search. Even though Addison wasn't a resident, the town had clearly adopted her. What had begun as a local story had since gained national attention, and people across the country seemed to breathe a collective sigh of relief at the way the events of the past few days had resolved.

The cruiser pulled to a stop in front of the JTF operations center's double-wide trailer, and Addison and Chase were escorted inside, where the full complement of law enforcement officers broke into applause as they entered. They were all apparently anxious to celebrate this success after witnessing some less-than-happy endings in the past.

Addison looked out the window at the Pend Oreille River flowing nearby. This little village on the banks of the beautiful river was not what she had envisioned as the end of her traumatic journey, but it was an ending she now relished. The warm welcome from the residents and law enforcement brightened her spirits.

***

Though Addison was a reluctant recipient of Cusick resident and law enforcement praise, Chase beamed as he watched his wife, and he enthusiastically joined in the cheering. No husband could be prouder than he was at that moment. He could already notice subtle changes in her as a result of the ordeal—her self-confidence and assertiveness chief among them—but all were positive.

When the cheering, handshakes, and pats on the back subsided, the door to the trailer burst open and in marched a waitress from the local diner who introduced herself to Chase and Addison as Flo. She'd brought other waitresses as reinforcement and announced the food and drinks were on the house, which brought another round of cheers, since many there hadn't eaten for a while.

Special Agent Sackett made sure Chase and Addison were properly cared for. Each gratefully accepted a sandwich and cold bottle of water. Sackett quietly motioned them toward a small conference room. He invited Ted and Floyd to join them. Sackett began to close the door when Chase suddenly jumped up.

"Wait, there's something we need to do before anyone leaves."

To the group's surprise, Chase grabbed Addison's hand and pulled her back out into the main section of the ops center with him. "Everyone! Can I please have your attention?"

The banter died down as everyone turned respectfully toward Chase and Addison. Bob, Ted, and Floyd looked on from the conference room doorway.

"We've already thanked many of you for everything you did to bring Addison home safely. But we would be remiss if we didn't thank the two brave officers who lay down their lives for us, as well as Gunner Archibald, the man who protected Addison and gave his life in the process. Nothing we could ever say or do will repay them or their families for that."

Chase's voice wavered. Tears streamed from his eyes. He coughed into his clenched fist in an effort to regain control. Beside him, Addison wept softly. Silence filled the room as the magnitude of their loss settled upon the group.

"We hope to meet with their families privately tomorrow, and we plan to attend their funerals. But, right now, we'd like to invite you to share a moment of silence with us in their honor . . . and to all those in uniform who have given, as Abraham Lincoln described in the Gettysburg Address, 'the last full measure of devotion.'"

After a couple of minutes of total silence, broken by the soft sobs of many in the room, Chase lifted his head. "Thank you all again." Then he and Addison turned and walked back to the conference room. Bob closed the door softly.

"That was very nice of you to do," he said. "You summed up what we've all been feeling. It was an experience none of us will likely forget. Thank you."

While the group outside the door relaxed and ate their fill, Addison and Chase recounted their experiences of the past few days. Bob, Ted, and Floyd asked follow-up questions as needed. A junior FBI agent videoed the dialogue as part of the police record.

Once the documentation was complete and follow-up questions had been asked and answered, it was finally time for Addison and Chase to go home. They were so tired they could hardly hold their heads up. Bob led them to the door, and they all stepped out into the cool evening air. They were surprised to see an air force helicopter sitting nearby, but Bob explained that Chase's commander had authorized the crew to fly them back to base so they could get home without delay.

Floyd offered to drive Chase's truck back that evening and leave it for him in the police department parking lot. As an added benefit, this plan would keep the press at bay for at least twenty-four hours since they couldn't come on base without permission. There would be time enough for them after the pair finally got a full night's sleep in their own bed.

The flight lasted thirty minutes, and they were once again met by cheering crowds, both their air force family and Addison's mother, Julia. Major White had been kind enough to call her with their arrival time and give her a ride to the base. Rick was still in the hospital, but Julia could not wait to embrace her daughter and son-in-law.

The celebration continued for another half hour before Major White insisted they all go home and give Chase and Addison a chance to recover from their ordeal.

"Chase," he said on the way out. "I don't want to see your ugly mug in the office for at least another week. Then we can talk about when you should come back to work. I want to make sure you and your family are fully recovered first. Is that clear?"

"Yes, sir. Thanks again for all you and the unit did. I'm not sure we would be here now if you hadn't helped as much as you did. Plus, I suspect you put your own career on the line a couple of times, asking for forgiveness rather than permission. I owe you and the unit a great deal."

"That's the beauty of being part of a military family. We all pull together whenever one of our own is in trouble. You would have done the same for anyone else if the roles were reversed."

They shook hands one last time, and the family left for home. The group was silent most of the way. They simply stared out the windows and enjoyed the peace of a quiet evening. It was a shame it often took life-changing events like this to help people appreciate what they had.

When Addison walked through her home's front door, she paused for a moment to drink it all in. Even with the early married home furnishings, she realized there was no place on Earth that could ever look as good.

CHAPTER 40

ONE WEEK LATER

"HI, MOM," ADDISON SAID WHEN she answered her phone.

"Hi, Addison. How's everything going?"

"Pretty well. We had a hard time getting through the funerals this week, but that's behind us now." There had been a funeral for Gunner and a combined funeral for the two officers.

"That's why I called. I can only imagine how hard it was, but I'm very proud of the way you and Chase stepped up and offered to speak at both events. I'm sure the families found your words comforting."

"I hope so. It was one of the most difficult things we've done, but we're so glad we participated. We wanted the three families to know how grateful we are for their sacrifices and to assure them that their selfless service will never be forgotten."

"I suspect they were completely different types of services, weren't they— law enforcement and then Gunner's?"

"Polar opposites, but both very sweet in their unique ways. The law enforce- ment funeral was a big production. Police from all parts of the country showed up and lined the streets in and out of the church." Both officers were Catholic, so the families had decided to combine their funeral masses in the Cathedral of our Lady of Lourdes. "It was such a beautiful venue for such a touching event."

"I'm sure it was," Julia replied.

"Chase and I both had the opportunity to share our thoughts, even though we aren't Catholic. Chase spoke of the sacrifices of so many men and women in uniform and how sacred their final acts of service are. He used the Savior's teachings from John 15, 'No greater love hath a man than this, that a man lay down his life for his friends.' And he talked about how heart-wrenching it was when he and Dad heard what happened over the police scanner, knowing immediately that the officers died trying to find and rescue me."

"I would have loved to have heard you both speak. How was your talk?"

"It was a very emotional and spiritual experience for me. I followed Chase, so I was able to refer to his talk and point out how much love Sheriff Mitchell and Trooper Hendricks demonstrated since they were willing to lay down their lives for someone they hadn't met before and who wasn't counted among their circle of friends."

"Wow. It sounds like both of your talks were not only poignant but uplifting to their families as well."

"We hope so. We've decided to try and stay in touch with the families and send them a thank you card every year on the anniversary of their family members' death. We don't want them to ever think we've forgotten their loved ones."

"That's a very kind gesture. I think it will bind the three families together in ways no one could have ever imagined. You and Chase are doing a wonderful and loving thing that will help the healing process for both families, as well as your own."

"I just wish we could do more. Nothing we will ever do can measure up."

"How about Gunner's service? Was that nice too?"

"His was nice, too, but a lot different. He doesn't have much family around here, just his aunt who owned the cabin that burned down. But his brother flew in from the Midwest to take him home for the funeral and interment. We asked him when he arrived if we could have a memorial service in Spokane before he took Gunner back home, and he agreed. We used the chapel on base, and one of the chaplains volunteered to conduct the service. Chase and I bought some flowers, and some of the women from church prepared refreshments. We just gathered around Gunner's casket and talked about him."

"Did his brother participate?"

"Oh yes." She chuckled. "He told quite a few stories about him when they were growing up and told us about their family. It turned into more of a wake than a memorial service, but it did give Chase and me a chance to tell his brother and aunt that he died a hero and how grateful we are for Gunner's willingness to help in my time of need. We told them how very impressed we were that he and some of his militia friends came back to help rescue me the second time."

"Was it very well-attended? With his family holding a service back home, I wouldn't think many would have come."

"There were more people there than I expected. His aunt was there, plus he had some colleagues from work, a couple of neighbors, and the members of his militia. Even the police and fire departments were represented. For a man who felt a little like an outcast, he was very well remembered and honored."

"That's wonderful. Well, I hope you know your father and I wish we could have been there, but I needed to get him back home so he can rest and heal. His part in this little adventure took a toll on him. And speaking of that, how are you and Chase healing up?"

"We're still a little banged up. We look like twins with our matching black eyes. My feet and muscles still hurt, and I don't have much energy. But otherwise, I'm doing well. Chase's nose is tender and a little crooked. I think it's kind of cute, but don't tell him I said that. He got the stitches out of his scalp, abdomen, and leg yesterday, so he's mending pretty well. The nurse told him they might leave scars, but Chase thinks that's pretty cool. He's already planning the stories he'll tell our kids and grandkids."

"Okay, so the physical damage is healing up. How about the emotional damage, especially yours? Have you been to counseling yet?"

"We both have an appointment next week with a family counselor with military experience. I doubt Chase wants to go, but he wants to support me. I still have some nightmares, and I know it will take a while to put this all behind me, but I don't think I suffered any permanent emotional scarring."

"Good to hear, but don't just rush through it to check off the box. I've found that those who put the most into it will get the most out of it, so keep an open mind."

"I will, Mom. But, like I told you before you left for home, I feel so much stronger now than I did before, and much more self-confident. It sounds a little crazy, but this has been a very positive growing experience for me, although I wouldn't recommend it to others. Most people are never tested like I was and may never know what their limits are. I know mine now; I know I can endure and overcome much more that I thought possible just a couple of weeks ago. I'll be fine."

"I know you will. Dad and I are praying for it and counting on it. Speaking of your father, I'd better go check on him. We love you and Chase."

"We love you, too, Mom. Goodbye."

CHAPTER 41

FOUR MONTHS LATER

"Hi, hon," Chase called out to Addison as she came into his air force office. "Hey, Angus, you old dog, you." He reached down to rub Angus's ears and pat his back. Angus was nearly back to full health after being shot, but he'd been retired from the force. Chase and Addison had immediately offered to adopt him, given their past relationship.

"Hi, Chase," Addison replied, giving him a quick hug. "Have you found out why Major White wants to see both of us? I'm a little nervous."

"Not yet, but there's no need to be nervous. He's a great guy. He's probably just following up with us to see how we're doing since the kidnapping."

"I hope you're right."

"We'd better get to his office. It's about time for our appointment."

They'd just sat down in the waiting room when the door popped open and Major White walked out. "Hey, you two. I'm glad you're here. Come on in."

Major White walked them into his office and gestured to a man who was probably in his mid-forties, with close-cropped brown hair and hazel eyes. He was dressed in a conservative suit and narrow, bland tie, looking very much like a typical Fed.

"Lieutenant and Mrs. Roberts," the major said. "I'd like you to meet Burke Summers, from the Department of Homeland Security."

The three exchanged handshakes and greetings.

"And I'm sure you remember Special Agent Bob Sackett, from the FBI."

"How could we forget?" Chase shook hands with Sackett. "Hi, Bob. It's great to see you again."

Bob then gave Addison a polite hug. "I have to admit, it's nice to get back together. I've missed both of you. Is that who I think it is?" Bob asked, nodding toward the dog.

"It sure is," Addison replied. "Angus recovered pretty well but had to be retired from police duty. I couldn't stand the thought of him going to the pound, or worse, so we offered to take him. Becka was kind enough to make the arrangements. After all, he helped save our lives, and it's good to have a dog around when Chase is out of town. Right, Angus?"

Angus let out a short bark to complement his already wagging tail.

Major White invited them all to have a seat and then offered refreshments. "So, how have the two of you recovered from your ordeal? Any lingering health concerns or other issues you're facing?"

"We're doing great now, and the doctors have assured us there are no medical restrictions. Our lives are pretty much back to normal," Chase responded. "How about the extended team? I haven't talked with Ted or Floyd lately, and we've been wondering how Gunner's aunt is doing. Have you heard anything?"

Bob chuckled a little. "Well, the last I heard, Gunner's aunt got some money from the insurance on her cabin, but it didn't cover replacement costs, so Gunner's old militia, the North Country Rangers, are supplying much of the labor to rebuild it."

"Maybe we ought to pay them a visit one of these weekends and give them a hand," said Chase. "How about Ted and Floyd?"

"We've stayed in touch by email, but I don't get over here often from Seattle. Whenever I do, I try to stop by for a short visit. Ted poked his head into my office a couple of months ago when he was in Seattle."

"How are the sheriff's and trooper's families dealing with their losses?" asked Addison. We visited them a few times, but we've drifted apart over the past month or two."

"I think they are doing as well as can be expected. It takes time to get through the grieving process before moving on."

"It's nice to catch up," Chase said. "But I'm sure this isn't just a social visit. May I ask why we've been invited here? We are more than a little curious."

Sackett responded, "I'm sure you are. Sorry for how mysterious this must look. Based on what I observed of the two of you a few months ago under very challenging circumstances, I've invited Burke to meet you. He's representing the Secretary of Homeland Security, with an offer you may find interesting and which we hope you'll seriously consider. Burke?"

"As Bob just said, I'm here at the request of the secretary to extend an invitation we hope you will favorably consider. But, so as not to put the cart before the horse, let me explain the opportunity first and give you a chance to ask questions, and then you'll have time to discuss it privately before you need to make a decision."

"Fair enough," Chase said, his curiosity piqued.

"I'm precluded from going into too much detail since much of this is classified, but what I can say is that the secretary, in conjunction with the secretary of defense and the attorney general, are creating an interdepartmental task force comprised of both military and federal civilian personnel for the specific purpose of rescuing U.S. civilian hostages being held by hostile forces in foreign countries."

Chase and Addison glanced at each other and then looked back at Burke.

"As you know from the news, the Islamic state, Al Qaeda, and their affiliates are targeting Americans much more frequently, and we need to be able to respond rapidly and decisively. The task force will include elements of the FBI's Hostage Rescue Team and selected members from our military counterterrorist units, like Seal Team Six and Delta Force. Since the team will be tasked with rescuing civilians, the FBI will take the lead. Special Agent Sackett has been selected to lead the team. He's asked for both of you to be members."

"What exactly would we be doing if we joined the team?" asked Addison.

"I can't go into specifics," Bob explained. "But, generally, Chase would continue primarily as a rescue helicopter pilot, and I'd like you, Addison, to organize and lead a team devoted to the interests and well-being of the hostages and their families—an advocate, if you will. I think you can see that both of you come uniquely qualified for this team."

Intrigued by the prospect, Chase nodded, as did Addison. Then Chase asked, "Will there be much travel? It sounds like there might be."

"Right now, we envision some travel associated with training, but we plan to house the team at a single location to keep you at home as much as possible. Obviously, the missions will require travel and how much of that depends on what happens around the globe. But, even on those missions, we will most likely be in and out as quickly as possible. Beyond that, circumstances will determine the volume."

"If we are interested, what's the next step?" inquired Chase.

"We don't want you to rush into a decision as weighty as this one, so the next step, if you give us the go-ahead, would be to conduct background investigations leading to both of you receiving Top Secret security clearances. Addison, you'd have to become a civil servant or contractor first. Then we'll read you in to this special access program so you know exactly what will be asked of you. When you are up to speed, you'll be able to make an informed decision. But first, we will need you to sign nondisclosure agreements so that what we do share with you remains protected and strictly under wraps."

He pulled out two one-page agreements and laid them on the coffee table. Chase and Addison quickly read through the details and readily signed. They stole another quick glance at each other and knew immediately what they would do.

Addison responded for both of them. "We would like to take the next step, and we're very interested in the opportunity as you've explained it. At least for a couple of years—until we start a family. Since our own experience, we've come to realize how utterly dependent we were on others for our own protection, rescue, and subsequent recovery. We'd love a chance to give back to others a portion of what we've received."

Addison looked down at Angus, who was lying next to her feet, his head resting on his front paws.

"But," she continued. "There is one condition."

"And that is . . . ?" Bob asked with a scowl on his face.

"That Angus also be part of this team. Maybe not as an attack dog anymore, but he just might make a great therapy dog for the victims. I'd feel better knowing he's around, especially if we are working overseas."

That brought out a smile on Bob's face, as Burke Summers laughed out loud.

"You drive a hard bargain, but it's a deal," Sackett said. "We'll begin the background investigations immediately. I can't tell you how happy I am that we may be working together again, helping others. Just imagine multiplying the relief you both felt when you were finally safe, by ten- or even a hundredfold. That's a huge motivator. At least, it is for me."

"We get that, Bob. Maybe more than you know," Chase said.

Then Addison added, "Even if it only results in one life saved, we know it will be worth it."

The group chatted amiably for a few more minutes, and then Bob looked at his watch.

"I can't believe the time. I have to get Burke to the airport." Then he turned to Chase and Addison. "It will take three or four months for the clearances to come through, but with two cabinet secretaries and the attorney general pulling for you, I'll bet they can speed things along. I'll email you the website where you'll begin your background checks. Until then, just keep doing what you're doing, and we'll let you know when we can dig a little deeper into the subject matter so you can make a final decision."

They exchanged pleasantries one more time and then watched as the two Feds walked out to their car and drove away.

"Well, that was quite an offer. What do you think?" asked Major White.

Again, Addison responded for both of them. "What's there to think about? Our country has asked for our help, and I can't think of many things that would give our lives greater purpose. Based on what we know now, we're very interested."

"Still, you have to be a little nervous about where this all might lead," White countered.

"Of course we are," Chase responded. "But that's part of the exhilaration. I'm sure at some point we'll have to reassess, especially when we want to begin a family, but we'll just cross that bridge when we get to it. In the meantime, we're young and anxious to make our mark on the world. I, for one, can't wait to find out where this path will lead us."

Addison wrapped her arm around Chase's waist and looked up at him. "That makes two of us!"

Angus barked again.

"Make that three of us," Chase said.

ABOUT THE AUTHOR

KENNETH M. PAGE HOLDS A bachelor's degree in management and a master's degree in business administration. He is a retired U.S. Air Force colonel and a retired Microsoft senior manager. His first book, *A Father's Blessing: The Power and Privilege of the Priesthood*, was published by Covenant in 2008. Two years later, he was a contributing author to another book published by Covenant, titled, *How Will Christmas Find Us?*, a collection of true Christmas stories by twelve authors.

Ken lives with his wife, Joni, in Kaysville, Utah. They are the parents of five children and the grandparents of fifteen grandchildren.